Ans	————————	M.L.	————————
ASH	————————	MLW	————————
Bev	————————	Mt.Pl	————————
C.C.	————————	NLM	————————
C.P.	————————	Ott	————————
Dick	————————	PC	————————
DRZ	————————	PH	————————
ECH	————————	P.P.	————————
ECS	————————	Pion.P.	————————
Gar	————————	Q.A.	————————
GRM	————————	Riv	————————
GSP	————————	RPP	————————
G.V.	————————	Ross	————————
Har	————————	S.C.	————————
JPCP	————————	St.A.	————————
KEN	————————	St.J	————————
K.L.	————————	St.Joa	5/09ESPIE
K.M.	1/10	St.M.	————————
L.H.	————————	Sgt	————————
LO	————————	T.H.	————————
Lyn	————————	TLLO	————————
L.V.	————————	T.M.	————————
McC	————————	T.T.	————————
McG	————————	Ven	————————
McQ	————————	Vets	————————
MIL	————————	VP	————————
	————————	Wat	————————
	————————	Wed	————————
	————————	WIL	————————
	————————	W.L.	————————
	————————		————————
	————————		————————
	————————		————————

Jeanne Whitmee is a highly successful author of romantic fiction. Before her marriage, she was actively involved in the theatre and now pursues a keen interest in drama and art. She has two grown-up children and lives in Lincolnshire.

POINT OF NO RETURN

When Imogen Jameson is injured in a London bomb blast and mistakenly reported as one of the fatalities, she takes the opportunity to escape from a violent marriage by assuming the identity of one of the victims. Imogen knows that her husband, William, only married her for her money. She leaves London to start again, and meets and falls in love with kind and caring Adam Bennett. But unaware that her new identity is that of an ex-con, Imogen has the criminal underworld searching for her, certain that she knows the whereabouts of a fortune in jewels. And William, a successful heart surgeon, doesn't believe that she was killed in the bomb blast — but he's determined to make sure that she *stays* dead . . . for good.

JEANNE WHITMEE

POINT OF NO RETURN

Complete and Unabridged

CHARNWOOD
Leicester

First published in Great Britain in 2000

First Charnwood Edition
published 2008

British Library CIP Data

Whitmee, Jeanne
    Point of no return.—Large print ed.—
Charnwood library series
1. Impersonation—Fiction
2. Romantic suspense novels
3. Large type books
I. Title
823.9'14 [F]

ISBN 978–1–84782–238–3

Published by
F. A. Thorpe (Publishing)
Anstey, Leicestershire

Set by Words & Graphics Ltd.
Anstey, Leicestershire
Printed and bound in Great Britain by
T. J. International Ltd., Padstow, Cornwall

This book is printed on acid-free paper

1

'Wait! Please — come back!'

As Imogen hurried after the girl she could already see the blonde head disappearing over the top edge of the packed escalator. Damn! There were so many people. If she didn't hurry she'd lose sight of her.

'I'm sorry, excuse me,' she pushed her way past the first few people on the escalator, craning to get a better view of the cream cashmere coat rapidly disappearing from view. 'Someone's taken my coat and bag,' she explained breathlessly. 'I have to catch her.'

'I've got my mobile. Want me to ring the police?' offered the woman she had just elbowed aside. She was already opening her handbag but Imogen shook her head. The last thing she wanted was to involve the police. William would be furious.

'No thank you,' she said. 'I'm sure it's a mistake.'

'I doubt that,' the woman said. 'These stores are full of thieves nowadays. Can't turn your back for a minute. They shouldn't be allowed to get away with it.' She pointed to the shabby brown coat draped over Imogen's arm. 'I take it that's the one she swapped yours for.' She smiled cynically.

'Yes.' Imogen was barely listening as she tried to see how close to the bottom the other girl was.

1

'Why not just let me call the police?' the woman was insisting. She brandished her mobile phone under Imogen's nose. 'After all, that's what we pay them for you know. To catch . . . '

'*Please*! Will you mind your own business!' Imogen pushed her way past the woman and struggled down the remaining steps. She had to catch the girl and get her things back. With relief she stepped off the escalator. She could still see the girl doubling back towards the stairs. She was heading up towards the Regent Street exit. Imogen's heart bumped painfully as she ran after her. Once on ground level and outside in the street it would be so easy to lose her in the crowds of Christmas shoppers. That woman had been right. There must be dozens of thefts at peak shopping times like this. If only she'd been more careful. Why hadn't she kept her bag under her arm? All her money, her cheque book and store cards were in it. And her rings and bracelet, taken off when she had her manicure! Her stomach lurched as she remembered that her return rail ticket was in it too.

Elbowing her way through indignant passengers she reached the exit in time to see the girl turn left towards Piccadilly. She was actually wearing Imogen's cream cashmere coat now, and moving fast. The pale colour shone out luminously in the dusk. She must have pulled it on while she was on the escalator.

The cold air cut like a knife as Imogen left the warmth of the station. It had begun to snow and she paused briefly to slip her arms into the shabby brown coat as she ran. Better than getting wet!

Some detached, impersonal part of her mind took in the street decorations that were now sparkling through the failing light — tiny bulbs twinkling like stars in the bare branches of the trees, huge glittering snowflakes suspended above the street. A weary-looking Santa was selling novelties outside Liberty's and a barrow on the corner was piled high with crimson poinsettias, holly and mistletoe.

At the traffic lights Imogen caught sight of the girl again. She was crossing the road. Greatly relieved she began to run, praying that the light wouldn't turn to green before she reached the crossing. Pushing her way to the front of the group of people waiting to cross she almost knocked an elderly lady off her feet and turned to apologise, grasping her arm.

'I'm so sorry.'

'Well, *really*!' The woman shrugged off her hand and glared at Imogen indignantly. 'People nowadays have no manners! No respect at all!'

Closing her ears to the woman's protests, Imogen stepped on to the crossing and ran to the central island. The girl was on the other side now. She'd reached the Conduit Street junction. The light had turned red again, but she could still get across if she was quick. She just *had* to get her things back.

She stepped on to the road and ran across, ignoring the frantic hooting and the obscenity yelled by an impatient taxi driver. Breathless, she reached the far side and craned for a glimpse of the girl — with just enough time to see her disappearing round the corner.

And then — it happened.

The explosion lifted her bodily from her feet and threw her against something very hard. All around her was scream-filled chaos that seemed to echo inside her head — the sound of breaking glass, running feet and falling masonry. It was as though her head was splitting. Then she was being sucked into a swirling vortex — around and down — down into the whining, spinning blackness at the bottom.

2

The first time Imogen saw William Jameson he was playing cricket. She and Chris had gone along to the charity match in the hospital grounds. St Aubrey's doctors versus Guys porters.

It was a warm Sunday in early June; a perfect day with wispy clouds sailing high in a sky of purest blue. Imogen had been on nights, so Chris had packed a picnic lunch and both girls were in a light-hearted mood.

From the moment he opened the batting for the doctors Imogen had eyes for no one else. Chris, on the other hand, wasn't so impressed.

'Never trust a man with looks like that,' she said scathingly. 'They're usually all too aware of the effect they have on the opposite sex. And being a doctor won't help one little bit!'

But Imogen wasn't listening. 'If he's a doctor at St Aubrey's I can't think why I've never seen him before,' she was saying dreamily. 'I know I wouldn't have forgotten him if I had.'

For that afternoon she had to content herself with admiring the tall young man in the spotless white flannels and shirt from a distance as he scored sixty runs for the doctors' eleven, and then turned out to be a bowler to be reckoned with as well. Later that week she discovered, after a little subtle probing of Jenny Douglas, the hospital administrator's secretary, that he had just transferred from the hospital in Edinburgh where he had trained, and that he was the new junior registrar on the team of Mr Edward Mayhew, one of the most brilliant and respected cardiac surgeons in the country.

It was three days later that she found herself working with him in A&E when a patient was brought in with severe chest pains. She found herself unable to take her eyes off the handsome face and the strong, skilful fingers as he examined the patient.

When the man had finally been sent up to cardiology to have an ECG he looked at her and smiled.

'Probably nothing more than mild angina,' he said. 'The trouble with chest pains is that the more the patient panics, the worse they get.'

Imogen blushed, enchanted by the attractive Scottish accent and racking her brain for some intelligent remark with which to impress him.

'He was a typical heart attack candidate though, wasn't he?' she said.

'Really?' His eyebrows rose. 'And what might that be?'

She blushed an even deeper shade of pink. 'Well — fifty-plus, overweight, a heavy smoker, too, by the look of those stained fingers.'

He shrugged. 'Last week we did an angioplasty on a young woman of thirty-five. Slim as a rail, never touched a cigarette in her life. Never think typical, Nurse.' He looked at her enquiringly. 'Nurse?'

'Kendrick,' she supplied. 'Imogen Kendrick.'

'Right, Nurse Kendrick.' He smiled. 'Still, it

was perceptive of you to notice those things.'

She was turning away when he asked, 'When are you off duty, Imogen?'

Surprised she turned back to look at him. 'In half an hour.'

'That's good.' His dark eyes were as warm as chocolate. 'Live far from here?'

'The nurses' home.'

'Fine. Pick you up in an hour.'

'Sorry?' She shook her head. 'What for?'

He was already starting to walk away. 'Dinner of course. What else?'

★ ★ ★

They had dinner in a small Italian restaurant where William was obviously well known. A smiling waiter showed them to a secluded table with a red-and-white checked tablecloth and a pretty shaded candle lamp. Imogen was enchanted and right from that very first evening she knew deep down that she was destined to fall in love. William listened intently to everything she had to say. He was kind and attentive and not a bit conceited, as Chris seemed to think. She told him about losing both parents in a car accident when she was seven; about Aunt Agnes and St Margaret's School and how lonely she had been until she met Chris. As she relaxed over her second glass of Chianti she told him about how her aunt had died a year before, naming her in her will as sole beneficiary.

'It was such a shock,' she told him. 'Inheriting her house and all her money. I always felt that

7

she didn't like me very much. She never seemed to know quite what to do with me or what to talk about.'

He smiled. 'You have to admit that it must have been a bit disturbing for an elderly unmarried lady, suddenly finding herself with a seven-year-old to bring up and educate,' he said. 'And you know, people who have never shared their life with anyone often find it difficult to express what they feel.'

'I suppose realistically, there was no one else to leave her money to,' Imogen said thoughtfully. 'After all, I was her only living relative.'

'There are always cats' homes!' he said with a wry smile. 'I think you underestimate yourself.' His fingertips met hers across the table and it was as though an electric current passed between them. 'I'm sure you must have brought a lot of sunshine into her declining years.'

Imogen blushed and drew her hand away. 'Oh — I don't know about that.'

His dark eyes looked searchingly into hers. 'Has anyone ever told you that you have a refreshing air of innocence, Imogen?'

She lowered her eyes, acutely aware of the compelling dark ones still intently on her. 'No,' she whispered.

'Well you have. Not many girls nowadays have your delightful freshness. And by the way, I find Imogen a bit of a mouthful. Would you mind if I called you Genny?'

'No, if you like that better.' Through her surprise she absorbed the implication that they were going to be seeing more of each other.

8

When she looked up at him she found it almost impossible to tear her eyes away from his steady gaze. The tension between them tightened like stretched wire and, flustered, she looked hastily at her watch. 'Oh! Is that really the time? I'm on an early shift tomorrow. I really should get back.'

Immediately she wondered why she had said it. It sounded so stupidly naive and, anyway, the last thing she really wanted was for the evening to end. She felt gauche and awkward and acutely aware that she was handling the situation ineptly. She stole a glance at him, expecting him to be offended by her unintentional abruptness. Instead he merely smiled and nodded.

'Of course. How thoughtless of me. I should have asked.' He paid the bill and took her arm, escorting her out on to the pavement. In the cab on the way back to the hospital he took her hand.

'You're a very nervous little person, aren't you, Genny?' The dark eyes smiled at her gently.

'No, not at all. Not usually,' she said.

'Oh! Is it me then? Do I make you feel tense?'

'Of course not. I've had a lovely evening.' In truth she knew she had been trying a little too hard to impress him. He was a registrar, she a newly qualified nurse. He must be — what — at least eight years older? What could they possibly have in common? What could he see in her? She couldn't see any reason why he would want to ask her out again.

He walked with her to the nurses' home. 'Do you like living here?' he asked.

She shrugged. 'It's all right. I've been looking

for a flat though. I can afford one now. As a matter of fact I think I've found just what I want, but I'll have to see what my friend thinks of it.'

'You friend?'

'Christine Day. We were at school together and we always said we'd share a flat one day. She works for the *Daily Globe*. She started as a typist but now she's training to be a journalist,' she added proudly.

'Personally I think it's a mistake to share,' he said. 'A lot of good friendships have been spoiled like that.'

She shook her head. 'Perhaps you're right, but Chris and I are very close. Neither of us would ever intrude on the other's privacy.'

In the shadow of the doorway he drew her firmly into his arms and kissed her gently and experimentally on the lips. 'Goodnight, little Genny,' he said softly.

'Goodnight. And thank you for a lovely evening.'

'So — when do I see you again?'

She looked up at him breathlessly. So she hadn't put him off with her childish inexperience after all. 'Well — I don't know.'

The dark eyes searched hers. 'Of course if you don't want to . . . '

'Oh but I *do*,' she said quickly. 'Very much.'

'That's more like it.' He laughed softly and bent to kiss her again. 'I'll ring you then. Maybe you'll show me this flat you've found.'

'Yes. I will — if you like.'

★ ★ ★

'Well if you really want to know, I think he sounds really patronising,' said Chris.

'Patronising! Why do you say that?'

'Well, telling you that you were having dinner with him instead of asking, for starters,' Chris said. 'And this 'Genny' thing. No one's ever called you Genny. How would he like it if you announced that you were going to call him Willy? Some girls would have told him to get lost!'

They were having a picnic supper on the living room floor in Imogen's new flat. She'd decided to take it on her own in the end. It was too good an opportunity to miss; conveniently close to the shops and within easy reach of the hospital. She'd felt a little awkward about not asking Chris to share, but it would have been too small anyway, having only the one bedroom. But if Chris had been disappointed by the change of plan she certainly hadn't shown it, helping enthusiastically with the preparation and moving-in process.

For Imogen it was heaven to have a home of her own, almost for the first time she could remember. Over supper that evening she gave Chris a glowing account of her blossoming relationship with William.

'He's not patronising at all,' she protested. 'He's just a very positive, firm person. He's very ambitious — means to get to the top of his profession.'

'By riding roughshod over everyone if I'm any judge.'

'That's not fair. You haven't even met him

properly. I expect he's used to giving orders. Anyway no one ever got to the top by dithering.'

'True.' Chris buttered the last of the French bread thoughtfully. 'Just don't let him walk all over you though. You're not one of his minions, at least not when you're out on a date with him!'

'I won't. He wouldn't anyway.'

Chris looked at her ruefully. 'Mmm, I wouldn't be too sure. You've always been vulnerable when it comes to people you like, Imo,' she said frankly. 'Don't take it the wrong way. You're nobody's fool. You're definitely in the right job. I can't think of anyone I'd rather have looking after me if I were ill, and I know you can stand up for yourself when you have to. But — '

'OK, let's have it. *But* what?'

'Well, you do tend to see only the best in people. You let them take you in.'

'Thanks a bunch for the character analysis,' Imogen said dryly.

'I'm only thinking of you. I don't want to see you getting hurt.' Chris looked at her, her head on one side. 'Is he the reason you didn't ask me to share the flat?'

'No!' Imogen knew that she protested just a little too firmly. If she were completely honest with herself she had to admit that it wasn't just that she felt the flat would be too small for two. She and William had been seeing each other regularly for a month now and she knew that once she had moved into a place of her own he would expect to take their relationship a step further. She found the prospect exciting, yet a little frightening at the same time. There was an air of danger about William; a feeling of suppressed passion that she found irresistible — hypnotic, almost, though she couldn't bring herself to admit it, not even to herself.

Chris grinned. 'Come on, don't look so guilty. I'm not annoyed. As a matter of fact I'm moving myself next week.'

'Moving?' Imogen looked up in surprise. 'You dark horse! You never said a thing. Well, it'll be my turn to help you this time and — '

'No, you don't understand,' Chris put in. 'I'm moving in with Max.'

'Max Lindsay?' Imogen knew that Chris had been going out with the senior reporter at the *Daily Globe* for some weeks now, but she hadn't thought it that serious. She hadn't met him but Chris talked about him a lot. She knew, for instance, that he was something like twelve years older than Chris — and that he had a wife.

'Don't look so shocked,' Chris laughed. 'It makes sense, economically as much as anything else. I've been staying over at his place several nights a week for ages now. Seems a waste to keep paying out two rents. We get along pretty well. So — '

'Isn't he married?' Imogen interrupted bluntly.

'Separated,' Chris said. 'There's a divorce pending.'

'I see. So — do you love him?'

Chris looked startled. 'Love? You are sweet, Imo. You've been at those romantic novels again, haven't you?'

'What do you mean?' Imogen was puzzled and not a little hurt by Chris's cynicism. 'I happen to

13

think love is important. I've always thought you did too.'

'Oh — when we were starry-eyed teenagers. Maybe I still do, but that's for the future — for settling down. Maybe one day I will love Max. Or some other man. I don't know. For now I prefer to reserve my judgement. Meantime, Max and I have a lot in common. We're compatible. Things are good between us.'

'Sex, you mean?'

'Since you mention it, yes — among other aspects.'

Imogen began to gather up the plates. 'Well, I hope you don't regret it.'

'We won't. If we do we'll cut our losses, call it a day and no hard feelings.' She looked at her friend. 'Imo — tell me to mind my own business if you like, but have you slept with William yet?'

Imogen shrugged non-committally. 'No. But — '

'But you want to and you will do soon, which is why you wanted this place?'

'Everyone needs some privacy. William has one of those grotty little bedsits at the hospital and — '

'Is he hard up?'

Imogen laughed. 'Show me the registrar who isn't.' Her smile vanished as she suddenly realised what Chris was getting at. 'Are you suggesting what I think you're suggesting?'

'No. Forget I mentioned it.' Chris scrambled to her feet. 'OK. You've moved in, so now when's the house-warming party?'

★ ★ ★

14

The house-warming was a small affair. Just half a dozen of Imogen's fellow nurses and their assorted boyfriends. The flat wasn't large enough to hold many people. Chris brought Max along. Imogen disliked him on sight. He was a large, rather intimidating-looking man with a shock of dark hair and a matching beard. He looked out of place in her neat little flat and gave every indication of wanting to get the whole thing over with as soon as possible. In the kitchen, as Chris helped her replenish the bowls of snacks, Imogen said, 'I think Max feels this is all a bit beneath him.'

Chris looked at her sharply. 'Of course he doesn't. Why do you say that?'

'He's got this look about him. Like a reluctant uncle at a kids' party. I think he's expecting a clown to arrive any minute and start handing out balloons.'

'Don't be so touchy,' Chris said. 'He's older than most people here, that's all. He can't help being sophisticated.'

'Sophisticated!' Imogen laughed. 'Is that what you call it? Well, if he was expecting some kind of orgy he's going to be disappointed.' Realising she'd upset her friend, Imogen was immediately contrite. 'Sorry, Chris. I didn't mean that the way it sounded.'

'I should damn well hope not!'

'Please — don't let's fall out.'

Chris turned to look at her, her expression softening. 'Don't be daft. We know each other far too well for that. Look, don't take this the wrong way, Imo, but if you take my advice you'll give

15

William the push while there's still time.'

'Oh dear.' Imogen sighed. It was childish of Chris to want to hit back. 'Look, I said I'm sorry . . . '

'I mean it. He's trouble, Imo.'

'Rubbish! How can you say that? He's an educated professional man — a surgeon for heaven's sake, not some lout!'

'I know all that. It makes no difference. I just *feel* it. There's something about him . . . ' Seeing she was getting nowhere, Chris turned and picked up a tray. 'Oh come on, let's get back with these. You're not even listening, are you?'

The party ended soon after midnight, though Chris and Max had left at eleven. William stayed on to help tidy and wash up. Imogen was busy at the sink when he came into the kitchen and put the tray of glasses he was carrying down on the worktop. She felt him standing behind her and her heart began to quicken as she felt his lips on the nape of her neck. She felt him untying her apron and as she turned to look at him he took her face between his hands and kissed her hungrily. As his mouth left hers she laughed, holding her wet arms out.

'You do choose your moments! Look at me. I'm all covered in soap suds.'

'I know.' He picked up a teatowel and dabbed at her arms. 'But I can't wait any longer. I've been waiting for this moment all evening.' He lifted her arms and placed them round his neck. Then he scooped her up and carried her to the bedroom.

The blood sang in Imogen's ears as he deftly

undressed her. This was the moment she had longed for, yet she dreaded it with a kind of delicious fear and now she was almost dizzy with a mixture of excitement and apprehension. She was so inexperienced. Suppose she disappointed him?

But William gave no sign of disappointment. He was an exciting lover, teasing and tantalising her with his lips and hands, stroking and caressing her until her body was consumed by desire. He was passionate yet tender, holding himself in check for as long as he could, and when at last he unleashed his passion their combined climax was shattering.

Afterwards as they lay together, their limbs entwined, Imogen felt as though she were dreaming. But it was no dream. Through half-closed eyes she could see the thick dark hair of his chest, beaded with sweat — could feel the beat of his heart as it gradually slowed once more in rhythm with her own.

Every fibre of her body tingled. She felt sleepy and languorous, yet as light as thistledown — as though she might float away. Making love with William had been like a revelation. Some primeval instinct had aroused in her a response she had not known herself capable of. She felt proud and happy and so much in love that tears filled her eyes and spilled over on to William's naked chest.

She turned her head to look up at him. Somehow she had expected him to look as drowsy as she felt; instead his dark eyes burned with triumph and his lips curved into a smile.

'I was your first,' he said, his arms tightening round her. 'Your first lover.'

'Yes,' she whispered, smiling.

'I feel honoured,' he said, kissing her. 'And so proud of you.' Swiftly and without warning he rolled her over and straddled her body possessively with powerful thighs. He looked down at her with an expression of fiery domination. 'You're mine now,' he said, his eyes shining. 'No one can change that fact. I've made you mine. Are you happy about that?'

'Yes!'

'I love you, Genny. Say you love me too.'

'I do.'

'No, say it. I want to hear you say it.'

'Of course. I love you, William.'

He made love to her again. Powerfully, assertively this time, taking her to even greater heights. Much later they both sank into an exhausted sleep, the duvet on the floor and the pillows scattered. At dawn he woke her to make love again — and again.

They were having breakfast together when he said, 'I want you to marry me, Genny. Say yes. Say you want it too.'

She looked up in surprise, her cheeks colouring with delight and excitement. 'Oh, William!'

'Well?'

'Yes. I want it too.'

'But first I have some things to tell you. When you know everything about me you might change your mind,' he said, his head lowered.

'When I know — know what?' Her heart

18

contracting, she reached across the table to touch his hand. 'William, before you begin I want you to know that nothing about you could ever make me change my mind,' she told him softly.

'Darling girl,' he sighed and stroked her fingers thoughtfully 'My parents split up when I was ten,' he said slowly. 'I had a baby brother who died when he was three months old. It was supposed to have been what they call a cot death, but ever since his birth my mother had been . . . strange — unlike herself. Post-natal depression, as we know it nowadays. And my father . . . ' He glanced up at her. 'My father believed that she had killed him.'

Imogen gasped. 'Oh, William! How awful.'

'He was convinced. There were months of rows — him shouting, her weeping hysterically. It was terrible. Eventually he left and later they divorced.'

'Your poor mother. What happened to her?'

His fingers tightened round hers. 'She slipped further and further into the depths of depression till eventually she had to go into a hospital for the mentally ill.'

'Poor William.'

'I loved my mother very much and I missed her terribly. Like you, I was brought up by relatives who didn't really want me. There was boarding school and then university and training.' He patted her hand and looked up. 'That's it, basically. I just felt you had a right to know.'

She clasped both his hands in hers. 'It won't

19

make any difference. I love you, William. You're like me. You lost your family at an early age. We've both missed out on home and family, been deprived of love and security. Maybe I can make up to you for all that.'

He raised her fingers to his lips and kissed them. 'You already have my darling. I'm so lucky to have found you.'

★ ★ ★

'*Married*? You're getting married — so soon?' Chris asked incredulously. 'But you've only known him a few weeks!'

'More like months. Anyway, why should we wait?' Imogen asked. 'We love each other and neither of us has ever been surer of anything.'

'But . . . ' Chris was shaking her head, almost lost for words. 'Where will you live?'

'At the flat, just to start with, but William has his eye on this lovely house in Richmond.'

'Richmond! That's a bit upmarket, isn't it?'

'It's not all that expensive,' Imogen said defensively. 'It's what the estate agents call, 'ripe for modernisation'.'

'Mmm — at what cost?' Chris said sceptically. She glanced at her friend. 'I hope you're not going to be the one footing the bill for it all.'

'If I am that will be my business,' Imogen said briskly. 'When you marry someone you share everything. It's one of the joys.'

Chris raised an eyebrow. 'Specially for the one who's got nothing.' She held up her hand at Imogen's outraged expression. 'OK! I've done it

20

again. Don't say it, I'm too outspoken for my own good!' She reached out and grasped Imogen's hands. 'Look, I'm happy for you love, of course I am, but won't Richmond be a bit far out for you? I mean, all that travelling can be very tiring, especially when you're on night duty.'

'It won't be a problem. I've given in my notice.'

Chris stared at her. 'You're *leaving* — giving up nursing? But it's barely six months since you passed your finals, and you've always been so keen! Imo, you're not pregnant are you?'

'No! There'll be a lot to do, getting the house in shape. Anyway, William thinks it would be best.'

'And what do *you* think?'

'I think so too — naturally. It's all going to be the most enormous fun, doing the house up, having a real home of my own.'

Chris's expression softened. 'I know love. I can see that. Look, I was going to ask you to come home with me for a weekend next month. Mum always loves having you to stay and it'd be like old times in the school holidays, remember? You could do with a break so why not come?'

'So that you and your mother can sit me down and talk me out of marrying William? No thanks. Look, Chris, I'm almost twenty-two. I know my own mind and I love William. I've never been happier and I'm never *ever* going to want anyone else.'

'OK.' Chris threw up her hands in surrender. 'You win.'

'Anyway, it's settled. We're getting married in

three weeks' time. It'll be a small wedding at a register office as neither of us has any family. We'll arrange a meal or something for afterwards. You're my best friend and I want you to be there. And Max of course. But naturally I'll understand if you don't approve.'

Chris hugged her. 'Shut up, stupid! Take no notice of me. I expect I'm only jealous really. Just you try and keep me away.'

★   ★   ★

Imogen made a radiant bride. She wore a cream silk suit and carried a posy of peach-coloured roses and forget-me-nots. Her long fair hair, she wore loose about her shoulders. To Imogen's surprise William had invited consultant surgeon Edward Mayhew, and his daughter, to the wedding. Edward was a tall, stooped man of about sixty with sparse grey hair and kind blue eyes. Imogen liked him at once. Carole Dean, his daughter, however, was quite another matter. Like her father, she was tall but that was where the resemblance ended. She was dark haired and vibrant looking, with flashing dark eyes and a full, sensuous mouth. Imogen learned that she was divorced and kept house for her father — in Richmond.

'They'll be our neighbours,' William told her happily. 'By a strange coincidence I find that they live quite close to our new house. In the next road in fact.'

Privately Imogen hoped she wouldn't have to see too much of Carole Dean. She knew

22

instinctively that they would not get on.

Imogen and William spent a week's idyllic honeymoon in Italy, at a little town on the Adriatic coast. Their hotel balcony overlooked the sea and as she lay in bed in the warm autumn nights, sated with William's lovemaking, Imogen felt convinced that she must be the happiest girl alive.

It was on the last night that it happened. They were dining at their favourite restaurant at one of the tables placed outside under a striped awning. The air was warm and caressing, rich with the scent of flowers and redolent of good food and coffee. The waiter, a young man who had served them regularly during the week, had been especially attentive, knowing it was their last evening. He had made sure that they did not wait between courses and that the wine was chilled just as they liked it. As he served them their dessert, he paused to pay Imogen a compliment.

'The signora has beautiful hair,' he said. 'Unlike Italian ladies. So blonde and soft. It is like silk.' He smiled at William. 'Signore is a lucky man.'

Instantly William was on his feet, his dark eyes blazing with anger. 'Who the hell asked for your opinion?' he shouted.

Imogen was acutely embarrassed. 'William,' she whispered, aware of the glances of the other diners. 'Mario was only paying me a compliment.'

The waiter was apologetic, backing away and waving his hands. 'So sorry, signore. I mean no offence. Please — '

'Bring me the bill,' William demanded. The man hurried away and Imogen shook her head at him.

'Don't spoil our last evening,' she begged. 'Poor Mario meant no harm. He was only being polite.'

William did not reply. Getting to his feet, he grasped her hand and pulled her after him. 'We're leaving,' he said abruptly.

Back in their hotel room he was still shaking with rage. 'You encouraged that lecherous lout,' he accused. 'You were openly giving him the come-on.'

She was shocked. 'William! I wasn't.'

'I know these Latin types. Give them an inch and they'll take a mile.' He glared at her. 'Want to get raped, do you?'

'That's a horrible thing to say! Stop it, William. You're over-reacting.'

'Over-reacting, am I?' He took her by the shoulders and pushed her towards the mirror. 'Look at you! Look at the way you do your hair. It's an open invitation. Anyway, it looks a mess.' Before she knew it he had pulled open the drawer and taken out her nail scissors. She tried to pull away from him.

'William. No! What are you doing?'

But holding her fast by the crown of her hair he snipped savagely at the long tresses, ignoring her screams, until most of it lay around her on the carpet.

She stared down at it in horror. In the mirror her distraught face stared back at her, framed by the jagged mess. 'Look what you've done!' she

24

sobbed. 'What's the matter with you?'

Suddenly calm, William sank to his knees, his arms around her waist. 'Genny! Oh my darling, forgive me. I'm sorry — so sorry.'

She tried to push him away. 'I'll never forgive you. How dare you behave like that? You have no right!'

But his arms tightened around her waist. 'I have *every* right to expect you to be loyal to me,' he said fiercely. 'You're my wife. You belong to me and no other man. I love you, Genny. I thought you loved me.'

She stared at him, fear making her stomach quake. It was beyond her comprehension. Why was he behaving like this — like some terrifying stranger? How could he treat her this way?

'There can be no love without trust, William,' she said. 'You accused me of something I would never do. And now . . . ' She fingered the ragged strands of hair, tears streaming down her cheeks. 'Look at me. Look what you've done to me.'

He stood up and stepped back from her, shaking his head. Then, without another word, he turned and left the room.

★ ★ ★

It was three hours later that he returned. Convinced that he had gone for good, Imogen cried herself to sleep, puzzled and distressed by his behaviour. She awoke to feel him slipping into bed beside her.

'Genny — are you awake?' he whispered, pressing close to her back.

25

She stirred and turned over. 'Where have you been?'

'Walking,' he said. 'By the sea, trying to come to terms with what happened.' He reached out to touch her hair. 'My God, Genny, I can't believe I did that to you. Do you hate me? Do you want to go home and get a divorce? I wouldn't blame you if you did.'

She touched his face. 'I just wish I could understand what made you so angry, that's all.'

He put his arms around her and pulled her close. 'It's because I love you so much,' he said huskily. 'I can't bear the thought of any other man — '

'There *is* no other man,' she told him. 'There never will be. How many times do I have to prove it to you?'

He cupped her face and looked into her eyes. 'Genny — I promise you faithfully that nothing like that will ever happen again. Forgive me, please?' He kissed her. Then his lips were on her eyes, her hair, her neck; travelling down to her breasts, his hands following, teasing, caressing. She felt the familiar excitement stirring, tightening her stomach muscles and quickening her heartbeat to a drumming frenzy.

'I — I forgive you,' she whispered, her fingers in his hair. 'I love you, William. I always will.'

And then he was on her, his weight crushing her deep into the bed. And inside her, thrusting, claiming, possessing; arousing her senses until she was oblivious to everything but the tumult of sensation that chased away all sanity and reason.

★ ★ ★

Next morning, before they caught the plane home, William took her to the town's smartest beauty parlour and she had her hair expertly cut in a short, bouncy bob. When she emerged his eyes shone with pride.

'You look beautiful,' he said, bending to kiss her.

3

Although Imogen had put down the deposit for the house in Richmond, it was William's name that was on the deeds. When she suggested that it should be in both their names he had told her dismissively that she did not understand these things and that, as he was paying the mortgage, this was the normal way of doing things. He said that it made no difference in the end because the house belonged to both of them. Finally she gave in. But when he tried to convince her that she should put all the money from her inheritance into their joint account she was adamant. His patience exhausted, he raged at her.

'For Christ's sake, Genny, what's the matter with you?' he ranted. 'Why can't you trust me? What do you think I'm going to do — run off with all your precious money? I had no idea you could be so bloody stubborn.'

'It's not that,' she told him. 'It's just that Aunt Agnes wanted me to have some independence. That was why she left me the money, so I think I should do as she said.'

He ran an exasperated hand through his hair. 'What the hell did your Aunt Agnes — some crusty old maid — know about finance? Listen, I can invest the money — make it work for us — for *you*. I know about these things.'

'But it's earning good interest now,' she argued. 'I'd really rather leave it where it is — at least for now. If I leave it for two more years I get a bonus.'

He shrugged, his eyes as hard as granite. 'All right. Have it your own way. But you'll regret it.'

Later she discovered what he meant. As he was leaving for the hospital he said, 'I'll be late home tonight. There's a meeting. I'll sleep in the spare room.'

He slept in the spare room for a fortnight without a word of explanation, but Imogen knew that it was his way of punishing her.

★ ★ ★

It had been Christmas before they moved into the house in Richmond and well into spring before the work on it was finally completed. Imogen was proud of their lovely home and during those first hectic months she didn't miss her job at all. But as time went by and life settled into a daily routine she began to miss the friendship of her fellow nurses and the busy life of the hospital. She'd even begun to make casual enquiries about vacancies at St Aubrey's — with a view to returning.

One afternoon in early May she was just about to start working in the garden when the doorbell rang. Opening the door she was surprised to find Carole Dean waiting outside.

'Imogen, my dear!' Carole smiled. 'I thought it was high time I called on you,' the consultant's daughter went on. Her smile slipped a little as she saw Imogen's obvious dismay. 'Oh dear, I suppose I should have telephoned first. Are you going out — expecting someone else?'

'No, no.' Imogen quickly adjusted her face, forcing a smile. 'Please come in. I'd have invited you round before. It's just that we've been up to our necks in builders' clutter till recently and the house hasn't been fit for entertaining.'

'So I hear from William. He tells me you'll be organising a house-warming party any day now.'

'Really?' It was the first that Imogen had heard of it. 'I mean, yes, of course we will.'

Carole was looking around the hall appraisingly. 'Well, well. Very nice. Did you choose the decor yourself?'

'Most of it.'

'Really?' The word was inflected with an incredulity that was almost insulting.

Imogen swallowed hard and tried to ignore it. 'Do come in. I'll make some tea,' she said.

'That would be lovely. I'm sure it's high time we had a girls' get-together.'

Imogen couldn't see any reason why they should. She couldn't imagine that she and Carole could possibly have anything in common, but she knew that as the daughter of William's boss, she was someone to be cultivated. William had made that very plain.

The drawing room, decorated in shades of ivory and moss green, had a view over the garden. Carole went to the French windows and exclaimed gushingly.

'Oh, how heavenly! Your view is almost nicer than ours,' she enthused. She turned to sweep her gaze over the decor of the room, her critical eyes darting into every corner. 'You've made this really quite nice,' she conceded. 'The lounge at my flat in Kensington was this colour. It was very fashionable at the time,' she added pointedly. 'That was where I lived before I moved back in with poor Daddy.'

She sat on the settee and accepted the tea that Imogen brought in, declining a slice of her home-baked sponge cake.

'I won't, if you don't mind. I try my best to keep in shape.' She appraised Imogen's slender figure, trying hard to keep the envy out of her eyes. 'You must join our health club,' she said. 'It would help you to build up a little firm flesh in the right places. Husbands prefer a woman to be — shapely, don't you think?'

Imogen made no reply. She was tempted to remark that Carole's husband obviously hadn't. But she kept the thought to herself.

'There's a waiting list of course, but I'm a member there,' Carole said. 'I'll introduce you if you like.'

'Thanks, but I think I'll be getting enough exercise out in the garden now that spring is here,' Imogen said.

'Oh dear! Don't you have a gardener?'

'Oh no. I don't want one. I'm looking forward to it. I've always wanted a garden of my own.'

Carole looked disapproving. 'Oh well, if you don't mind getting dirt under your nails and ruining your manicure. Each to his own, I suppose. Personally I find my social life is too busy for that kind of thing.' She sipped her tea, looking speculatively at Imogen over the rim of her cup. 'You're very lucky. William is a brilliant surgeon, and an absolute poppet,' she giggled girlishly. 'But obviously you already know that. How thrilling for you to have worked with such a dedicated man.'

'I never actually worked with him,' Imogen told her. 'Except in Casualty. I only did a brief spell in the theatre during my training.'

'Oh? What a pity. I always think it must be wonderful, working alongside a gifted surgeon, especially when he's also your husband. I can tell you that he's *very* popular, among the staff as well as the patients.'

Imogen smiled. 'I'm sure you're right.'

'Daddy thinks very highly of him. He relies on him more and more as the months go by. When he retires I wouldn't be at all surprised if — ' She broke off with a simpering smile. 'There I go again, opening my mouth and saying too much.'

Imogen smiled. 'It's nice to know that William's valued.'

'Oh he is. Very much so.' She paused. 'And it must be wonderful to know that it's within your power to help his career.'

'Have you finished your tea?' Imogen asked, not sure what the other woman was driving at. 'Would you like another cup?'

Carole looked at her watch. 'No. Actually I must dash. It's our daily's day off and I have to prepare dinner tonight.' As she stood up she asked, 'Do you play golf?'

Imogen shook her head. 'Afraid not.'

'That's a pity.' Carole frowned. 'Don't take this the wrong way, Imogen — I may call you that? — it's just that with William climbing the

32

professional ladder, so to speak, it might be wise of you to try to socialise a little more. You should try to interest yourself in his work and his leisure activities more.'

Imogen blushed, deeply indignant. 'I have been rather busy,' she said coolly. 'With the house and everything.'

'That's another thing. Maybe you should try to delegate more. You know, look around for a cleaning woman, gardener — that kind of thing. It would give you more time to get about and meet people; the *right* people if you see what I mean. Create the right ambience.'

Imogen bit back a sharp reply. 'Well, I won't have much time when I go back to nursing,' she said.

Carole stared at her. 'Go back? You're going back to nursing! But why?'

'I like my job. It isn't all that long since I qualified and it seems a waste to give it up. And now that the house is finished there isn't really enough for me to do at home,' Imogen explained.

'Oh, I see.' Carole looked disapproving. 'Well of course if you feel you have some sort of vocation.' She paused. 'Still, I'd have thought it was the last thing William would have wanted.' She drew on her gloves. 'Oh well, perhaps it's in your blood.' She made it sound like some kind of disease. 'Was your father a doctor?'

Imogen shook her head. 'As a matter of fact my parents ran a newsagent's shop — until they were both killed in a car accident.'

'Oh dear!' Carole frowned. 'How awful for you.'

Somehow her expression and tone of voice managed to convey that she felt it far more 'awful' for Imogen's parents to be newsagents than to be dead.

'Well — it's been lovely meeting you again and I shall look forward to that house-warming party!' She flashed her smile, reminding Imogen of a piranha fish. 'Meantime, I'm sure we'll be seeing a lot of each other now that we're almost neighbours.'

As Imogen closed the door behind her, she let out her breath explosively. 'Not if I can help it!' she said aloud.

That evening over dinner she recounted Carole's visit to William. She was sure that William must find Carole Dean as overbearing as she did and she tried to make the encounter sound entertaining. But he made it clear that he did not share her amusement.

'Genny, I'm sure I don't need to remind you that Carole's father is my boss.'

'Of course. She didn't let me forget it for a moment.' She looked at him. 'By the way, she said that you'd mentioned a housewarming party to her.'

He glanced up at her. 'Just an idea.'

'You never said anything to me.'

'I was waiting for you to suggest it. After all, it's your province.'

'Maybe we should have one later, when we've had time to get to know our neighbours better,' she said. 'Meantime, we could invite a few friends round for a meal one evening.'

'Who, for instance?'

'Chris and Max for starters, and Mr Mayhew and Carole too.'

'Together? I don't think so.' He laid down his knife and fork. 'Genny — I think it's time to drop certain people, don't you?'

She frowned. 'Who?'

'Your friend Chris and her — live-in lover,' he said scathingly.

'Forget my friends? Why would I want to do that?'

He sighed. 'Do I really have to spell it out for you?'

She felt her cheeks colouring. 'Yes, I'm afraid you do.'

He shook his head. 'To begin with — that man — Max Lindsay, the newspaper hack. He's hardly the kind of man you'd want to be seen associating with, now is he?'

'Why?'

'Why? He looks like some sort of vagrant. All that hair. And his clothes. The man's a lout!'

'I happen to know that he got a first at Cambridge,' Imogen said. 'And he does have a very good job on a national newspaper.' She wasn't keen on Max herself but not for the same reasons as William. 'Anyway, if Chris thinks he's all right that's good enough for me!'

'Well, if you're going to entertain people like that you'd better do it when I'm not here,' he told her icily. 'And certainly not at the same time as the Mayhews.'

His remarks stung, but in the end Imogen

decided that it would perhaps be more comfortable to have the Mayhews to dinner on their own.

The date was chosen and the invitation accepted and Imogen spent all afternoon in the kitchen, nervously preparing the meal. She studied all her cookery books carefully and chose three fairly simple courses; dishes she knew she could cook successfully. She didn't intend to give Carole anything to find fault with.

Everything seemed to have gone well until they reached the coffee stage. Then Carole suddenly looked up at her and said, beaming her piranha smile, 'So when are you planning your return to work, Imogen?'

Imogen stole a glance at William. She hadn't yet discussed her intention to return to work with him. 'I don't really know,' she said. 'So far it's just an idea.'

Carole looked at William. 'How does it feel to have such a dedicated wife, William?' she asked. 'So many women would be perfectly happy to sit back and enjoy a lovely home like this, but Imogen tells me she can't wait to get back to the drama of hospital life, can you dear?'

William glowered at Imogen across the table and Edward Mayhew put in quickly, 'We can certainly do with all the nurses we can get at St Aubrey's. This steak and kidney pie is delicious, Imogen. The pastry is as light as a feather.'

The moment they had closed the door on the departing Mayhews, William turned on her. 'What the hell was all that rubbish about you going back to nursing?'

'It was just something that came up in conversation, that afternoon when Carole came round for tea.'

'I see. I suppose it didn't occur to you to ask what I thought before spreading the good news far and wide!'

'I was going to,' she said defensively. 'Carole made it sound as though it was cut and dried. It was only an idea.'

'Well it's one you can forget,' William said arbitrarily. 'If you'd mentioned it before I'd have put a stop to it there and then.'

Imogen caught her breath. 'Don't I get any say in it at all?'

He rounded on her. 'I'd have expected you to know what's expected of you as my wife, Genny. When you didn't I had to get Carole to come and tactfully brief you. But even now it doesn't seem to have sunk in.'

She frowned. 'You — asked *her* to come and speak to me?' She was remembering Carole's puzzling remarks about mixing with the right people and social climbing. 'You asked *her* . . . Why couldn't you have told me what you wanted?'

'I thought it would come better from another woman,' he said. 'But I didn't expect to have to ask another woman to instruct my wife in the duties she should be expected to know.'

'Well if Carole Dean is such a wonderful wife how is it her husband is out of the picture?' She gasped with shock at the dark expression in his eyes as he took a step towards her.

'Carole is a very clever woman,' he told her. 'She's an accomplished hostess and a great asset to her father's career.' His eyes glinted. 'And while we're on the subject, that meal you served this evening was pathetic. I was ashamed and humiliated.'

Imogen recoiled. She'd worked so hard on the meal and thought everyone had enjoyed it. 'But — Mr Mayhew said it was delicious,' she said.

'Huh!' He gave a bark of mirthless laughter. 'What else could he say? I could see him struggling to get rid of it. What Carole thought of it I dread to think. She has a gourmet diploma. Steak and kidney pie followed by lemon mousse. I ask you! It was like something dished up in a factory canteen!'

'Well then in future perhaps you'd better get a caterer in,' she said warmly. 'Or take them out to a restaurant.' She turned away, but William caught at her arm and jerked her round painfully.

'Don't speak to me like that. And don't turn your back on me! First thing tomorrow, you'd better enrol for some cookery classes!' he instructed. 'And while you're at it get yourself signed up for some schooling in simple etiquette too. You behave like a guttersnipe sometimes.' He grasped her shoulders as she made to move away. 'And you think you have time to go back to nursing!' he said with contempt. 'Think again, Genny. Bloody well *think* again!' He strode off into his study and slammed the door.

She wept as she got ready for bed, deeply hurt by William's behaviour. She had done her best to make this evening a success. What was more she knew that Edward Mayhew had enjoyed his meal, whatever William said. But the idea of William discussing her with Carole and asking her to pass on tips was the worst humiliation. It was almost too shaming and hurtful to contemplate.

She climbed into bed. William had not come up. She imagined he would be sleeping in the spare room again. But she had only just turned off the light when the door opened and he came in. He had already undressed and climbed silently into bed beside her.

'Turn over, Genny,' he said into the darkness. She turned, expecting an apology, a kiss or some tender remark of remorse for his harsh treatment. Instead he straddled her swiftly and pushed up her nightdress. Shocked, she tried to push him away.

'No! William — don't!'

But he pushed her thighs apart with one powerful knee and took her, violently and painfully, his hands cruelly kneading her flesh while his mouth crushed hers with brutal disregard for her protests. When it was over he rolled away from her, ignoring her sobs, to lie with his back to her.

For several minutes she lay shaking, tears streaming down her cheeks, then, unable to lie there any longer she slipped out of bed and went into the bathroom. Standing under the shower she let the warm water soothe her bruised body till her trembling ceased and she was able to relax again.

When she came back into the room he was standing by the bed. She flinched and turned away, but he crossed the room to pull her into his arms.

'Genny — Genny. Forgive me,' he whispered. 'Never allow that to happen again.'

'Why did you do it?' She burst into fresh tears. 'Why did you want to hurt me like that?'

'It's because I get afraid,' he whispered. 'Afraid and angry when you want to shut me out — when you want to do things without me, without telling me. Promise you won't do it again, Genny.'

'But I didn't *do* anything, William,' she said, her whole body trembling with shock. 'The things you said — and what you did — I don't understand.'

'I want you to be here for me, Genny. All the time. I want you to be my wife and — and nothing else. It's not too much to ask, is it?' He held her away from him and looked into her eyes, his own as dark as night, the pupils pin-points of fire. 'Well, is it?'

There was something here that was beyond her comprehension and for the first time she knew stirrings of real fear.

'If ever I try to do anything like that again I want you to promise you'll stop me,' he said urgently. 'Hit me — slap my face — anything to bring me to my senses. Say you'll do it.'

'All right. I will.'

'Say you love me, Genny,' he urged. 'You haven't said it lately.'

His arms around her were like steel bands, crushing the breath out of her. 'I — I love you,' she faltered, almost inaudibly.

'*Again*. Say it again.'

'I love you.' She could hear the tremor in her own voice.

'That's better. Let's go back to bed.'

In the darkness she lay tense and rigid, feeling the intimidating heat of his body, listening as his breathing deepened and he fell asleep.

It was next morning at breakfast that he said suddenly, 'There is a way you could help me, Genny.'

She looked up. 'In what way?'

'I know you want me to be successful.'

'Of course.'

'Once I get a consultancy I'm going to need to have a surgery here at home. I'll need a consulting room — something impressive.'

'Yes.'

'It's something we could be doing now, Genny — so as to be ready. We could put that money of yours to good use.'

'I see.'

'I'll need a better car too. Something that will raise my status. A Mercedes or a BMW. It's for our future, Genny — for both of us.'

'I know,' she conceded. 'It's just that we've spent all the available money on furnishing the house. The rest is tied up.'

'Tied up! For how long?'

'Five years.'

'But you could still get at it?'

'I suppose so.'

'Better go and see to it then.'

She looked at him. 'William, I'd like to learn

41

to drive too. And maybe buy a little car of my own.'

He turned to her sharply. 'Whatever for? There's no need.'

'But I'd like to.'

'It would be a waste of money. Much better to stick to public transport. There are plenty of buses and the station is only five minutes' walk away.'

'But I'd like to drive.'

'I doubt if you'd take to it. Driving nowadays is too hazardous. The traffic in London is horrendous.'

Imogen was stunned by his arbitrary dismissal of the idea. It was so mean of him. She thought about it all that day, knowing that she really should assert herself on the subject. After all, it would be her own money she was spending.

She made an appointment to see the manager of the building society as William had suggested, but he strongly advised against withdrawing the money, reminding her of the sizeable bonus she would earn by leaving it where it was until the investment matured. She agreed.

When she told him, William was furious. 'You said you'd take the money out. You promised.'

'But I'll lose so much, William. And there's only a few more months to run. Couldn't we wait and have the work done next year? After all, there's no real hurry, is there?'

He drew in his breath impatiently. 'But I've already booked a builder to start next week! Now I'll have to take out another mortgage on the house. It's too bad, Genny! How can you let me down like this? How can you be so selfish?'

He hardly spoke through dinner and spent most of the evening in his study, going out later and not returning until the small hours.

★ ★ ★

Carole raised herself on one elbow to look down at William.

'Daddy told me you took over for him in theatre today. Managed a difficult and complicated by-pass on your own.' She smiled. 'He's always saying how brilliant you are. He's getting quite frail, William. He'll retire within the year and you'll get the job for sure. I'll see to that.' She kissed him hungrily, exploring his mouth with a rapacious tongue. 'Do you know what I'd like?' she whispered in his ear.

He laughed. 'I think I can guess.'

'No, not that.' She ran her fingers over his chest. 'At least not for the moment. What I'd really enjoy would be to watch you operate.'

'Would you? Well, that can be arranged. Although you'd probably have to be content with sitting in with the students and seeing it on CCTV.'

'No. I want to be there, in the theatre: seeing you make the incision; getting the close-up views and feeling the tension.' Her eyes glinted and she shivered with excitement. 'The atmosphere of it all.' She bent her head to nibble the smooth flesh of his shoulder. 'The thought of having a human life right there, in your hands — having a life balanced on the edge of extinction . . . ' She bit

43

him hard, making him wince. 'Mmm. It would be a real turn-on.'

'As if you needed one!' He pushed her back and rolled over her. 'I've never known a woman like you, Caro, you're absolutely insatiable.'

She smiled up at him. 'So — could you fix it?'

'I don't know. I'll see.' He paused to glance at his watch and she groaned.

'God! Married men are all the same, one eye on the clock all the time!' She pushed him away. 'Can't you wait to get back to *her*?'

'You know it's not that.'

'Did she come across with the cash for your surgery?'

'She will,' he said non-committally. 'And till then I've obviously got to tread carefully.' He began to get out of bed but she grasped his arm and pulled him back.

'Are you still sleeping with her?' she demanded.

'Well of course I am. I can hardly avoid it, can I? But you know it's only a matter of time.'

'How do I know that?'

'Because I tell you!'

'Why should I believe you? Sometimes I think you're just stringing me along.'

'I've told you, I'm working on it.'

'In what way? Why can't you tell me?'

'I just am. That's all you need to know. If you don't believe me you'll bloody well have to do the other thing!'

'Give her hell, William,' she said, her eyes glittering. 'Make her suffer. She deserves it!'

'Shut up about it, can't you? Just shut up!'

He looked angry and her flesh tingled with excitement as she goaded him further. 'Do you still make love to her?' When he turned away she grabbed at his shoulders and held him fast, her long red fingernails digging into his flesh. 'You *do*, don't you? How can you bear to, William? Perhaps you shut your eyes and pretend it's me. What's she like in bed? Is she as pathetic as she looks?'

'What do you think?'

'Does she do this to you? And this?' She pushed him back and went to work on him, her hair sweeping his naked skin as her greedy mouth sought out his most sensitive and erogenous places. As she teased him with her tongue, her sharp teeth and her expert fingers, he fought to control his arousal, till at last the urge was too strong for him. With a cry he seized her, throwing her on to her back and taking her swiftly in the tempestuous frenzy of lust she relished so much.

Later she watched him sleepily through narrowed eyes as he hurriedly dressed. She was so glad she had persuaded William to rent the Kensington flat for their meetings. She lived for the snatched moments she spent with him, loving the battle of wills that took place every time they were alone together. The animal intensity of their shared passion was exhilarating; the most thrilling thing in her life. She knew that one day he would be hers and that when he was she would conquer him. She looked forward to the challenge. Some day she would be in control of him just as she was in control of her father. It was no fun with Daddy any more. He was old and tired. He just gave in and let her have whatever she wanted. William now — ah, William was different. With William the battle was everything. He was strong — a virile and exciting opponent. Eventually of course she would win as she always did. But not yet — not too soon.

4

When Chris rang and suggested lunch Imogen was thrilled.

'Oh, Chris, that would be lovely!'

They hadn't met since the disastrous occasion six months before when Chris and Max had come to lunch and William had come home unexpectedly. He had made his displeasure clear by turning on his heel and walking straight out of the house again, not returning until after they'd left. Since that day she'd spoken to Chris regularly on the phone, but had avoided inviting her again. She felt guilty about it.

'You're sure William won't mind?' Chris was asking.

'Of course not. Why should he?' Imogen had said bravely. But quite how William would feel about her going up to town to meet her old school friend she hardly dared guess. In the end she decided not to tell him. She'd be home before him anyway, so there was no need for him to know. Lately she'd taken to indulging in these little deceits. It did William no harm not to know if she went for a day's shopping or to see a film. He could hardly expect her to sit at home waiting for him all day. It was lonely and boring. And now that the builders were hard at work, building the extension that was eventually to become William's private consulting room, she was

47

beginning to find the house noisy and claustrophobic too.

William played golf with Carole most weekends. Imogen had suggested to him that perhaps she should learn. He had dismissed the idea abruptly.

'I think not.'

'Why not, William?' she asked. 'It's something we could share.'

He sighed with studied patience. 'Genny, Hayesmere Golf Club is exclusive. They'd never let someone like you loose on their greens, hacking up the turf and getting in everyone's way.'

'But they must have learners there,' she argued.

'Perhaps, but I have no intention of my wife being one of them,' he said. 'I won't have you making me look a fool, Genny.'

Then there was the worrying business of her sleep walking. As far as she knew she had never suffered from sleep walking in her life, not even as a child when she had suffered the trauma of losing both parents. Now, according to William, she did. She would wake during the night with the covers off, feeling cold and shivery. Then William would tell her that it had occurred again.

She had no memory of what she did during her bouts of somnambulism, but when things began to go missing it was assumed that she had hidden them. First it was William's favourite pen; then his cufflinks — a book, one of his golf clubs. It worried her a lot, especially when the things were eventually found at the bottom of the ornamental pond in the garden.

More recently, and most upsetting, there had been the business of the kitten. Imogen had found the little black stray in the garden; tiny with huge blue eyes and four white feet, and fallen in love with him. Although she had telephoned the police and put an advert in the evening paper, no one came to claim him. William seemed to like the little creature, too, and was quite happy for Imogen to keep him. She named him Twinkle and spent hours playing with him.

When he went missing she was devastated. She looked everywhere and spent two days combing the neighbourhood for him. William was unconcerned, insisting that cats often behaved like this and that Twinkle would eventually turn up.

Days went by and there was no sign of him. On the fourth day Imogen was weeding the rockery that surrounded the pond in the garden when something lying on the bottom caught her eye. When she reached into the shallow water to pull it out she screamed with horror. The kitten had obviously drowned some days before and had been lying at the bottom of the pond ever since.

She buried the pathetic, bedraggled little creature at the bottom of the garden and when William came home she broke the news to him, tears running down her cheeks.

'How could it have happened?' she asked. 'He hated water. He was afraid of it. He never went near the pond.' The answer was clear to see in William's eyes. She shook her head, gasping with horror and disbelief. 'No! I couldn't have. Oh my God, William, tell me I didn't. Tell me it wasn't me!'

He drew her into his arms and held her. 'I think you should see someone, Genny,' he said. 'And maybe we'd better not replace poor little Twinkle. At least, not yet.'

The incident had shaken her badly, making her fear so much for her sanity that she put off making an appointment with her doctor, afraid of what he might tell her. When Chris rang and suggested meeting, she was relieved to have something to look forward to. Something that would take her mind off the disturbing events in her life.

★ ★ ★

They met at their favourite restaurant on The Strand. Ordering a glass of wine each, they settled down at their corner table to catch up on their news.

'Long time no see,' Chris said cheerfully. 'What have you been doing with yourself all these months?'

Imogen shrugged. 'Oh — I don't know. I always seem to be busy. I told you we're having an extension built. And time flies, doesn't it?'

Chris eyed her with some concern. It was almost two years since Imogen's wedding and six months since their last meeting. She could see a disturbing change in her friend. She was used to

50

the new short hairstyle that altered her appearance, but apart from that she had changed her style of dressing. The clothes she wore looked expensive, but oddly out of character and too old for her. She was wearing an over-sweet, heavy perfume too, instead of the light flowery one she had always liked.

'You're thinner,' she said. 'What is it? All this building work getting you down, or aren't you eating properly?'

'I don't think I've lost any weight,' Imogen said defensively. 'I'm as fit as anything — apart from — '

'Apart from what?'

Imogen shook her head. 'Nothing — a bit of sleep walking, that's all.'

Chris took a sip of her wine. 'OK, I admit it. I'm jealous. You know me. However hard I diet I never could get down to your weight. I bet I'm the only woman on earth who can put on weight on a diet of fresh air! I ought to be in the *Guinness Book of Records*!' She laughed. 'It's a good job Max likes his women well upholstered.'

'How is Max?'

'He's great. He's left the paper by the way. He's freelancing now. It's a precarious way to make a living but he seems to think he can earn more money. And I have to admit that he has a nose for a good story — *and* a ruthless streak too, which helps,' she said with a slightly wistful air. 'That's my one failing where this job is concerned. I care too damned much.'

Imogen smiled. 'Don't ever let anything change that.' She sipped her wine. 'Did Max's divorce come through yet?'

Chris shook her head. 'No, unfortunately. There are endless disputes with his ex over maintenance.'

Imogen looked up in surprise. 'He has children? You never said.'

'That was because I didn't know,' Chris said wryly. 'Plays his cards very close to his chest over some things, my Max. He has two boys. Both in their teens and about to embark on expensive education. Neither of them wants anything to do with their dad, yet they still expect him to fork out for their needs!' Chris looked up with a resigned smile. 'Still we're getting it all sorted. You don't want to hear about that. Tell me about you.'

'Me? Oh, I'm fine.' Imogen played with the stem of her wine glass.

'Great! William?'

'He's fine too.'

'And what about all your posh new neighbours? Film stars and all sorts, I bet.' Chris held up her hand. 'Don't tell me, let me guess — they're fine too.' She grinned. 'Jazzing it up with the rich and famous every night of the week?'

'Not really.'

'Right. So much for all the news.' Chris peered closely at her friend, noting the fine lines of strain around her eyes and the way her coat hung loosely on her thin frame. 'Imo,' she touched Imogen's hand. 'You are all right love, aren't you?'

'Of course I am.'

'No you're not. Look, we've known each other far too long for you to pull the wool over my eyes. There's something wrong — want to tell me about it?'

Imogen shook her head. 'We've come out to enjoy ourselves. You don't want to listen to me complaining.'

'So there *is* something to complain about?'

'No! It's just . . . ' Imogen hesitated. She longed to tell someone about her fears. Her bewildering mental state and the way her marriage seemed to be heading for disaster — and yet . . .

'You mentioned sleep walking,' Chris probed. 'What's all that about?' To her horror, Imogen dissolved into tears. 'Oh God, Imo, I didn't mean to upset you love.' She watched helplessly as Imogen searched her handbag for a tissue and struggled for control. 'Listen,' she said decisively. 'I'm going to get you a brandy, and then I want to hear what's bothering you. You obviously need to talk to someone.'

Imogen sipped at the brandy and felt its warmth relax her. Haltingly and painfully, she told Chris about her sleep walking and about Twinkle, something which still hurt and disturbed her deeply.

'Oh, Chris, he was such a sweet little thing. So helpless. I loved him. If I could do that to him what am I turning into?'

Chris frowned. 'Look, Imo, I'm not an authority on sleep walking but I can't believe that you'd ever do anything asleep that you wouldn't be capable of while awake. It surely must be a bit like hypnotism. No one can hypnotise you into any action contrary to your nature. I did an article on hypnotism recently and I do know that.'

Imogen shook her head helplessly. 'William thinks I should see a doctor. Perhaps I should.'

'Maybe it isn't such a bad idea at that,' Chris said thoughtfully.

'So you think I'm ill too — mentally ill?'

'No, I don't! And I think a doctor would confirm that.'

'I try so hard to please William,' Imogen went on. 'I go to the cookery classes he wanted me to go to. I gave up the idea of going back to work. I even tried to get my investments released before the term was up.'

Chris's eyes widened. 'He asked you to hand over the money your aunt left you?'

'Not hand over — just make available for the building work. To save him having to borrow,' Imogen said. 'William isn't mean. He's really very generous. He's always buying me presents — makeup, perfume. He bought me this coat.'

'Do you ever get to choose the things you like?' Chris inquired wryly.

'Well, no — he likes to surprise me.'

Chris regarded her friend across the table for a moment. The cream cashmere coat she was wearing looked expensive, but it wasn't 'her'. And the heavy perfume was one she'd always said she hated. Clearly William was manipulating her. Chris could see that she was already regretting unburdening herself. She'd started to clam up — smooth things over. Recognising that she would get no more out of her friend today, Chris smiled. 'Listen love. You know I won't say anything about what you've told me. And if you ever need me — for whatever reason at all — just ring me.' She patted Imogen's hand. 'Day or night,' she added. 'I'm always here for you.'

★   ★   ★

When Imogen arrived home, at first she thought that the builders had packed up and gone for the day, but when she walked through to look round the newly built extension, she discovered one carpenter still working on, trying to finish. He looked up with a smile as she came through.

'Mrs Jameson. Hi! Not long now,' he remarked cheerily. 'Just got to finish these cupboards and the bookshelves and you'll be all ready for the decorators.'

'It's taken longer than we thought,' Imogen said.

'Usually does.' The man stood up and looked around him. 'Still, big job, this. Consulting room and office, extra bathroom.' He smiled at her. 'What kind of doctor is hubby then?'

'A cardiac surgeon,' she told him. 'Hoping to be a consultant soon.'

He nodded. 'Ah — heart jobs and all that. Wonderful isn't it, what they can do nowadays? Transplants and by-passes — everything. Live to be a hundred these days. No problem!'

'Yes.' Imogen smiled. 'Would you like a cup of tea before you go home — er . . . ?'

He smiled. 'Craig's the name. Thanks. That'd be very nice.'

'Good. I'll put the kettle on.'

But when he came through to the kitchen a few minutes later Craig was holding a bloodstained handkerchief round his thumb. 'Cut it on a chisel,' he explained. 'I was just putting it away when it slipped out of my hand. Caught it in mid-air.' He gave her a wry grin. 'You'd think I'd have more sense, wouldn't you? It's not as if I didn't know how sharp it was.'

'Hold it under the tap.' She was reaching into the cupboard for the first-aid kit she kept there. 'I'll put a dressing on it for you.'

'No really, it's okay, Mrs Jameson. I'll be fine.'

'Do as you're told,' she commanded. 'That hanky doesn't look too clean to me. It's all right, you can trust me. I used to be a nurse.'

She cleaned the wound and dressed it for him, then poured him a cup of the tea she'd just made. He watched her admiringly.

'You said you used to be a nurse,' he remarked as he took the cup from her. 'If you don't mind me saying so, you look too young to be a *used* to anything.'

She laughed. 'I qualified about six months before I was married,' she explained.

'It's a waste if you ask me,' he said. 'Got a real gentle touch, you have. And lovely soft hands.' He drained his cup and stood up. 'Well, better be going I suppose.'

'Let me see if that bandage is tight enough.' As she took his hand and bent over the injured thumb she heard the slam of the front door. She was still adjusting the bandage when the door opened and William stood in the doorway glowering.

'What's going on?' he thundered. 'What the hell do you think you're doing?'

'Craig cut his thumb.' Imogen explained. 'I was dressing it for him.'

'If you're as badly injured as all that, *Craig* — you'd better get yourself off to the nearest Casualty!' William said sarcastically. He crossed the kitchen and held the back door open, glaring ominously at the man as he scuttled through it. Slamming it forcefully behind him, he stared at Imogen.

'Pity I came in and ruined things for you,' he mocked.

'I don't know what you mean. The man cut his thumb. I cleaned it for him and gave him a cup of tea.'

'It's what you were *about* to give him that bothers me!' He advanced until he was towering over her. 'Another minute and you'd have invited him upstairs, wouldn't you?' he accused. 'Ten more and I'd have found the two of you in bed together!'

Seeing the look in his eyes her heart began to thump. 'That's rubbish!' She made to walk past him but he grasped her arm.

'Rubbish, is it? Perhaps I've got it the wrong way round. Maybe you'd just come down!'

'William, don't be absurd.' She hated it when he was in one of these completely irrational moods. Like this, he was capable of believing

57

anything. 'I've been out,' she told him. 'I've only just come in.'

'Been out? Where?'

'Just shopping.'

'Don't give me that! You don't dress up like that to go shopping. Or was it to impress your labourer friend?'

'If you must know I went up to town to have lunch with Chris.'

'Oh!' He laughed. 'I see, Chris. That explains a lot.' He took off his jacket and threw it, along with his briefcase, on to a chair. 'Now if you don't mind I'd appreciate something to eat. I'll be late tonight. There's another meeting at the hospital.' He turned. 'I'm going up to have a bath and change. I'll eat when I come down.'

Numb with despair, she picked up his briefcase and jacket and took them through to the cloakroom. As she was hanging the jacket up she heard something rustle in the pocket. Reaching in, she took out a crumpled sheet of paper. Straightening it out she saw that it was a hastily written note.

All set for tonight. Pick me up at the usual place — same time. C.

Imogen pushed the note back into his pocket. It didn't take more than one guess to work out who C was. She thought of all those other 'meetings' at the hospital. And all the weekend golfing sessions — the way William had prevented her from joining in. It was fairly clear that there was something going on between William and

Carole. What was more, she suspected that Carole wanted her to know about it.

She prepared William's meal and laid a place at the table, her mind spinning. It was time to act. She had to say something now, before things went any further.

When he came down William was freshly bathed and shaved. She brought in his food and sat down opposite. He looked across at her.

'What's this, not eating? Oh, for God's sake, Genny, you're not sulking again, are you?'

'I'm not hungry.' She took the note out of her pocket and put it on the table between them. 'I found this,' she said. 'There is no meeting at the hospital, is there? You're going to meet Carole. You've been seeing her.'

He stared at the note and then at her, his eyes dark with anger. 'What on earth are you raving about? That note is from Charles Jenkins. He's a paediatrician at the hospital and I always give him a lift when there's a meeting. You're hysterical, Genny! Calm down.'

She hesitated, unsure for a moment. Was it possible? Was she behaving like a hysterical wife? But in her heart she knew he was lying. She knew that Charles Jenkins lived on the other side of London. William couldn't possibly be giving him a lift.

She tried hard to stick to her guns but the hesitation had been her undoing. 'I don't believe you,' she said. But sensing that William knew he had won she got up and walked into the kitchen, her knees shaking as she heard him following.

'What is all this about?' he asked. 'And why

59

are you going through my pockets? Christ, Genny, I thought your nocturnal habits were odd enough, but this ... The sooner you get an appointment with a doctor — preferably a psychiatrist, the better!'

Suddenly anger and fear collided explosively inside her. 'There's nothing *wrong* with me!' she shouted. 'It's you! You're trying to make me believe I do these things; trying to undermine my confidence. Now you're having an affair with Carole Dean. I know you are so don't deny it!'

It was then that he hit her hard across the face with the back of his hand, the blow sending her spinning into the worktop.

'Don't you *dare* speak to me like that!' he growled. 'I can see what this is. It's the influence of that whore you went to see today. She's put you up to this! She's jealous. Can't you see that? Are you too stupid to recognise envy when you see it? You're not to see her again. Do you hear me?' He took a step towards her. 'Well — do you?'

She nodded, one hand still holding her stinging face. A trickle of blood was beginning to run from her lip where his signet ring had caught it.

He stared at her in disgust. 'You're seriously disturbed, Genny. No, don't look at me like that. It's time you faced up to the fact. Get yourself cleaned up. You look revolting.' He turned on his heel. 'I'm going. I probably won't be back tonight, so don't bother to wait up.'

She went into the hall and watched from the window as he drove away. In the hall mirror she caught sight of herself. Her lip was cut at the corner and one eye was beginning to discolour. Across her swollen cheek were the distinct tell-tale marks of William's fingers. Go to the doctor, he had said. Would he really want the local GP — a man he played golf with, to see her like this?

★   ★   ★

By the following week Imogen knew that she could not push aside the suspicion that had been nagging at her for weeks. At the chemist's she bought a pregnancy-testing kit and later that day her suspicion became a reality. Staring at the tube, now displaying the feared pink strip, she felt stunned, her mind churning with mixed emotions. Before they married she and William had never actually discussed the possibility of having a family, but she had always wanted children.

Since their row over Carole the previous week she had felt unhappy and insecure. The atmosphere between them had gone beyond marital tension. There were things about William that disturbed her deeply. And their marriage was not a healthy one. Should they be taking on the responsibility of parenthood? On the other hand, perhaps a child would help to mend their unravelling relationship.

When he came home that evening she was waiting, her heart beating unsteadily and her stomach fluttering. She'd prepared a special meal. An arrangement of flowers adorned the table, a single candle glowing in its centre.

William smiled as she put the first course in front of him. 'This looks good. It's not a special occasion, is it?'

Imogen smiled. 'It is as a matter of fact. I've got a surprise. But I'll keep it for later.'

'Sounds intriguing.'

They finished with a special dessert, the recipe for which Imogen had learned at the cookery classes. William was appreciative.

'You've come a long way since the steak and kidney pie days,' he said. 'That was delicious. Now — what's this surprise?'

Imogen poured two cups of coffee then sat down apprehensively, aware of the suspense she was creating. 'William,' she said. 'I'm pregnant.'

'You're *what*?'

'Pregnant. We're going to have a baby.'

He put down his coffee cup with a bang and stared at her. 'You can't be!'

She laughed. 'Well, I am. The baby is due next summer.'

He was shaking his head. 'Is this the surprise you were talking about?'

'Yes.'

He gave a snort of derision. 'And I thought you were going to tell me you'd taken the money out to pay the builder. My God, Genny! How could you do this to me? It's completely the wrong time. God!' He threw down his table napkin and got up to pace the room. 'I thought you were taking care of things. How *could* you be so careless?'

Her heart sank. 'I thought — I hoped — you'd

be pleased,' she said unsteadily.

'Pleased? Pleased! Are you mad? We can't afford to take on any more commitments. I'm up to my neck in debt as it is.'

'My money will be available next month.'

'Do you think I don't know that? Christ! I've been counting the days! I'm going to need all of that and more to pay off what I owe.'

'All of it? All of my money? But — how do we owe all that?'

'How do you think? The new extension — the car. Never mind how. We *do*! You stupid little fool, Genny!' He stopped pacing to stare at her. 'Have you seen a doctor?'

'No. I got one of those kits from the chemist.'

'So — how far on are you?'

Her throat was tight and she felt the familiar nausea churning her stomach. 'About eight weeks, I think. I've missed twice.'

'Right, it's not too late. There's only one thing for it. You'll have to have a termination.'

She stared at him in horror. 'An abortion, you mean?'

'Yes. We'll get it done as soon as we can. I know a clinic in — '

'I won't do it, William!' She was on her feet. 'I won't kill our child. You can't make me.'

He sighed and ran a hand through his hair. 'Oh, don't be so melodramatic. It's not *killing* a child, it's just putting right a mistake.'

'Not to me it isn't. I won't do it, William.'

He stepped up to her and grasped her by the shoulders. 'You'll bloody well do as I say!'

'Not this time.' Her voice trembled but her

eyes held his determinedly. 'I won't kill the baby. If that's what you want you'll — you'll have to kill me first!'

For a long moment he stared at her with eyes that chilled her to the heart. His hands left her shoulders and moved up to encircle her neck, the thumbs pressing against her adam's apple, constricting her windpipe so that she could scarcely swallow. Her heart seemed to freeze in her chest and her legs began to shake. In that breathless moment she truly believed him to be capable of murder. And the last vestiges of her love for him shrivelled and died. But she stood perfectly still, holding his gaze steadily till at last his hands loosened and dropped to his sides.

'It has to go,' he said coldly. 'If you won't do it my way you'll have to think of something else. But don't expect any support from me.'

★   ★   ★

From the bedroom window she watched him drive the silver BMW out through the gates. Heaven knew where he'd gone or when — *if* — he'd be back. Picking up the receiver she dialled Chris's number.

'Hello. Chris Day speaking.'

The familiar voice brought tears to her eyes. 'Chris, it's me, Imogen.'

'Imo! Are you all right? You sound funny.'

'Chris, I'm pregnant.'

'Darling! That's wonderful. Aren't you pleased?'

'I was. But William is so angry. He says it's the wrong time — says I have to have an abortion.'

'He *what*? What's wrong with the man?'

Imogen poured it all out — all she had kept hidden for so long. She hadn't meant to, but her unhappiness overwhelmed her. It was too much to contain. At the other end of the line, Chris was shocked and concerned.

'I knew there was something. Imo, listen — leave him.'

'Leave? I can't.'

'Yes, you can. You've got to. And make sure he doesn't get his hands on your money. He can't, can he?'

'No. It's tied up till next month.'

'Right. You can come to me.'

'I couldn't. Anyway, what about Max?'

There was a pause at the other end. 'Max and I are splitting up.'

'Oh, Chris.'

'It's for the best — a long story. Never mind that now. Look, you want to have the baby, don't you?'

'Of course I do.'

'Right. I'm moving into a new flat next week. There's room for you — the baby too when it comes. It's vacant now so you could stay there. Just pack your things and come. I'll give you the address. Have you got a pencil?'

Imogen hastily scribbled down the address. 'I can't promise anything, Chris,' she said. 'You don't know what William's like. He won't rest with things as they are. I realise what it is now. He needs to be in control.'

'Well tough! He'll just have to *need*, won't he? Move into the flat, Imo,' Chris urged. 'I've got a couple of days off next week to move. You'll love it. It's at Chiswick, quite close to the river.'

'Maybe I'll come and help you move,' Imogen said. But even as she said goodbye and rang off she knew it would be no use. If she tried to leave William, he would come and find her. He would make her come back and then things would be worse than ever.

5

Through the weeks that followed Imogen wished many times that she had taken up Chris's offer. She was wretchedly sick every morning. Desperately in need of loving care and reassurance. But William ignored her most of the time. He hadn't mentioned her pregnancy again. He moved into the spare bedroom and spent most of his evenings out, sometimes remaining away all night. She knew that he was waiting for her to give in — agree to have the abortion. She was equally certain that she could not do it. The situation could not continue but she had no idea what to do about it. One morning at breakfast she decided to try to talk to him about it.

'What do you want, William. Would you like us to separate?' she asked.

He looked up, his face dark with anger. 'Separate?'

'You don't want the baby,' she said. 'You don't seem to want me either very much. Wouldn't it be better?'

'You'd like that, wouldn't you?' he said. 'You'd like to make a show of yourself; make a lot of adverse publicity for me and wreck my career?'

'No! No one needs to know why. It would be between us. I wouldn't say anything.'

He shook his head. 'We're staying married, Genny.'

'I'm sure we'd both be happier apart.'

'It would make *me* happier if you tried to cooperate,' he said. 'All you can think of is yourself and what you want.'

'That's not true, William.'

'Isn't it? You could have fooled me! All I ever asked was that you wait to start a family.'

'But I'm pregnant and — '

'Termination is nothing nowadays,' he interrupted. 'You'd be home the same day. No worse than having a tooth out.'

'We're not talking about a tooth, William. It's a child — our child. Can't you understand the emotional trauma of it? Don't you care about what I feel?'

'When did you ever care about what *I* feel?' White with anger, he got up from the table. 'You can forget any ideas about separation or divorce,' he told her. 'There'll be no gossip to set tongues wagging at the hospital, do you understand? We're married and we're going to stay married. And if you persist in going ahead with the pregnancy you'll have to take the consequences.' He paused in the doorway. 'And don't think of leaving because I'd find you wherever you went. I won't forget your stubbornness over this, Genny.'

* * *

She was almost three months pregnant when she received the letter. She was surprised when she saw that it was addressed to her. Hardly anyone wrote to her. William had not been home the previous night so she was breakfasting alone. She carried the letter through to the kitchen and slit open the envelope. As she read the crudely printed capitals, her mind froze with shock. She spread the cheap notepaper on the table and read it again.

IF YOU WANT TO KNOW WHERE YOUR HUSBAND SPENDS HIS NIGHTS AWAY FROM HOME TRY 21 NELLIGAN COURT KENSINGTON. OR ASK MRS CAROLE DEAN!

The letter wasn't signed. Imogen looked at the envelope. It bore a London postmark, which told her nothing. All through that day she thought about it, taking it out and reading it again and again as though somehow the words might change themselves into something innocuous. In the afternoon, she telephoned William at the hospital, something he strictly forbade. His surprised secretary informed her embarrassingly that this was his day off. After dinner she rang the golf club and learned that he had been playing golf all afternoon with Mrs Dean, but that he had left an hour ago. As he hadn't returned home she assumed that he must still be with Carole.

For almost an hour she moved restlessly from room to room in an agony of indecision. It had to end. She could not bear this situation any longer. She must face him; tell him she had had enough, ask for a divorce if necessary. She telephoned for a taxi and went upstairs to get ready.

The flat was in a large block. At the main entrance there was an entryphone and she stood for several minutes, wondering what to do. She could hardly ring the flat and announce her arrival. Then, just as she was about to turn away, a woman came along and inserted her card. Seizing the opportunity, Imogen slipped into the building behind her before the heavy door closed.

The entrance hall was carpeted and hushed. An imposing marble staircase with a wrought iron baluster curved upwards; next to it was a lift that rose up through the stairwell. To her relief the woman had disappeared into one of the ground floor flats. Studying the board by the lift, Imogen saw that number 21 was on the fourth floor. She got into the lift and pressed the appropriate button.

The moment she slid back the lift gate, she saw that number 21 was directly opposite. She paused, her courage wavering. Was she really prepared to find William here with Carole? How would she handle the situation? What would she say? What would he do? But she knew that she couldn't just turn and go away. Not now. Having come this far she must see it through. Taking a deep breath she rang the bell.

For a long time she thought no one was coming. It was almost a relief. Then her heart quickened as she heard someone on the other side of the door. A moment later she found herself looking into William's astonished eyes.

'My God! What are you doing here?'

'I could ask you the same question!' Catching him off guard seemed to bolster her courage and she pushed the door open and stepped inside. He wore a towelling bathrobe and his expression was a mixture of shock and anger. He opened his mouth to speak, but before he could say anything she opened her handbag and thrust the anonymous note at him.

'Someone was kind enough to send me this,' she said. 'Is it true?'

'Who is it, William? What do they want?'

Imogen turned to see Carole in the doorway of one of the rooms leading off the hall. She too wore a dressing gown. She looked at Imogen indolently and without surprise, then at William who was still studying the crudely written note. Without a word he handed it to her. She took it, read it, then looked up with a frosty smile.

Imogen's heart froze. 'It was *you*, wasn't it?' she said. 'You wrote it. It *is* true then.'

William spun round to stare at Carole. 'You stupid bitch!' he shouted. 'Why couldn't you leave it to me? Why do an idiotic thing like this?'

Imogen looked at him. 'You accused me of causing gossip — of trying to wreck your career, when all the time you were having an affair. You lied to me.' She took a deep breath. 'I want a divorce.'

'Don't be ridiculous. You're over-reacting.'

'*Over-reacting!*' Imogen felt herself losing control. Hysteria began to bubble up inside her and the feeling she had suppressed for weeks came pouring out. 'If you refuse I'll go to the hospital — the BMC. I'll tell them about you; how you hit me, and about your adultery. I'll tell them how you tried to make me end my pregnancy.'

'*Pregnancy?*' Carole's smile vanished. 'She's having your child? You swine! You told me — '

'Of course she isn't!' William snapped. 'It's all in her mind. I've told you often enough. She's completely mad!'

Imogen felt as though she was suffocating as she looked from one to the other. It was unbelievable — like the worst kind of nightmare. How could he treat her like this? How could she argue — how could she compete with such evil duplicity? She had to get away from here — from him; go anywhere — now, as quickly as she could.

She wrenched the door open and ran out of the flat just in time to see the lift descending out of view. She made for the stairs, William following, shouting angrily to her to stop. Panic-stricken, her heart racing, she recalled the feel of his fingers around her throat and gave a cry of alarm as she felt his hand grab her arm.

'Genny! Wait.'

'Let me go!' As she pulled away from him her heel caught on the top stair and she overbalanced. She cried out, clutching wildly at the rail, but she was too late to save herself. The next moment she was falling, rolling over and over; the hard edges of the marble stairs striking her back, her head, her shoulders, battering the breath from her body. She was aware of doors opening — people rushing out — voices. She saw their shocked faces along with William and Carole's staring down at her from above. Then her head struck something hard. There was a blinding pain. And she knew no more.

★   ★   ★

'Are you with us, Mrs Jameson?'

Imogen opened her eyes to see a smiling face. She was surprised to find herself in bed in a small white room. 'What — where?' She frowned, her head still hurting. The nurse patted her shoulder reassuringly.

'You're in hospital,' she said. 'You had a nasty fall. You're a bit concussed and you've got some nasty bruises, but there's nothing broken.'

'Your husband is here, Mrs Jameson.' The nurse looked round and William came into view at her shoulder. He smiled down at her.

'You gave me such a fright,' he said. 'Getting up in the night and falling downstairs like that.'

'No!' Bewildered, she shook her head. 'I didn't. It wasn't like that. I was at Carole's flat,' she said. 'You were there.'

'No, no.' He took her hand and held it tightly. 'It was one of your bad dreams. You walked in your sleep again. Like before, remember?'

Imogen felt confused and afraid. Her whole body felt sore and bruised and suddenly she remembered the child she was carrying and her heart lurched. 'The baby,' she said feebly.

'I'm afraid you lost the baby, Genny. But you

73

were lucky not to have injured yourself more severely.'

'You've won,' she said, tears welling up in her eyes. 'You didn't want it and now — now it's dead.'

'Shh. Don't try to talk. Just rest now,' he said. 'I'm taking you home tomorrow. It's Christmas soon, so there's that to look forward to. Maybe in the New Year we could take a little holiday.'

But Imogen wasn't listening. She'd been at Carole's flat. She hadn't dreamed that. She knew she hadn't. And she could prove it! 'The note,' she whispered. 'I had a note. I showed it to you. It was about — it said — '

'Quiet now.' He bent over her and kissed her, stopping the words. 'I told you, Genny. It was all a dream.' His lips were cold and hard and there was a sharp warning edge to his voice.

'Better let her rest now, Mr Jameson,' said the nurse.

Suddenly Imogen realised that the nurse was still in the room. His words had been for her benefit. He bent and kissed her again.

'See you tomorrow, darling. Sweet dreams.'

Sweet dreams! She hardly dared to sleep, let alone dream. Turning her head from side to side on the pillow she tried to unravel the tangled thoughts in her troubled mind. She'd had the note. She remembered getting it in the post. She'd gone to the flat — found them there together. She'd confronted William. Asked for a divorce — threatened — yes, threatened him with the BMC. And then — then she had run

74

away. But why? Closing her eyes in concentration she tried to remember the conversation. Then William's words came back to her like the replaying of a tape.

'Of course she's not pregnant. It's all in her mind. I've told you often enough. She's completely mad!'

But she had been pregnant. And now she wasn't. Tears rolled down her cheeks. And William was saying it was her fault, that she had walked in her sleep and fallen down the stairs. It wasn't true; she knew it wasn't. But who would believe her?

She remained in hospital for three days, then William came to take her home. As they drove she stared dully out of the car window at the shop windows ablaze with Christmas colour. Lights twinkled on trees in people's gardens and already the odd Christmas tree glittered bravely in front room windows. She turned away from the sight. She had never felt less like celebrating.

At home life was bleak. She spent most of her time alone. Chris rang one day and as there had been such a long lapse since their last conversation, she assumed Imogen and William had made up. 'Is he happy about things now?'

'No, Chris. I've been in hospital. I lost the baby.'

Chris was shocked. 'Oh, Imo! I'm so sorry, love. How did it happen?'

'I — had an accident. I fell.'

'You poor love. Are you all right? Can I come and see you?'

'No,' Imogen said quickly. 'Better not. I'll be

fine. I'm getting over it.'

'But how did it happen? Imo, I can't just leave it like that. Are you having counselling?'

'No.'

'Well — do you want to talk to someone about it? You must be feeling dreadful.'

'Look, when I'm feeling up to it I'll give you a ring and we'll meet somewhere,' Imogen told her.

'Well, if you're sure.' There was a pause, then Chris asked, 'Imo — is William treating you all right?'

'Yes, yes. We're fine.' She knew Chris's concern was genuine but it grated her raw nerves. She couldn't face telling her friend about all that had happened. The mere idea of going into it all exhausted her. Better to leave it, to wait for a healing skin to grow over the confusion of the past few days until it was all blocked out and she could get some peace again.

* * *

When she had been home about a week, Carole came to see her, bearing a huge bouquet of flowers and keeping up the charade that William had created. Neither of them mentioned number 21 Nelligan Court but it wasn't long before Carole brought up the subject of Imogen's accident.

'You really should see a doctor about that sleep walking of yours,' she said solicitously. 'It could be dangerous. Next time you could hurt yourself badly.'

'I did actually lose my baby,' Imogen said. 'But perhaps you think that's trivial.'

Carole ignored the remark. 'William tells me you've been having some strange dreams,' she went on. 'Saying some really paranoid things. I'm sure you know in your heart of hearts how much he loves you. He'd never dream of being unfaithful to you. You should be careful who you speak to, Genny,' she said gravely. 'You know, you have an absolutely brilliant husband, but you could do his career a lot of harm and I'm sure that's the last thing you want.' She looked thoughtful. 'And maybe the carpet on the staircase could do with tightening up. You don't want to trip on it again, do you?'

Imogen thought dully that she detected a veiled threat behind Carole's words, but she couldn't summon up the energy to worry about it. She shrugged and said nothing.

Every day she woke up thinking about the baby. Would it have been a boy or a girl? Now she would never know. When she slept she dreamed of holding her child in her arms; of feeding it, bathing it, playing with it. Those precious first words, first steps. Now she would never know the joy of them. The grief of losing her baby hurt so badly that it was almost too much to bear. And the fact that William hadn't wanted the child — didn't care, made no attempt to comfort her — made the pain so much worse. She hauled herself through each day, lethargy dragging at her feet like lead weights.

Then there was the bewildering business of

where her accident happened. At first she'd been so certain that she'd received a letter — gone to the flat. And that it had all happened there. To begin with she had known for sure that it was no dream. But William kept insisting that what she thought she remembered was nonsense until at last her confidence became eroded. He insisted that she had been sleep walking — that she walked that night, and that she had continued to do it. Nothing seemed certain any more. Perhaps he had been right; perhaps she could no longer rely on her memory. Perhaps she was going mad.

He brought sleeping tablets home from the hospital for her, advising her to take them, but she refused. If she walked in her sleep; if she had strange inexplicable dreams, then so be it. She would not start depending on drugs. She was already too zombie-like.

On more than one occasion, when despair dragged her down, she had emptied the bottle and looked longingly at the contents. The little heap of harmless-looking tablets that offered escape — oblivion — beckoned invitingly. But each time she had resisted the temptation to swallow them all and in the end she had tipped them all down the lavatory. At the centre of such desperation her core of strength, forged in those early days after her parents were killed, was still strong. It saw her through. *Somehow* — she promised herself — *somehow I will get through this. After Christmas I'll feel stronger. Next year I'll make a new start. Maybe then I'll have the courage to stand up to him — and leave.*

Christmas loomed like a black cloud. She

knew that William would be expecting her to prepare, yet she'd done nothing. One morning at breakfast he said casually, 'I've invited Edward and Carole to spend Christmas Day with us, so you'd better start doing something about it.'

She stared at him. 'You invited them — without asking me?'

He shrugged impatiently. 'I knew if I asked you you'd make some excuse to get out of it. This way you're going to have to make the effort. It's time you pulled yourself together, Genny.'

'I've just lost my baby,' she said. 'You're glad about that, aren't you? But do you think it's easy for me? Do you really think I can throw it off like you can?'

'Clearly not,' he said coldly. He got up from the table. 'But I'm afraid you're just going to have to try. Life goes on, Genny. And time's getting short. You'd better start making some preparations.'

After he'd left, she sat at the table for almost an hour. Her mind was numb. How could she do it? How could she entertain anyone — let alone Carole — when she felt so unhappy, so exhausted and inadequate? She could imagine Carole's sneering face and pointed, sarcastic remarks. And she would have to sit there and take it all. Tears stung her eyes. How could she bear another day of it — another minute?

The sudden ringing of the telephone made her start. Wearily she got up and went into the hall to answer it.

'Hello?'

'Imo, is that you? You sound odd.' It was Chris's voice.

'Yes, it's me. Hello, Chris.'

'Listen, I've got a few days off. Why don't you come up and stay with me? It would give you a break.'

Imogen sighed. 'I can't. I've got too much to do.' She went on to explain to Chris about the Christmas arrangements William had made.

'You're joking! I can't believe you actually let him get away with it.'

'What else can I do?'

'Tell him to get stuffed, that's what! OK, OK, I know you won't do that. Listen, tell him you're staying up in town to do some Christmas shopping, that it's not worth coming home each night. He can hardly complain after dropping you in it like that, can he?'

Imogen was about to make another excuse when she suddenly asked herself why not. Why shouldn't she get away for a few days? William obviously didn't care whether she was here or not. And after all, she had all the Christmas shopping to do. She glanced at her watch. She might even still catch him on his mobile phone before he reached the hospital. If not, she could leave him a note. After all, he had told her she should make a start on the Christmas preparations.

Suddenly she realised that this was the first time she'd felt even mildly enthusiastic about anything since her accident. 'All right, why not?' she said at last. 'I'll come.'

'That's my girl!' Chris was clearly delighted.

'We'll have a couple of days to ourselves. Just the two of us. It'll be like old times. I can't wait!'

★ ★ ★

Seated behind the glass observation panel in Theatre Three at St Aubrey's, Carole watched, enthralled as William began the tricky by-pass operation. The observation room, with its closed-circuit TV monitor, was normally reserved for students and surgeons observing new procedures. But William had managed to get permission for her to be there today and she had the room to herself. When he came into the theatre he had glanced up to where she sat and they had smiled at each other in mutual acknowledgement.

She thought he looked magnificent in his theatre greens; tall and commanding. His eyes, the only part of his face visible over the mask, looked dark and mysterious, focused intently on the task ahead of him. She shivered in anticipation as she watched the long skilful fingers make the first incision.

The patient was an elderly man. Seeing him lying there, still and helpless — at the mercy of this man with the power of life and death at his fingertips — thrilled Carole to her very bones. Everyone knew that William was the most promising and the most popular surgeon at the hospital. Her father was leaving more and more of the work to him nowadays and soon William would take over from him as St Aubrey's cardiac consultant. It was already a foregone conclusion. The staff liked and respected him

81

and the patients revered him; trusting him to make them well again, and in all but the most hopeless of cases, he did. Grateful families and relatives thought him no less than godlike.

But although the thought had never been outwardly expressed between them, Carole knew that surgery gave William more than just the satisfaction of a professional job well done. She could tell instinctively that he enjoyed the same buzz from performing it as she did from watching. And she sensed that most of that thrill came from the control he had as he operated.

Both of them were all too aware that one small nick of the scalpel a fraction of a centimetre out of place and the patient would never wake again. It was a powerful, almost intoxicating feeling. To have that kind of choice at the tips of one's fingers — even though one might never use it — must feel a little like being God.

Carole quivered with an excitement that was almost sexual as she looked into the patient's opened chest, at the pulsating heart. Already she was anticipating the mood of exhilaration that William would be in when they met later. He was always on a high after surgery; the kind of high that made him want her with an animal intensity. She smiled to herself, imagining the sparks that would fly between them.

Today was to be special. Today they would not be meeting at the flat. He had rung her just an hour ago to say that Imogen was going to stay with a friend for a few days. Today, after he had completed his list, they would go back to the house.

Carole pictured them making love in *her* bed, showering together in *her* bathroom. That particularly noxious little fly in her otherwise delicious ointment. Her eyes narrowed. She still had to pay William back for making Imogen pregnant and then lying about it. He wasn't going to get away with that lightly. How could he have made such a stupid mistake? If only he had the same control over his wife as he had over the patient lying there so limp and dependent on the operating table.

For all her fragile looks Imogen was proving unbelievably tough and hard to get rid of. And of course William couldn't simply dump her. He couldn't let her dump him either, too afraid of his precious image, she supposed. The caring, compassionate surgeon. It would never do for people to know he'd tried to make his wife have an abortion; made her so unhappy that she'd left him. But there had to be a way if only she could think of one.

If only Imogen could have killed herself when she fell down the stairs that evening at the flat, Carole mused dispassionately. Even when, at her suggestion, William had put the means into her hands — a hundred double-strength sleeping tablets — the stupid little fool had failed to do what was expected of her.

She watched as William completed the operation and began to suture his patient. She could see that in the end one of them was going to have to do something drastic — make something happen. And the sooner, the better.

* * *

Chris was seriously disturbed when she saw Imogen. She'd been thin before but she was little more than skin and bones now. She had a gaunt, haunted look about her that frightened Chris. And although she chatted animatedly enough as they ate the lunch that Chris had prepared she knew that deep down there was something seriously wrong.

At last, little by little, Chris coaxed it all out of Imogen: William's mental and physical brutality; the anonymous letter; her visit to the flat where she had confronted him with his mistress; the fall that had cost her the child. But even worse than all that was the brainwashing — persuading Imogen that what had happened was all in her mind.

'You've got to leave him,' she said when Imogen had finished.

'I've tried. I've asked him for a divorce — a separation — but he won't hear of it.'

'But why? He obviously doesn't love you. He didn't want the baby and he's got someone else.'

'It's the gossip,' Imogen told her despairingly. 'Nothing must ruin his career, or his image. I suppose he just wants things to go on as they are.'

'But they can't. You'll be ill. Just walk out — leave him,' Chris said. 'Nothing could be simpler. Then he needn't take the blame. He can say it's all you.'

'You don't understand,' Imogen said. 'I threatened him. That night at the flat. I'd had enough and I went a bit wild. I said I'd go to the hospital, the BMC.' She broke off in mid-sentence, her eyes widening. 'Chris! I've only just realised — that *proves* I was at the flat. If I'd fallen downstairs because of a dream — sleep walking — how would William know about the threats I'd made?'

'It's still only your word against his though,' Chris said. 'You still have no concrete proof.'

'It proves it to *me* though,' Imogen said. 'That's so important to me. I was beginning to doubt my sanity.'

'I still say leave him,' Chris urged.

'I've tried to get him to agree to separate, but he won't hear of it. He says that if I leave he'll come and find me. He means it too.'

Chris stared at her, lost for words. 'What will you do, Imo?'

'I don't know. I feel trapped.'

Chris sighed. 'We'll think of something, don't you worry,' she said with a conviction she didn't feel. 'Meantime we're going to have a couple of days' holiday. Just the two of us. For forty-eight hours, we'll forget everything — William, Max, the lot of them. Right?'

Imogen sighed. She hadn't felt so relaxed for months. 'Tell me about Max,' she said. 'What went wrong between you two?'

Chris pulled a face. 'It was all to do with

his family. He still puts them first, Imo. Every time we arranged something his ex-wife would ring and ask him to change his weekend for seeing the boys; usually because she wanted to do something herself and it suited her.'

'It must be difficult for him,' Imogen said.

'Difficult my foot! The moment she knew that he and I were together she started all this. She's jealous. And he just can't say no to her. I wouldn't be at all surprised if deep down he still loves her.'

'Oh, surely not.'

'Well, anyway, it was causing so many rows that we decided to call it quits — for a while at least.'

'That's a shame.'

Chris gave her a wry smile. 'You've changed your tune. You didn't even like him.'

'That doesn't mean I want you to break up. I'd rather see you happy.' Imogen reached out to touch her friend's hand. 'How do you feel about it, Chris?'

'I don't know. He has a ruthless streak that I don't like either — except when it comes to his family. That was another thing we couldn't agree on. I know in journalism the scoop is everything, but I still think you should respect people's feelings. A good story is one thing; exploiting grief and tragedy is something else.'

'So — do you think you'll get back together again?'

Chris lifted her shoulders. 'Who knows? We still see each other occasionally, as friends. Even if we did patch things up it might not work.

Probably better to let it die a natural death.'

The telephone rang. Chris got up to answer it and came back to the room looking apologetic.

'That was the paper,' she said. 'Seems there's been a coded phone call from a terrorist group, warning of a bomb primed to go off in an Islington supermarket this afternoon. They've cordoned off the area, and the police, fire brigade and bomb disposal lads are out in force.'

'And they want you to cover the story,' Imogen finished for her.

Chris nodded. 'Sorry love. That's one of the drawbacks with journalism. You can never really rely on anything you've planned.' She was already collecting her gear together and checking her camera for film.

'Don't you have any photographers at the *Globe*?' Imogen asked.

'We do, but they can't be everywhere at once so we have to be prepared in case we miss something.' She snapped her camera case shut and pulled on her leather jacket. 'Look, I don't suppose I'll be all that long, love. You can put your feet up and make yourself at home here. Or . . . ' Her face brightened. 'I know. Why don't you go up to Dickins & Jones and treat yourself to the works in their beauty shop? They're advertising a free manicure when you have a hairdo and facial. It's just what you need to cheer you up.'

Imogen gave her a wry smile. 'Is that a polite way of telling me I look a mess?'

Chris laughed. 'Just remember you said that, not me! Either way, I should be back in a couple of hours. If I'm not, you'll know I've been blown up!' she joked.

Imogen shivered. 'Chris, don't say things like that.'

'Don't worry, it'll probably be a hoax,' Chris said lightly. 'Nine times out of ten these calls are. Sometimes they give you a location when it's somewhere completely different.' She slung her bag over her shoulder. 'See you later. Tell you what,' she called out as she opened the door, 'pop into the food hall while you're in D and Js and bring in something nice for dinner. My treat.'

When she'd gone Imogen wandered round the flat for a while. Passing a mirror, she stopped and took a long look at herself. Chris had been right. She was in need of some grooming. It was ages since she'd had her hair restyled and her nails were a disgrace. Perhaps she'd do as Chris had suggested.

When they first came to London she and Chris had occasionally treated themselves to a hairdo at Dickins & Jones in Regent Street. Usually you could get in without an appointment. If she went now, she'd have time for a cut and blow-dry, and a manicure. She checked her handbag. She hadn't had time to go to the bank and she wouldn't have enough ready cash on her, but she could always pay with her credit card.

She took a taxi up to Regent Street. Upstairs in the beauty salon at Dickins & Jones she was delighted to find that Cindy, the girl who had always done her hair when she was working in London, was still here. It was almost like old times, having her hair professionally cut. For an hour she almost forgot the trauma of her married life and some of the old light began to come back into her eyes as she watched herself being transformed under Cindy's expert hands.

At the desk, she dropped her coat and bag on to a chair and took out her credit card. The receptionist processed the card and gave her the slip to sign.

Then it happened in a flash.

As she turned back to the chair for her things, a young woman appeared from nowhere. She snatched up the coat and bag and made for the escalator at a run.

Imogen cast a frantic, disbelieving look at the receptionist who was as stunned as she was. Then she gave chase, calling as she went,

'Wait! Please come back!'

★　★　★

William and Carole were in the shower when the doorbell rang. At first they didn't hear it above the sound of the water, until the loud banging caught William's attention.

'What the hell is that?' William turned off the tap and listened. 'Good God! It sounds as though someone's trying to break the door down.'

He stepped out of the shower and pulled on a robe. 'I'll have to go down and answer it.'

When he reached the hall he could see the

dark shape of a uniformed figure through the glass panel of the front door. He opened it.

'Yes?'

'Good evening sir. Mr William Jameson, is it?'

'That's correct. What can I do for you? Excuse me for not inviting you in but I've just got out of the shower.'

'I think it would be better if we spoke inside, sir,' the policeman said.

Reluctantly, William opened the door and ushered the policeman into his study. 'Now — what is this all about?' he asked a little tetchily.

The policeman removed his helmet and cleared his throat. 'I don't know if you're aware of it, sir, but there was a car bomb incident this afternoon in the West End — just off Regent Street, to be precise.'

'Yes — and . . . ?'

'There were a number of casualties and five fatalities. I'm sorry to have to tell you this, but one of them appears to be your wife.'

'Oh, God!'

'Are you all right, sir?'

William swallowed hard. 'I'm fine. It's all right.'

'I'm afraid I have to ask you to come along to the hospital and identify her body. She's at St Aubrey's.'

'Of course. I'll get dressed and drive right over.'

Carole stood at the bend in the stairs, her ears strained to make sense of the words, but she could only pick up the barely audible buzz of voices through the closed door of the study. She stepped smartly back out of sight as the door opened and William came back into the hall with the policeman. By the time he had closed the door she was halfway down the stairs.

'That was the police, wasn't it? What did they want?'

William's face was chalk white as he looked up at her. 'There was a car bomb this afternoon in Regent Street,' he said flatly. 'Imogen is dead. She was killed in the explosion.'

★ ★ ★

Chris climbed the stairs to the flat wearily. What a waste of time. Almost three tiring, boring hours spent in that supermarket looking for a non-existent bomb! They'd turned the place upside down. These people should be hung, drawn and quartered for wasting public money, she told herself; not to mention the time and energy.

As her head came level with her floor she saw a pair of jean-clad legs leaning against the wall outside her door and her heart jumped when the rest of the body came into view. It was Max.

'Chris! Thank God. I've been waiting ages,' he said. 'I thought you'd never come.'

She shrugged. 'I've been out for the paper on some bloody hoax bomb call. 'If you'd rung the bell Imogen would have let you in. She's staying with me for a couple of days and — ' She broke off when she saw his expression. 'What is it?

What's the matter?'

'Look, Chris, can we go inside?'

'Yes, of course.' She was fumbling in her bag for the key. 'What's wrong? Imo must still be out, I should have thought she'd — '

He bundled her inside and took both her hands, holding them tightly as he looked into her eyes. 'Listen, Chris, there's no other way to give you this, but straight. Your friend Imogen Jameson was killed this afternoon in an explosion. A car bomb went off in the West End.'

She gasped. 'No! Oh my God, is *that* where it was? Oh Christ, it can't be true. Say it's not true, Max!'

He pulled her into his arms and held her close. 'I'm sorry love, but it is. I was there. I had a tip-off from a guy I know in bomb disposal. A policeman found the device but unfortunately they couldn't get to it in time. It was all hell let loose. She was killed instantly — must have been very close to the car when it went up. Couldn't have known a thing about it.' He looked down into her stricken face and wiped away a tear with his thumb. 'I came as soon as I could. I wanted to be the one to tell you.'

'Thanks, Max,' she whispered.

'I know how close the two of you were and I didn't want you to hear it on some damned news bulletin or through the paper.'

'Oh, Max, I can't believe it,' she sobbed, her face pressed against his chest. 'If it wasn't for me she'd be alive still. It was me who sent her there. They rang me to go out on this wild goose chase and I suggested she went up West to have her hair done. Oh God, I'll never forgive myself!'

'No, no.' He held her tightly. 'You can't blame yourself. I know how you must feel.' He tipped up her tear-stained face to look at her. 'Chris, do you want me to stay with you tonight?'

She hesitated, then shook her head. 'No. You have things to do. I'll be fine.'

'Are you sure?'

'Yes.'

'Is there anything I can do?'

She looked at him for a long moment. *You can come back, Max,* she longed to say. *You can say you love me — and only me. You can make a commitment.*

Imo had been right when she'd said that love was important, she told herself dully. But she thought she knew best. She'd thought she was strong enough to wait — to handle Max's casual, capricious outlook on love. Now she knew she'd been hopelessly wrong. She'd allowed her heart to be broken and she had no one to blame but herself. Now she'd lost the best friend she'd ever had and she'd never be able to tell her that she'd been right all along.

6

Imogen's eyelids fluttered, then closed again against the glare of brilliant light. She heard someone say, 'I think she's coming round.' Someone raised one of her eyelids and shone a pencil light into her eye.

'Seems OK,' she heard a man's voice say. 'Concussion certainly, lacerations and bruising. Looks like she's one of the lucky ones, but we'd better admit her — do a CT scan on that head injury to be on the safe side. As soon as there's a bed, get her up to the ward.'

Imogen opened her eyes again in time to see a broad, white-coated back disappearing through the cubicle curtains. A young nurse patted her shoulder and smiled down at her.

'Hi there. How do you feel?'

Imogen blinked and winced as a pain knifed viciously through her head. 'Awful,' she muttered. 'What happened?'

'A car bomb,' the nurse told her. 'Just off Regent Street.' She shook her head. 'Christmas week! I ask you. I don't know how these people can live with themselves. Dozens of casualties. We've been rushed off our feet all night.'

'All night? What time is it?'

'It's about six a.m. Shift's almost over, thank goodness.'

Imogen tried to look at her watch but it wasn't there. Instead her left hand and arm was bandaged. 'Oh! What . . . ?'

The nurse took her arm and gently tucked it back under the blanket again. 'You've had a nasty bump on the head and you've got a few cuts, Sylvia,' she said. 'Flying glass. And you weren't wearing a watch. Don't worry though, your handbag is safe along with your clothes.'

Imogen frowned. What had she called her? Sylvia? She felt confused and disorientated. Where were her rings — her other pieces of jewellery? But the nurse was smiling reassuringly.

'Your injuries? Nothing serious. The crack on the head is the worst.' She smiled. 'You've got the makings of a couple of lovely shiners. But the cuts on your hand and arm will soon heal and your face is — '

'My face!' Imogen tried to sit up and groaned as the pain in her head struck again.

'All right, it's only superficial,' the nurse said, gently pressing her back against the pillow. 'Just one little cut here on the cheek and another couple on your chin. We cleaned them up and applied Steristrips before you came round.' She smiled. 'No need to worry, honestly. You won't even have scars.'

The curtains parted to reveal a grinning porter.

'Any more for the Skylark then?' he enquired cheerily.

'We're going to get you up to the ward now, Sylvia,' said the nurse. 'I'll come with you and see you settled, then if I were you I'd try and have a nice sleep.'

Imogen opened her mouth to tell them her

name wasn't Sylvia but, as the trolley was turned round and wheeled out of the cubicle, the ceiling spun and she was so overcome with dizziness and nausea that she had to close her eyes. Had anyone telephoned William? He thought she was with Chris. He wouldn't know. She tried to form the words as they went up in the lift, but somehow her tongue had grown too big for her mouth and, although she thought she was speaking, no sound seemed to be coming out. Finally, as they eased her into the bed and tucked her in, she surrendered to the buzzing confusion inside her head, too weary to bother.

★   ★   ★

Next time she woke up it was daylight. The ward around her was all bustle and she soon realised that lunch was in progress. The ward sister noticed that she was awake and came over to her.

'Hello. How are you feeling now? She took the thermometer from its holder above the bed and slipped it between Imogen's lips. As she did so she looked at the card clipped to the bed rail. 'Feeling better, Sylvia?'

The thermometer in place and Imogen unable to speak, she simply nodded.

'Fancy something to eat?' the nurse asked. 'Lunch is nearly over but I'm sure I could find you something; a bowl of soup?' As Imogen shook her head she said, 'OK. Later perhaps. Nice cup of tea? I expect you're thirsty by now. I'll see that you get one.' She took out the thermometer, studied it, then shook it down and replaced it in its holder. She bustled off and a few minutes later a young nurse arrived with a cup of tea, helping Imogen to sit up.

'What happened to the others?' Imogen asked, sipping the hot tea.

'Others?'

'There must have been others — caught in the bombing — casualties. Were there any — was anyone killed?'

'Yes, I'm afraid there were five fatalities. Terrible, isn't it? Just at Christmas too. There were about thirty others injured too — some quite serious — three are up in ICU.' She smiled at Imogen. 'Your scan was OK. You got off quite lightly.'

Imogen frowned. Scan? She didn't remember anything about it.

'Would you like your handbag,' the nurse asked, 'so you can freshen up and comb your hair? It's here, in the locker. I'll just draw your curtains round if you like — give you a bit of privacy.' She took the bag from the locker and put it on the bed. 'Go easy on your head,' she advised. 'You took a nasty knock.' She tucked another pillow behind Imogen's head. 'You're lucky you know. One of our doctors here has lost his wife in the bombing,' she said.

Imogen looked at her sharply. 'Where am I? I mean which hospital?'

'St Aubrey's.'

Imogen's heart missed a beat. 'One of your doctors?'

'Yes. Doctor Jameson. He's Mr Mayhew's

senior registrar — on the cardiac team. Ever so popular with everyone. It's shaken all the staff, I can tell you.'

As she drew the curtains and left, Imogen sat staring at the unfamiliar handbag, the nurse's words echoing in her head. They were talking about William. What on earth did it mean? Why were they calling her Sylvia? And who did this strange handbag belong to? It certainly wasn't hers. Then slowly, in her confused mind, the events of the previous day began to fit back together again like shreds of torn paper.

Chris had gone off on an assignment so she'd come up West to have a manicure and hairdo in the beauty department of Dickens & Jones. She'd taken off her rings, bracelet and watch to have a hand massage — slipped them all into her handbag. Then, as she was paying at the reception desk, a blonde-haired girl snatched her coat and handbag and ran off with them.

She recalled sickeningly the breathless chase down the escalator and through the store out into the street. She remembered pushing people out of the way; crossing the road when the lights were against her — even the taxi driver swearing at her. After all that — nothing. That must have been when the bomb exploded.

As she stared down at the cheap plastic handbag on the bed in front of her, the truth hit her. That girl — wearing her coat and carrying her handbag — must have been killed in the blast. And she'd been wrongly identified — as *her*!

She stared down at the shabby imitation

patent handbag, steeling herself to open it and inspect the contents. Inside was a purse with a small amount of loose change, some make-up, a comb and mirror and the other detritus all handbags contain: used bus tickets, shop receipts, crumpled tissues. In a zippered pocket, she found a medical card. Imogen stared at the name. Sylvia Tanner — date of birth 7 April 1974. One year younger than her. There were three East London addresses, two of them crossed out.

She felt her blood chill. Somewhere, probably in this same hospital, Sylvia Tanner lay cold and lifeless with a name tag that bore her name: Mrs Imogen Jameson. It was grotesque — bizarre! She must tell someone — put it right at once.

She drew back the covers and put her feet to the floor, but the moment she put her weight on them her knees buckled and her head swam. Sweating and weak, she crawled back into bed and lay there, her head spinning nauseously. It was ridiculous, but there was no need to do anything. The mistake would be discovered soon enough, even if she didn't point it out to them. William would certainly be asked to identify the body and then, of course, he would know. Her heart lurched. Then she would be in trouble. He would blame her for being stupid — for causing him so much trouble and anxiety — making him look foolish. She must try to get a message to him somehow. But try as she would the disabling weakness overwhelmed her, turning her legs to jelly and her brain to a confused jumble. There was nothing she could do about it. She was too tired. She lay back against the pillows and gave up the fight.

* ★ *

'Feeling better, Sylvia? You've had a lovely long sleep.'

A nurse — a different one this time, a middle-aged auxiliary in a green uniform — looked round the curtain. 'Oh, look, your bag has fallen on the floor. Well, never mind.' She picked up the bag and put it in the locker. Twitching at the sheets, she said, 'Sister's asked me to get the name of your next of kin dear. Is there someone you'd like us to contact for you?'

Imogen shook her head. There was only William and she didn't feel strong enough to face him at the moment. She hadn't worked out what she would say. When she first woke up she'd hoped that the bizarre mix-up between her and the girl was a dream. Now she knew it was real. Did he know yet? Had anyone told him?

'Have the people who — who were killed been identified?' she asked haltingly.

The nurse frowned. 'Now, now, dear. You mustn't worry about things like that,' she said. 'Don't want you getting depressed, do we?'

'No, but the other nurse said that one of the casualties was the wife of one of the doctors here. Was she — brought here, to this hospital?'

'Well — as a matter of fact, yes.' The nurse said hesitantly. After a pause she leaned forward and lowered her voice confidentially. 'Seems she was one of the first to be brought in and identified. Well, she would be with her husband being right on the spot, wouldn't she?'

Imogen's heart leapt. Maybe it was some other Doctor Jameson. Of course. If it *was* William, he would have known . . .

'Must have been a terrible ordeal for the poor man,' the nurse went on, shaking her head. 'Her injuries were terrible. Part of the car or a bit of concrete or something had hit her on the head, poor soul. A nurse I know down in A&E said that her face was . . . ' Seeing the colour leave Imogen's face she broke off. 'Well you can probably imagine. Must have been instantaneous though, so that's a blessing — couldn't have known much about it.'

Imogen swallowed, feeling her stomach heave. 'But — how did they — did he — ?'

'Identify her? Oh well, they recognised the name right away down in A&E when she was brought in — from what was in her handbag, you see,' the nurse went on. 'Her wedding ring and stuff was all in her bag too. Funny she wasn't wearing it though. If you ask me — '

'Nurse!'

Sister's head came round the curtain. She looked very angry. 'Nurse Potter! I asked you to get this patient's next of kin, not to stand there gossiping.'

'Sorry, Sister.' Looking shamefaced, the auxiliary shuffled off. Sister stepped up to the bed and peered at Imogen.

'Are you feeling all right?'

'Yes — I think so.' Imogen felt the nausea return and closed her eyes. Sister pulled a tissue from the box on the locker and dabbed at her brow.

'Take no notice of Potter's ghoulish stories,' she said. 'She means well but she does tend to let her tongue run away with her. Try not to worry about the others. As I said, you're one of the lucky ones. Now, can I just have your next of kin?'

Imogen heard herself say, 'There's no one.'

'No one at all? No friend — someone you'd like to see?'

'No one, thank you.'

★ ★ ★

It was warm in the ward. Too warm. And dark. Just the dim light shining through from the corridor and the desk lamp at the nurses' station. Imogen was wide awake now. She felt she had had enough sleep to last the rest of her life. Her mind was clear now. Crystal clear.

In the quiet dimness memories flooded back: her parents' sudden devastating death in a car accident when she was seven; going to live with Daddy's Aunt Agnes in Edinburgh; the rigid routine of the dark old house that had never known a child's laughter — or tears; the desolation of her first weeks at boarding school; and Chris, who rescued her from the cruel taunting of the bullies.

Dear Chris, the best friend she'd ever had, with her laughing eyes and copper hair. She remembered the tension and excitement of passing their 'A' levels and coming to London with Chris; she to St Aubrey's to train, while Chris got a secretarial job with the *Daily Globe*.

Her mind turned then to Aunt Agnes's death and the surprise of finding herself the sole beneficiary of her estate. Everything could have been so different. She could have had so much fun — like she did in that first year with Chris.

But all that was before she met William. William, her first love; the most exciting — most thrilling — and the very *worst* thing that had ever happened to her. She closed her eyes, picturing his handsome face; the dark eyes that could melt you with desire and — she discovered later, *too* late — burn with fury and malevolence.

Wide-eyed, Imogen stared up at the ceiling. At first she'd surprised herself, telling Sister she had no next of kin, but now she knew that she'd been stalling for time. Deep inside her mind an idea was taking shape; an idea that was heart-stoppingly terrifying — and so impossible that she refused to accept it. But try as she would, the idea refused to go away. Its presence was almost tangible, a persistent voice whispering urgently to her through the darkness.

Yesterday had been pre-ordained, it said; a chance that fate had blown her way and dropped into her hands. It was a gift, the kind of chance that came only once in a lifetime. If she let it go now she would never be free and God knew where it would all end.

But could she — *dare* she take it? The idea beckoned determinedly. When she closed her eyes, she could still hear its seductive voice tempting her. *Do it, Imogen. Do it — now! Seize the chance — before it's too late!*

She opened her eyes and stared up at the ceiling. It wasn't impossible. She *could* do it. If she were brave enough. She could escape. She would have to begin again from scratch — with no money and nowhere to go. That was frightening. But not nearly as frightening as the prospect of returning to William.

He already thought she was dead.

So why not stay dead?

7

It was two days later before Chris could bring herself to go out to the shops. Ever since Max had broken the news of Imogen's death to her she had felt numb with shock. Yesterday's news bulletins on TV had been full of the Regent Street bombing. A terrorist group had claimed responsibility and already today two arrests had been made. But the death toll had risen to six and nothing could alter that.

Chris still blamed herself. If only she had urged Imogen to stay where she was. She wondered vaguely if William had been notified. Of course he must have been by now. She wondered how he felt — whether he was suffering remorse for the way he had treated her. Poor little Imo. She hadn't had much of a life. William had been her first serious love affair and she'd fallen for him so hard that she'd been blind to everything else. Love was important but it could do as much harm as good, she told herself wryly. Maybe she was better off without Max. If only she could make herself believe it.

She shopped for her few needs and returned to the flat through dusky streets already lit by the street lamps. It was dark on the stairs and when she reached the landing she put down her shopping and fumbled for the light switch. Just as her hand found it, a voice from the shadows startled her.

'Please — don't switch it on.'

Chris spun round. In the dimness a figure emerged and she gasped with shock.

'Imogen! Oh my God!'

'Yes, it's me. Please, can we go inside?'

Inside the flat Chris switched on the light and stood staring at Imogen. Her heart was thumping so hard that she could hardly breathe. 'I — I don't understand,' she whispered. 'You're supposed to be — Max came the night before last. He told me you were . . . ' She peered at her friend, taking in the bruised and cut face, the pallor of her skin and the sheer exhaustion in her eyes. 'Oh, my poor Imo. Thank God! Come here.' She drew Imogen into her arms and held her close. 'I don't know what this is all about and I don't care. You're alive, that's all that matters.'

'Chris, I need your help,' Imogen said. 'Someone else — another girl was identified as me. It's a long story and I — I . . . '

'Where have you *been*?' Chris asked. Imogen's cheek was icy cold against hers and she could feel her shivering through the thin material of the shabby brown coat she wore.

'In hospital — till early this morning. Then I left. Discharged myself. I was afraid to stay any longer — terrified I might run into William. I've been walking around all day. I daren't come here until it was dark because . . . ' She swayed, her eyes glazing. 'Because . . . '

'Never mind that. Tell me later,' Chris said. 'You look wiped out.' She led her friend gently to the living room and made her sit down on the settee. 'You're not to utter another word till you've had something to eat and drink.'

Half an hour later, after a bowl of hot soup and a cup of strong coffee, Chris tucked a rug round Imogen's legs and settled on a stool beside her.

'OK, now you can tell me,' she said. 'I want to hear everything — all of it, from when you left here the day before yesterday, right up to today.'

Haltingly, Imogen told her about her trip to Dickins & Jones; the girl who snatched her coat and bag in the beauty salon; the chase through the store and down the busy street — the explosion.

'When I woke up in hospital, I gradually worked out that they'd mistaken her for me and by the time I realised fully what was happening William had identified this other girl's body and everyone was calling me Sylvia.'

'I see.' Chris was puzzled. 'Well, I don't. I mean, how could William identify this other girl as you?'

Imogen swallowed hard. 'Apparently she had a very severe head injury. From what I could make out she was virtually unrecognisable. It was just — '

'The coat and what was in the handbag. I see.' Chris looked thoughtful. 'So what happened then? Did you tell the staff at St Aubrey's? Have you contacted William?'

'No.' Imogen sat up. 'And I'm not going to. Chris, don't you see, it's fate. This is a new start for me. A chance to be free.'

Chris stared at her. 'What on earth do you mean?'

'Everyone thinks I'm Sylvia Tanner. So from now on — I *am*!'

'But — you can't do that, Imo. Why should you want to?'

'I can't go on as before, Chris. I can't live with William any more.'

'Then divorce him!' Chris was on her feet now. 'Listen, you've had a terrible shock. You've had a head injury — two head injuries in fact. There was the other one when you fell down the stairs.'

'I'm not *crazy*,' Imogen interrupted. 'I've thought it through, Chris, and I know what I'm doing. William would never let me go. He said as much. He thinks of me as his property — someone over whom he has complete control. You have no idea what it feels like to be dominated like that, not to be able to call your soul your own. This is my only chance to escape.'

Chris shook her head. 'What William has done to you is criminal,' she insisted. 'Never mind whether he'd *let* you go. You have strong grounds for divorce. Look, ring him now. It's not too late. Tell him you've been unconscious — confused, and you've only just realised what happened.'

But Imogen was shaking her head. 'I can't, Chris. I *won't*. You don't know what the past two years have been like. He's done his best to undermine my confidence — my sanity even. I really began to believe I was going out of my head. I think I would have done if I'd stayed with him much longer. Just let him think I'm dead. It's the only thing he'll accept. And it's so simple.'

'But it *isn't!*' Chris said. 'This girl whose identity you're planning to take; she could be married, have a husband and kids who are missing her. Can you let them suffer? She's probably got an employer who'll be waiting for her to turn up for work — friends, family. Don't you see? It won't be long before she's reported missing and then there'll be a hue and cry. The police will be looking for her.'

Imogen bit her lip. 'I have thought of all that,' she said slowly. 'And that's where I thought you might be able to help me.'

'You want me to . . . ' Chris was staring at her, comprehension dawning. 'Oh God, Imo. You can't be serious about this.'

'You're a journalist,' Imogen said quickly. 'You know how to go about these things.' She opened the handbag that had been Sylvia's. 'There's an address in here. And her medical card.'

Chris took the card and looked at it. 'You mean you actually want me to — ?'

'Look, Chris, I'll make a deal with you. If you make enquiries for me and find she's got a husband and family, I'll give the idea up and go to the police. If not — '

'If not, you'll expect me to collude with you in taking her identity.'

'I wouldn't ask you — wouldn't implicate you — if I wasn't so desperate to be free of William, Chris. There's no one else I can go to; nowhere else to turn.'

Chris sighed and sat down on the settee beside her friend. 'I can see that, and you know I'd do anything to help — ' She broke off, shaking her

109

head. 'Look, Imo, what do you intend to do? I mean, even supposing this crazy idea of yours is workable. What about your money for instance, your bank account? You realise, don't you, that as your next of kin William will be able to claim everything?'

'I don't care about the money. He can have it.'

'But you must try to look at this sensibly, Imo. What do you propose to live on?'

'I do have some money in a current account,' Imogen said. 'When I got my clothes back this morning I found my credit card in the pocket of my skirt. I must have pushed in it there when my bag was snatched. I withdrew as much as I could from a cashpoint this morning. I can get the rest out the same way.

'But won't that be recorded — with the date and everything?'

Imogen shrugged. 'They'll just think someone found my card.'

Chris conceded that this was feasible. 'So — where would you go?'

'I'll go right away somewhere — get a job.'

'As what? As Imogen Kendrick you were a qualified nurse. You can't claim qualifications as this Sylvia Tanner person.'

'Then I'll do something else. I'll scrub floors if I have to. Anything would be better than going back to *him*.'

Chris took her friend's hands and looked into her eyes. 'Imo, please don't do this. You're *you*. You're Imogen, my dearest friend. However hard you pretend, you can't change that.'

'I *must*, Chris. I have to,' Imogen said

110

desperately. 'I don't want to *be* Imogen Jameson any more. But it's more than just being William's wife. I don't want to be *me*. Can't you see? I'm a total failure. I despise myself. I want to leave myself behind along with all the mess I've made of things. Start again.' She looked pleadingly into Chris's eyes. 'Please help me, Chris. If you don't, I don't know what I'll do.'

For a long moment Chris looked into her friend's tear-filled eyes, then aching with compassion she put her arms around her and hugged her. 'Of course I'll help, love,' she said. 'I only hope to God it's the right thing we're doing.'

⋆ ⋆ ⋆

25 Canning Terrace turned out to be a run-down B&B off Hackney Road. Chris parked her car and fed the parking meter, looking up at the crumbling three-storey building without enthusiasm.

In the narrow hallway a reception desk was crammed into a recess at the bottom of the stairs. Chris rang the bell on the counter. The man who emerged from a room at the front of the building had greasy collar-length hair. He wore a grubby waistcoat over his shirtsleeves and regarded her through the smoke rising from the half-smoked cigarette between his lips.

'Mornin'.' He shifted the soggy brown cigarette from one side of his mouth to the other. 'What can I do for you?'

'Does a Miss Sylvia Tanner live here?'

'Who wants to know?'

'Does she?'

The man smiled revealing nicotine-stained teeth. 'Who shall I say is callin' — police or the Social?'

'Neither. I'm a friend.'

'*Friend*, eh?' He sneered. 'That's a new one. Well you're out of luck darlin'. She ain't in. In fact she ain't been seen for two days.'

Chris's mind went into overdrive. 'As a matter of fact she won't be coming back,' she said glibly. 'She asked me to pick up one or two things for her, so if I could just have the key to her room.'

''ang on a minute.' The man's eyes narrowed. He took the cigarette end from his mouth and ground it out in an overflowing ashtray on the counter. 'First you ask me if she lives 'ere. Now you say she ain't comin' back. Which is it then?'

Chris sighed. 'It's very simple really. She's staying with me. I said I'd pick up her things for her, but I thought she just might have got here before me.'

'Oh, you thought that, did you? Well you was wrong, wasn't you?' The man paused to light another cigarette, regarding Chris suspiciously through the rising smoke. 'I s'pose she didn't 'appen to mention that she owed four weeks' rent?' he said.

'Actually no.' Chris stared him out. 'But if you let me have her key I'll clear her things out. Then perhaps we can talk about it.'

'That's more like it.' He took a key from a drawer under the counter and slapped it down hard. 'First floor front,' he said. 'Number 6. I'll be 'ere when you've done.'

Chris climbed the stairs, glancing over her shoulder in the fervent hope that the man wasn't about to follow her up. On the landing a young woman stood by an adjacent door with a baby on her hip. She watched as Chris inserted the key in the lock of the door marked 6.

'Matter o' fact it's only two weeks,' she said quietly.

Chris turned to look at her. 'Sorry?'

'Sylv only owed that slimy little sod *two* weeks' rent, not four,' the woman said. She took a step forward. 'Is she all right? I been really worried about her. Ain't seen her for days. I thought maybe the bastard had got to her again.'

Chris let herself into the room and looked around. It was a soul-destroying place, furnished with the bare minimum of furniture. A sagging bed, scratched table and chairs, a single battered armchair. Grimy curtains adorned the smeared window and a curtained-off corner of the room served as a wardrobe.

'She's stayin' with you then?' The young woman had followed Chris into the room and stood in the doorway.

'What?'

'Stayin' with you — Sylv?'

'Oh — yes.'

'All right, is she?'

'Not really. She was involved in the Regent Street bombing.'

'Christ!' The woman's eyes widened. 'Poor kid. Is she hurt?'

Chris looked at the woman. 'Her memory's

affected. Look, I'd be really grateful for anything you can tell me about her.'

'You're not from the Social, are you?'

'No. I promise you. As I said downstairs, I'm a friend. I'm trying to help.'

The woman looked guarded for a moment. She regarded Chris appraisingly as she shifted the baby to the other hip, then, appearing to come to a decision she nodded. 'Can't talk here,' she said with a quick glance over her shoulder. 'Look, there's a pub on the corner of the next street — Prince of Wales. How about I meet you in there in half an hour? I'll get the old gel upstairs to have my Darren for a bit.'

'Fine.' Chris took down the clothes from behind the curtain and threw them on to the bed. She looked around for a suitcase, but didn't find one.

'I can let you have a couple of bin bags for that lot if you like,' the woman said helpfully. 'Oh, and by the way, her giro came. I kept it in my room. If that greasy little git downstairs had got his paws on it he'd've hung on like grim death so I grabbed it quick. Daresay she'll be glad o' that.'

The Prince of Wales was warm and quiet. Chris found a corner table where they could be relatively private and ordered herself a mineral water. After about ten minutes the woman arrived and joined her.

'What will you have?' Chris asked.

'Can I have a whisky and ginger?' the woman asked. 'Keeps out the cold a treat, in this weather.'

Chris fetched the drink and sat down again

opposite the woman. 'I don't know your name,' she said.

'Maureen. Maureen Sullivan, but everyone calls me Mo.' She took a sip of her drink. 'Ooh, that's lovely. Thanks,' she said with satisfaction. 'Now — what d'ya want to know?'

'Tell me about Sylvia, Mo,' Chris said. 'You said back at the house that you were afraid that that bastard had got to her. Who did you mean?'

'She ain't told you about Phil then?'

'I told you, her memory's affected.'

Mo pulled a face. 'Just as well if you ask me. I reckon Phil Morgan's one person she'd rather forget!'

The name rang a bell somewhere inside Chris's head. There was a case involving a man of that name a couple of years ago. She hadn't covered it herself but she remembered it causing quite a stir at the time. Mo took another sip of her whisky and said, 'Phil was Sylv's boyfriend. Potty about him, she was, till he wanted her to go on the game. Then the rot set in.'

'You mean he was her pimp?'

Mo shook her head. 'No. She wasn't havin' any. Brought up real strict, Sylv was, in one o' them C of E kids' homes. You know the kind of thing — church every Sunday, mornin' prayers and stuff. That was in the Midlands. She come up to London to work as a nanny when she was eighteen, but she lost her job because the dad of the kid she was lookin' after kept makin' passes at her an' his wife found out.' She took out a packet of cigarettes and offered Chris one. She shook her head.

'No thanks. So what happened then?'

'Well, she never got no reference so it was hard to get another job nannyin'. She lived in a hostel for a while, on the Social. Then she got a job behind the bar of a club up West, in Soho. That's where she met Phil.'

'And fell in love?'

Mo drew hard on her cigarette. 'Tell me about it! Quite a looker, Phil. Smooth with it. He was in the money at the time and they had a posh flat up West. I don't know what he was into except that it definitely weren't legal. Anyway, something went wrong and it all fell apart. That's when they moved to the East End and Sylv got a job in the same supermarket as me. That was when we chummed up. I found her cryin' her eyes out in the ladies one day. She told me he wanted her to go on the game.'

'What happened when she refused?'

'That was when he started knocking her about. She tried to leave him but he kept finding her and bringing her back. Then he planned this job — robbery. There was this old gel, widow of a wealthy businessman Phil used to know. He got to hear that she had a whole heap of jewellery, all kept in a safe at home. He got Sylv to get a job cleanin' for her. It worked a treat. She trusted Sylv enough to give her a key. After that they was all set. Phil's plan was to walk in there one night and clear the safe out.'

It was all coming back to Chris now. Max had covered the case and it had been quite sensational. 'I believe I remember something about it from the papers,' she said.

'That's right. Made headlines for a couple of weeks. It all went pear-shaped 'cause the old girl was a light sleeper. She woke up and heard a noise — come down and found them. When she tried to phone the police Phil panicked and clouted her. Trouble was, the poor old gel had a weak heart and she died in hospital next day.'

'From the injury Phil Morgan gave her?'

'That and the shock. That was why they couldn't pin a murder charge on him, 'cause of her bad heart, see? And he kept sayin' she'd tripped and hit her head on the fireplace. But it was him all right. Manslaughter, that's what he got sent down for.'

Chris was remembering now. 'Didn't the girl — didn't Sylvia turn Queen's evidence at the trial?'

Mo nodded. 'That's right. Wasn't like Sylv to shop anyone, but by then she hated Phil. She was horrified by what he done to the old gel. She'd been good to Sylv and she had a soft spot for her. Turning Queen's evidence meant that she only went down for two years, while Phil got seven.' She stubbed out her cigarette and tossed back the last of her whisky. 'Sylv come out of prison six months ago. Poor kid's 'ad nothing but hassle ever since.'

'Want another of those?' Chris nodded towards Mo's empty glass.

'Oh — well, thanks very much.'

By the time Chris got back to the table Mo had lit another cigarette and looked all set to continue. 'What kind of hassle?' Chris asked.

'Phil Morgan's got this brother — Rex. Real

nasty piece of work. He was on to Sylv soon as she got out — threatenin' and that.'

'What does he want?'

'Don't know, revenge mainly. I think he just wants to make her sweat. Sylv's not one to moan. She's close too. Keeps things to herself. I reckon I'm the only person she ever confided in, an' if I can do anything to help her you can count on me.'

'I'm sure she's grateful for your friendship.'

'Can I come an' see her?'

Chris looked up in alarm. 'I — er — don't think she wants to see anyone right now, Mo,' she said. 'Between ourselves, I think she might be planning to go away for a while. But I'll give her your best wishes.'

Mo was nodding. 'Best thing she can do — get away.'

'I'm sure you're right. And obviously from what you tell me, the fewer people who know where she is, the better.'

'That's true.' Mo glanced up at the clock behind the bar. 'Better get back,' she said. 'My Darren'll be wantin' 'is dinner. Nice to meet you, Miss . . . '

'Knight,' Chris said, snatching at the first name that came to her. 'Nice to meet you too, Mo. And thanks for all your help. I'll give Sylvia your regards.'

'Do that. Tell her that she can drop me a postcard when she gets settled. Needn't put the address on it. I'd just like to know she's OK. Bye then. And thanks for the drinks.'

Chris sat on for a few minutes after Mo had

departed. She'd told more lies in the past hour than in the last ten years. Max would have been proud of her. He always said she had too much integrity for her own good. So far, so good, she told herself. Her next job would be to go back to the office and have a rummage through the archives — look up the case in question and see if she could fill the gaps in Mo's story.

At the newspaper office Chris found the report of the case. The old lady who had died was called Mrs Enid Jarrold. She was the widow of a highly successful businessman who was reputed to have had a finger in some rather dubious pies, though nothing illegal was ever pinned on him.

Morgan had never actually succeeded in opening the safe on the fateful night of the robbery. But in actual fact it turned out to be empty anyway. Had Sylvia Tanner tipped the old lady off in some way? Where had the jewellery gone? It had never been located.

Sylvia Tanner had been convicted as an accessory and sentenced to two years imprisonment. Chris calculated that she would have done about eighteen months. She also managed to confirm from the transcript of the trial that Sylvia had no relatives and few friends. Everything that Mo had told her seemed to be correct.

At the trial Phil Morgan's brother, Rex, had given him an alibi — said that Phil had been with him on the night in question. In fact he had tried to pin the robbery on Sylvia, pointing out that she had a key and probably knew the combination of the safe. The jury had dismissed his accusations, but Chris sat back thoughtfully. Could it be that this Rex Morgan really believed that Sylvia knew the whereabouts of Enid Jarrold's jewellery, and that he was harassing her for that reason? Could he have been following her on the day of the bombing and she had taken Imogen's coat and bag in a desperate attempt at disguising herself? Could it even be that Rex Morgan had been right and Sylvia *was* the real culprit — that she had incriminated her lover as revenge for his ill-treatment of her? It was all very intriguing. But now they would never know.

'Doing some research?'

Chris hadn't heard anyone come in and she jumped violently, quickly switching off the microfiche monitor.

'Hey! You're jumpy. What were you looking up?' Max leaned over and switched the monitor back on again. 'Oh, the Jarrold case. That was an interesting one. What's your interest in that?'

'Nothing really,' Chris said dismissively. 'Just comparing it to another similar case.' She switched off the monitor and swung round on her chair to face him. 'Anyway, what are you doing here?'

'Just dropped a piece in,' he said. 'A spin-off from the Regent Street bombing as a matter of fact. One of my spies gave me some info about a new device they've got for detecting car bombs. I think the old man's quite taken with it.' He reached out to touch her cheek. 'Come and have lunch.'

'Not today, Max,' she said. 'I've got some urgent things to do.'

'Not so urgent that you can't find time to eat.'

'No, but I — already have,' she lied.

His fingers traced the line of her jaw and his eyes were tender as they searched hers. 'I miss you, Chrissie.'

'Do you?'

He smiled. 'That's your cue to say you miss me too.'

'I've had to learn to live without you,' she said.

'Oh, come on. We were good together — weren't we?'

She stood up. 'Max, if you don't mind I have to get on now.'

'I'm really sorry about your friend,' he said. 'It must take some getting over, a thing like that.'

'Yes.'

'Why can't you let me help you?' He grasped her shoulders and pulled her close. For a moment she held herself stiffly, but the touch of his lips on hers was too much to resist and she found herself responding in spite of herself. When his mouth left hers she shook her head at him.

'That wasn't fair, Max.'

'Maybe not. It was good though. You're not going to deny that. Your lips told me otherwise. Chrissie — we have to talk.'

'We've already talked more than enough,' she turned away.

'Let me come round — tonight.'

'No!' The refusal had come out far more stridently than she had intended. The last thing she needed was for him to find Imogen at the flat.

'OK!' He took a step backwards, his eyebrows rising. 'OK. I get the message — loud and clear. I take it there's someone else.'

'In a way. No, not really. Look, Max, I really need some space. Let's just leave it for now, eh?'

He lifted his shoulders. 'If you say so.'

'You've got your family problems and I've — well I've got things on my mind too.'

'So it seems.' He looked at her for a long moment, then he turned. At the door he looked round at her. 'By the way, you might be interested to hear that Janet — my ex — is planning to re-marry.'

Her heart almost seemed to stop and she gasped. 'I see. So now that there's no chance of getting back with her you're prepared to make do with second best.'

He winced and his eyes darkened with pain. 'Well done, Chrissie,' he said thickly. 'You finally learned how to punch below the belt.'

Chris stared with brimming eyes at the door he slammed shut behind him. 'Shit!' she said.

★   ★   ★

'I don't know whether to say it's lucky or not,' Chris said as she and Imogen sat together over their evening meal. 'The only person who's on the lookout for Sylvia Tanner is a violent criminal with murder on his mind!'

Imogen shrugged. 'It's not me he's looking for though, is it? Even if he tracked me down he'd just assume he'd got the wrong person.'

Chris nodded, conceding that she was probably right. 'Look, Imo, you are going to tell me where you're going, aren't you? You wouldn't just take off into the blue?'

'Of course I'll tell you. I have to trust someone and who else but you?' Imogen said. 'I've been thinking about it and I've made up my mind. There's this little place where Mum and Dad took me on holiday the summer before they were killed. I loved it and I've always promised myself I'd go back some day. This seems like the perfect opportunity.'

'Right. So where is it?'

'It's a little place on the border of Norfolk and Suffolk; on the coast. It's called Craybourne-on-Sea.'

'Is there likely to be much in the way of employment there?' asked Chris doubtfully.

'I hope so. If not I'll have to move inland a bit, Norwich or maybe Ipswich, but I'd like to settle in Craybourne.'

Chris was silent, understanding the connection for Imogen with her late parents and her need to look back on happier times. She felt desperately sorry for her friend and was still uncertain that Imogen was doing the right thing. 'Look, Imo,' she said. 'You are sure about all this, aren't you? Absolutely sure?'

Imogen was nodding. 'One hundred per cent, Chris. And believe me, I'm really grateful to you for what you've found out for me today. I wouldn't have dared risk it without knowing all that about Sylvia.'

'And you will stay in touch. Maybe I could even come and visit you?'

Imogen smiled. 'That would be marvellous.'

'So — when do you plan to go?'

'As soon as possible. Tomorrow.'

'Tomorrow? Are you sure you're fit enough?'

'I've got to be, Chris. The longer I stay here with you the more I'm going to lose my courage.'

'Well, you're looking better.' Chris nodded towards the two bin bags full of Sylvia Tanner's belongings. 'What do we do with all that? I take it you won't be wanting her clothes?'

'No.' Imogen shivered. 'Perhaps you could dispose of them. I'll get you to buy me a toothbrush and nightie. The rest I can pick up as I go along. While you were out I enquired about trains. There's one to Ipswich at seven ten tomorrow morning. I can get a bus to Craybourne from there.'

Chris swallowed hard. So she was serious. She was actually going to do it. Until now she hadn't really faced the fact that it would really happen.

'You'll need luggage of some sort,' she said. 'It'll look odd if you turn up with nothing. We're about the same size. I can fix you up with a few things to tide you over.'

'Right. Thanks.'

The two girls looked at each other, both aware of the enormous step Imogen was about to take.

'Right then,' Chris said at last. 'Better get some sleep if we're to be up by six.'

8

As Imogen sat on the bus on the last leg of her journey to Craybourne-on-Sea her stomach churned with apprehension. Last night after she had made the difficult decision to leave the security of Chris's flat, she had looked at herself in the dressing table mirror and her heart had plummeted.

'Look at me, Chris,' she wailed. 'How can I possibly go looking for work like this?' The skin around her eyes was still discoloured and the cuts on her cheek and forehead still bore the adhesive strips applied at the hospital. She turned to her friend despairingly. 'I've got no references either — and no one I can ask. I'm kidding myself, aren't I? This just isn't going to be possible.' She sank down on the edge of the bed and buried her face in her hands. 'Oh, Chris, what am I going to do? It isn't going to work, is it. It's all just a silly pipedream.'

'Now you listen to me!' Chris pulled her hands away from her face and looked into her eyes. 'I'll admit that I thought you were mad at first but now, God help me, I think you should stick to your guns.'

Imogen looked at her in amazement. 'You do?'

'Yes. If nothing else it might buy you some time to get your thoughts straightened out.'

'But what about the way I look?'

'I'll do your hair for you. We'll arrange it to

125

hide the cut on your forehead. And I've got some concealer; careful make-up will disguise your eyes. Those bruises will be gone in a couple of days now anyway. How long have you had the Steri-strips on?'

Imogen counted. 'Five days.'

'Right, they must be ready to come off then, mustn't they? You're a nurse, you can do that yourself.' She took Imogen's arm and led her through to the bathroom. 'Come on, Imo. You've taken your life into your own hands. This is the first real decision you've made since you married William. You can't look back now.'

Imogen looked at her. 'Chris, what about my — Sylvia's — prison record?'

Chris shook her head. 'You're under no obligation to mention that. Sylvia served her sentence and paid her debt — such as it was. She'd have been entitled to lay that part of her life to rest, and so are you.'

'Are you sure?'

'Positive. Now, let's get to work.'

Imogen smiled ruefully to herself as she remembered how Chris had shampooed and blow-dried her hair, remarking what a good thing it was that she had just had it expertly cut. When she gingerly removed the Steri-strips the cuts on her face looked much better; obviously healing well. As Chris had said, a few more days and her injuries would hardly be noticeable.

This morning Chris had supervised her make-up carefully, lending her the concealer to apply around her eyes. The finished effect was encouraging.

'You look almost like the Imogen I know and love,' she said, giving her friend a hug. 'Ready for anything — yes?'

Imogen had nodded, managing a smile in return despite the fact that her insides were turning to jelly at the mere thought of what she was about to do.

As she walked out of the bus station, to her surprise Imogen saw that Craybourne-on-Sea looked much the same as she remembered it: the same bustling shops clustered round the medieval church; the narrow little streets with their quaint tumbledown shops still meandering seawards towards the cliffs.

It was still only mid-morning but she was desperately tired. Last night she'd hardly slept and the train and bus journey had shaken and jolted her still bruised body till she felt as though every muscle was strained to its utmost. Saying goodbye to Chris had been painful. It had felt like severing her last link with her old self.

'Promise me you'll keep in touch.' Chris had said, biting her bottom lip. 'You will ring me — often?'

'Of course I will.'

'And promise me that the minute you feel able to face William and ask for a divorce you'll come back. You can stay with me and you know I'll support you all I can.'

'I know you will.' Imogen had hugged her friend, vowing silently to herself that that day would never come. She had reached the point of no return. There was no way she could ever let William know of the deception she'd played on him. Knowing William as she did, she knew that the retribution would be terrible.

The day was bright and frosty, and the little town looked festive with its decorated Christmas tree standing by the church gate and the shop windows abundant with colour. She was reminded that there were only three more days to go before Christmas. But the thought did nothing to cheer her. There was little hope of finding work now until after the holiday. Anyway, her first priority was to find somewhere to stay.

She'd forgotten the harsh winds that blew in from the North Sea, gusting down the narrow side streets to catch the passers-by unawares. As a particularly icy blast buffeted her she turned up the collar of the warm tweed coat Chris had given her and turned towards the town centre where, she remembered, there used to be a taxi rank. To her relief it was still there.

Leaning in through the window of the first taxi in the line she asked him if he knew of a reasonably priced hotel.

'Mrs Perkins in Acacia Avenue does B&B if that'll do you, love,' he said. 'You won't find anything cleaner or more comfy. Number 24, it is. Want me to take you there?'

'Yes please.' Imogen climbed into the car, thinking longingly of a cup of tea, a hot bath and a long sleep.

Mrs Perkins turned out to be a motherly, middle-aged woman of about fifty. The moment she opened the door and set eyes on the exhausted Imogen, her plump face softened sympathetically.

'Bless you m'dear, I've got plenty of rooms vacant this time of year,' she said in answer to Imogen's anxious query. 'I only do bed and breakfast, mind.'

'That'll be fine, thank you,' Imogen said, following her wearily up the stairs. The room was pleasant and comfortably furnished and the bed looked irresistibly soft and inviting. Mrs Perkins watched thoughtfully as Imogen took off her coat.

'I can make you a few sandwiches and a pot of tea if you like,' she said. 'You look all in dear, if you don't mind me saying so.'

Imogen smiled. 'Thank you, that would be very kind. I've been travelling since early this morning and I'm too tired to go out.'

She ate the sandwiches Mrs Perkins brought her and drank the tea gratefully, then she undressed and climbed into the bed, falling into an exhausted sleep almost at once.

When she woke up it was mid-afternoon. Downstairs she found Mrs Perkins in the kitchen. The woman looked up with a smile when she tapped on the half-open door.

'Oh there you are then, dear. Had a nice rest, have you?'

'Lovely, thank you.'

'There's plenty of hot water if you'd like a bath.'

'Thanks, I would.'

Mrs Perkins dried her hands on a towel, looking thoughtfully at her guest. 'Pardon me asking, but how long were you planning to stay?'

Imogen took a deep breath. 'I'm hoping to

129

stay in Craybourne permanently,' she said. 'If I can find a suitable job, that is.'

The older woman looked doubtful. It was a strange time to be settling in a new place, even odder to be looking for a job two days before Christmas.

'I see. Well, you're welcome to stay on here for as long as you like. But I daresay you'll be looking for a little flat or something.'

'Once I've found a job,' Imogen said. 'You wouldn't know of anything, would you?'

'In what line dear?'

'Anything,' Imogen said hopefully.

'Well now, if it was something temporary you were after I daresay you could do worse than try one or two of the big hotels on the cliffs,' Mrs Perkins said. 'There's always extra help needed in the hotel business at Christmas. Though I'd imagine most of them will be fixed up by now.'

'Thanks, that's a good idea. I'll try them.'

'You'll be here for the holiday then? I mean, you won't be spending it with your family?' Mrs Perkins asked.

Imogen shook her head. 'I have no family. My parents were killed in a car accident some years ago and I was an only child.'

'Oh, you poor dear.' She smiled gently. 'I know how it feels. My husband died last year and we never had a family. I'd be lonely if it wasn't for this place and my guests. A job in a hotel might be just the thing for you too,' she said cheerfully. 'Plenty of company.' She peered at Imogen, curiosity getting the better of her. 'Nasty gash you've had there, dear. Bruises too. Accident, was it?'

Imogen nodded. She was about to mention the Regent Street bombing, which Mrs Perkins must have heard about. Then she changed her mind. The less she was associated with that, the better. 'I was in a friend's car when it ran into a lamp post,' she said. 'Not serious, luckily.' She bit the inside of her lip at the glib way the lie had slipped out. But then from now on her whole existence was to be a lie. She'd better get used to it, she reminded herself.

'Accidents shake you up more than you realise at the time,' said Mrs Perkins sympathetically. 'Let's hope you have more luck with your job hunting.'

But although Imogen tried every one of the smart hotels along the cliff walk the following day, walking till her back ached and her feet were sore, none of them had a vacancy of any kind. There was just one hotel she hadn't tried and she decided to leave it till the next morning. After that it would be Christmas Eve and there would be no hope of a vacancy until after the holiday.

The Imperial was a tall white stuccoed building at the far end of the cliff walk. It was half past ten when she arrived there the following morning. Later than she'd intended. When Mrs Perkins had caught sight of her white face and the dejected droop of her shoulders as she climbed the stairs last night, she had insisted on making her supper. And this morning when Imogen came downstairs she found a hearty breakfast waiting.

'That'll set you up for the day dear,' Mrs P beamed. 'Nothing like a good breakfast, I always say. Helps boost your energy.'

Imogen climbed the front steps of The Imperial and went through the glass doors into the lush warmth of the reception hall. Her feet sank into the deep-pile carpet and the ambience and comfort of the place seemed to wrap itself round her. The furnishings were elegant, yet simple; the Christmas decorations kept to a tasteful minimum, consisting only of evergreens embellished with frosted fir cones and festive flower arrangements in the mirrored alcoves on either side of the fireplace and behind the reception desk. Large windows looked out on to a wonderful sea view and comfortable chairs were grouped invitingly round the open fireplace where a blazing log fire gave off a wonderful scent of wood smoke. Through double glass doors beyond the curving staircase she could see a dining room. Tables were laid with snowy cloths, silverware and crystal, and a chandelier glittered overhead. It was quite the nicest hotel Imogen had seen in Craybourne. Luxurious, yet warm and inviting at the same time.

She walked up to the reception desk, but the moment she caught sight of the exquisitely groomed blonde receptionist behind the desk, her confidence wilted. Stupid of her to imagine that there would be vacancies here the day before Christmas Eve, she told herself. The management of a place like this, so well organised and well run, would have made sure they had enough staff for the holiday months ago. It really was useless, looking for a job at this time of year.

'Can I help you?' The receptionist was looking expectantly at her and suddenly Imogen made up her mind.

'Can I book a table for lunch please?' It could be the last treat she'd have for some time, she told herself. And in spite of Mrs P's breakfast she was certainly hungry enough to do justice to it.

'Certainly,' the girl said. 'What time would you like it for? We start serving at twelve thirty.'

'I think one o'clock would be best,' Imogen said.

'Right. A table for how many?' The receptionist looked at her enquiringly.

'Oh — just for me — for one.'

She went back to Acacia Avenue and changed into the one dress she had, an almost new black jersey shift that Chris had given her, protesting that she had put on weight since buying it. On the day of the bombing, Imogen had been wearing her pearls. They were part of her Aunt Agnes's legacy and as she clasped them round her neck she reminded herself that she might need to sell them soon if no job turned up. The few hundred pounds in her current account wouldn't last long.

At five to one she arrived at The Imperial and walked once more into the opulent atmosphere, now redolent of luxurious food that made her mouth water. In the dining room she was shown to her table by an immaculate waiter. She was a little disappointed to find she had been allocated a small table right next to the kitchen, but when her soup arrived and she tasted it, she soon forgot her disappointment.

She was halfway through her first course when she heard a loud crash and an agonised yell from the kitchen. Through the swing door she could hear sounds of panic and when her waiter appeared again she asked him if anything was wrong.

'Not at all.' He shook his head, but nevertheless he looked agitated.

'But I heard a scream,' she insisted. 'Look, if anyone is injured I might be able to help. I'm a nurse.' The words were out before she'd had time to think. The man hesitated, biting his lip. 'One of the girls in the kitchen has upset a pan of boiling water over her feet,' he explained in a whisper. 'Perhaps if you could just take a look. It's this way.' He led her through to the kitchen.

A plump girl of about seventeen sat on a chair surrounded by a group of agitated kitchen staff. Tears ran down her cheeks and her white face was contorted with pain. Someone had taken down a first-aid kit and the contents lay strewn on the kitchen worktop but no one seemed to know the correct treatment. When Imogen arrived their relief was obvious.

Kneeling down beside the girl, she took her hand and asked her name.

'Glenda,' the girl said through chattering teeth. Imogen saw at once that both the girl's feet had been severely scalded and knew she must be in agony.

'Don't worry, Glenda,' she said. 'I'm going to take your shoes and tights off as carefully as I can, then we'll see if we can ease the pain.'

Over her shoulder she said, 'She needs to go to hospital as quickly as possible to be on the safe side, so could someone please telephone for an ambulance? And can I have a bowl of cold water and a cool drink for her, please? She should have some fluids at once.'

She worked quickly, removing her shoes and tights as gently as she could and immersing the scalded feet in cold water. By the time the ambulance arrived Imogen had covered the cooled scalds with clean towels and after she had helped the paramedics to get the girl into the ambulance, the kitchen staff crowded round to thank her.

'Please go back to your table and let me bring you some fresh soup,' her waiter insisted. 'Yours will be cold by now.'

She returned to her table and enjoyed her meal, a little embarrassed by the special attention she received from the waiter. She was finishing her coffee when he appeared again at her side and cleared his throat.

'Er, excuse me, Miss, but Mr Bennett, out proprietor, has asked me to tell you that your lunch is on the house,' he said. 'And when you have finished he would be pleased if you would step into his office for a moment. It's just off the reception hall.'

'Oh. Thank you.' Imogen blushed, dismayed. The last thing she had wanted was to draw attention to herself. She thanked the waiter again and as soon as she thought no one was looking she got up and walked quietly out of the dining room. In the reception lounge a few people were chatting over their coffee.

Outside it had begun to rain. The wind from the sea had strengthened to gale force and was buffeting the windows with pulses of rain. She paused to put on her coat, turning up the collar and wishing she had an umbrella. The walk back to Acacia Avenue would take her about twenty minutes and she looked forward to it without enthusiasm. Her hand was on the door, about to brave the weather when a voice behind her said, 'I believe I owe you my thanks.'

She turned, embarrassed at being caught sneaking out. A tall, well-built man stood in the doorway of the office behind the reception desk. He wore a dark grey suit and his brown hair was frosted with silver. Under heavy, well-shaped brows his hazel eyes were smiling warmly at her. She felt herself blushing.

'Oh — not at all. Thank you for my lunch. There was no need.'

'On the contrary, it was the least I could do. I hope you enjoyed your meal.'

'Oh, I did — very much. Thank you.'

He held out his hand. 'I'm Adam Bennett and I own The Imperial. Please — will you come and join me in a brandy before you go? It's cold outside.'

Imogen hesitated. 'Well . . . '

'Please . . . ' He stood aside and held the door open, making refusal impossible.

In the office he indicated a chair and opened a

cabinet, taking out a decanter of brandy and pouring two glasses.

As he handed her the glass he said, 'The unfortunate incident in the kitchen could have been much worse and I'm very grateful that you happened to be on hand to deal with it. Mrs Lane, our housekeeper, has a first-aid certificate but she's away today having some dental treatment. There really should be some back-up for such occasions. I shall have to see to it.' He smiled at her over his glass. 'I took this place over only recently and I thought I'd reorganised efficiently, but that's an important area I've clearly missed out on.'

'Accidents happen. I was happy to be able to help,' she said.

He was looking at her closely, his quick, perceptive eyes taking in the cut on her cheek and the slight discolouration around her eyes. 'Are you new to Craybourne, Miss — er, Miss . . . ?'

'Tanner,' she said quickly. 'Sylvia Tanner. Yes, I only arrived here the day before yesterday.'

'Staying for the holiday? You have family here?'

'No. I'm hoping to settle here.' She smiled wryly. 'If I can find work, that is.'

'That surely won't be a problem. All the hospitals are desperate for nurses, aren't they?'

She blushed, taking a sip of her brandy to hide her confusion. 'I'm not actually a nurse,' she said. 'I mean I — did the training but — never qualified.'

'That's a pity. You're obviously efficient. I'd

have thought you could still go back. Finish your training perhaps?'

'I don't want to go back,' she said quickly, wishing he would drop the subject. 'I — I'd rather do something else.'

He smiled. 'Well, if you're really desperate, we're going to be short of kitchen staff now.'

Her heart quickened. 'Do you mean it? Is there really a vacancy? Would you consider me?'

His smile vanished and he looked shocked. 'I was *joking*, Miss Tanner!'

'I wasn't,' she said bluntly.

'But surely you'll be looking for something more — well something better?'

'I'd be happy to take anything for the time being,' she said. 'And of course I realise that it would only be temporary — until Glenda — at least until after Christmas.'

'Well, that's right — although Glenda was only working here in her school holidays, so I daresay that under the circumstances she won't be coming back.'

'And I've no experience and — no — no references,' she said glancing at him sideways. 'So if you think — I mean, I don't want you to feel you owe it to me or anything.'

His eyebrows rose. 'Miss Tanner, you're obviously an intelligent young woman. I think I can trust you to manage a menial job like preparing vegetables and washing up! In fact I feel it's a poor way to repay you for what you did today. The money is hardly . . . '

'It'll be fine. At least for now,' she assured him. 'When would you like me to start?'

'Well — would this afternoon be too soon?' he asked, taken aback by her obvious eagerness.

'Not at all.'

'Then why don't you report to Peter McKenzie — he's the chef and everyone calls him Mac, at about three o'clock.'

'Fine. I will.'

For a moment they stared at each other, then Adam said, 'You are sure about this? I mean, absolutely sure?'

'Yes, of course.' She stood up awkwardly, backing towards the door. 'Well, I suppose I'd better go home and change.'

He got up from his desk and watched from the window as she went down the steps and lowered her head into the driving wind. *Well! What was all that about?* he asked himself. Why was she here at this time of year, searching so desperately for a job that she'd take hotel kitchen work? She was attractive, articulate — obviously well educated. She didn't look hard up. He'd noticed the fine string of pearls she wore and the soft white hands that definitely weren't accustomed to kitchen chores. But the anxious look she'd darted at him when she mentioned that she had no references hadn't escaped his notice. Was she running away from something? He sincerely hoped he hadn't just taken on someone with a police record. He'd had enough trouble to last him for a while without that! No. The girl's clothes had looked good — expensive. Yet somehow they hadn't looked quite *right* on her. The tweed coat had been too heavy for her delicate frame. The wide fur collar that she turned up against the harsh wind almost obscured her heart-shaped face.

Frowning, he turned away from the window. He'd always prided himself on being a good judge of character. Mustn't get carried away by deceptively innocent looks. He remembered the recent lacerations and, if he wasn't very much mistaken, the remains of a couple of black eyes; faint, but unmistakable. A battered wife? But he'd noticed that she wore no rings. Battered girlfriend? He hardly thought so somehow. He shook his head and turned back to his desk. Oh well, it was none of his business. She wasn't likely to cause him any trouble in the few days she was likely to be there. And after all, they were short-staffed.

★　★　★

Chris had been relieved when Imogen rang her to say she had got a job. She'd tried to keep the dismay out of her voice when she heard that her friend was to work in a hotel kitchen all over the Christmas holiday. Privately she thought that the man who owned the hotel had a damned cheek, offering a job like that to someone who had helped him out of a difficult situation. It was pretty bad, not having anyone on hand who knew any first aid. He'd be lucky if the girl's parents didn't sue him. But she said nothing, not wanting to spoil Imogen's obvious pleasure.

Secretly she wished that Imogen could have stayed to share Christmas with her. She could have taken her home. Her mother would have been delighted to see her. But of course that wasn't possible under the circumstances. To everyone but herself, Imogen was dead. She had to remind herself of the fact a dozen times a day and she prayed that she wouldn't forget and let something slip while she was at home that would give her friend away. She was still uneasy about Imogen's decision to adopt the dead Sylvia Tanner's identity. Some day she would have to come back and face the truth. Sylvia had a police record — had been to prison. In spite of her reassurances to Imogen she wasn't at all sure what effect the discovery would have on a future employer's opinion of her.

Max rang her on Christmas Eve, just as she was setting off for home. He wanted to know whether she was covering the inquest on the victims of the bombing which was to take place the week after Christmas.

'No,' she said. 'I asked if someone else could cover it.'

'I think you should do it, Chris,' he said. 'It might help you to face up to Imogen's death. You'll be going to the funeral, of course.'

'What funeral?' The moment she'd said it she bit her tongue hard. 'Oh, you mean Imogen's. No, I shan't go.'

'Why not?'

'Because I don't happen to like William Jameson,' she told him.

'That's you all over, isn't it, Chris? You just can't face up to anything unpleasant. You'll never make a good journalist until you toughen up.'

'Thanks for the advice,' she said crisply. 'At

141

least no one could ever accuse *you* of not being tough and hard.'

'I am when I have to be,' he said quietly. 'That's the difference between you and me.' There was a small silence, then he asked, 'How are you, Chrissie?'

'I'm absolutely fine, thanks.'

'I know you must still be missing her — Imogen.'

'Yes.'

'What are you doing for Christmas?'

'I'm going home for a couple of days,' she told him. 'In fact I'm just off. You only just caught me.'

'Good. I'm glad.'

She paused, frowning. 'Why, what are you doing?'

'Oh — nothing much.' She knew by the hesitation in his voice that he would be spending at least part of the holiday with his family. 'Come on, Max, where's all that tough ruthlessness? Why can't you just tell the truth?' she asked acidly. 'I don't give a damn what you do with Christmas or any of your free time any more. I'm surprised you even *care* what I think about it anyway.'

'I *do* care, Chris,' he said. 'As a matter of fact I was wondering if we might have dinner together on New Year's Eve. See in the New Year together, just the two of us. I thought it might be nice.'

'Sorry, I'll be working till late and anyway I already have a date,' she lied.

'You could always cancel it. It doesn't matter

how late it is. I'd like to see you, Chris.'

She caught her breath. 'You really do have the most colossal nerve, Max,' she told him coldly. 'I'm supposed to sit around here waiting till you deign to call me, then cancel everything I've planned when you do. Well the answer is a very definite no!'

'Come on, Chris, you know I have my priorities,' he said wearily. 'The boys have to come first — at least until they're standing on their own feet.'

'Well I have news for you, Max,' she said. 'I might just not be around when that happy day dawns, so don't rely on it.' Slamming down the phone she stood staring at it, tears in her eyes and her hands trembling. Why couldn't he just go away and leave her alone? Every time she thought she was getting over him he'd surface again and open all the old wounds. Damn him to hell!

★　★　★

Christmas passed in a blur of frenzied activity for Imogen. She had never realised how many vegetables were consumed in a hotel dining room. It seemed to her that she prepared a small mountain of brussels sprouts, carrots and potatoes for every meal, not to mention the out-of-season things; fiddly mangetout and fine beans, sweetcorn and spinach.

Most of the washing up was taken care of by the huge dishwasher in the kitchen, but Mac, the chef — or 'Mac the Knife', as the rest of the staff called him behind his back, insisted on having his pans and ovenware scrubbed by hand in the massive stainless steel sink. Imogen's hands soon became red and chapped. If the pans were anything but clinically spotless Mac would return them to be done again, accompanied by an explosion of volatile criticism, liberally peppered with colourful swear words. She couldn't handle the large pans wearing the slippery rubber gloves provided and the steel wool pads and scouring powder soon demolished her nails and roughened her skin to the texture of sandpaper.

The one good thing about the job was that all her food was provided. And wonderful food it was. Mac was an excellent chef and he saw to it that the staff ate as well as the guests.

Imogen soon made friends with other members of staff too. Three of them in particular. There was Paulo, the waiter, who had served her on the day of Glenda's accident. He was Italian and studying languages in his spare time. Then there was Maggie, the motherly middle-aged waitress who had returned to work to help her son through university. And Connie, Mac's assistant chef, whose ambition was to get a job on a cruise liner and see the world. They were all kind and good humoured, helpful and not at all nosy.

The work was hard and tiring but, for Imogen, it was good to mix with ordinary people once again; to be able to relax mentally, free from the constant fear of unwittingly offending William.

The greatest relief of all was that there was no one questioning her sanity a dozen times a day. Not once since the bombing had she walked in her sleep and she was beginning to question whether she ever had, suspecting that it had been dreamed up by William, like all his other forms of mental torture, to undermine her confidence and destroy her self-esteem.

After work at night she walked back to Acacia Avenue with Paulo, whose bedsit was two streets away. He wouldn't hear of her making the journey on foot alone. Mrs Perkins was always waiting up with a freshly brewed pot of tea, eager to hear about all that had happened during her day. It was wonderful to be with people who cared about her again. And although Imogen knew that the job was only temporary, she was happy that at least she had taken that first frightening step into the Unknown.

★　★　★

There were many members of St Aubrey's nursing staff at the funeral of Imogen Jameson; girls who had trained with her and knew her well. They were waiting in the church as William followed the coffin, accompanied by Edward Mayhew and his daughter Carole, the only other mourners. William looked pale and dignified in his immaculate dark suit and the hearts of all went out to him, their most brilliant and popular surgeon. It must have been so traumatic for him, having to wait so long before he could lay his young wife to rest.

145

Outside the church they lingered in subdued little groups, talking quietly amongst themselves and admiring the huge heart-shaped wreath of red roses which was William's tribute. Some reached out a sympathetic hand to him as he passed on his way to the cemetery, a gesture he responded to with a faint smile and a nod.

The interment was private; just William, Edward and Carole. Afterwards the undertaker stepped up to him and cleared his throat. 'Might I have a word, sir?'

William nodded to Edward and Carole. 'It's cold. You go back to the car. I'll be with you in a moment.' He turned to the man. 'What is it?'

'I thought you might like to have this.' The man took a small box out of the pocket of his black overcoat. 'It was the one piece of — er — jewellery that hadn't been removed.'

Frowning, William opened the box and found a small gold ring nestling on cotton wool. He looked at the man. 'I don't understand. I have all my wife's jewellery. This can't be hers. It's an earring. She didn't have pierced ears.'

The man shuffled his feet, looking acutely embarrassed. 'No, sir, not an earring. I expect it has escaped your memory. It was removed from the deceased's — er — navel.'

William stared at the man for a long moment, then, recovering himself, he quickly slipped the box into his pocket. 'Of course,' he said. 'I'd forgotten. Thank you for being so discreet.'

'Not at all, sir. Fashions come and go, don't they? Please accept my sincere condolences.' Replacing his hat the man walked away towards the empty hearse leaving William staring after him.

9

William lay staring at the ceiling. Although his eyes were open he was reliving that day in the hospital mortuary when he had identified the body as Imogen's. Although he was a surgeon and accustomed to the sight of the human anatomy at its most vulnerable and defenceless, the viewing of that smashed and mutilated body had turned his stomach. He had taken only a cursory glance as the mortuary assistant had turned back the sheet. They had done the best they could to tidy up what was collectively termed 'severe head injuries' but any resemblance the pathetic remains had even to a human being had been hard to see, and even harder to view.

His identification had been a mere formality. Although the coat she had been wearing had been torn and stained it was unmistakably Imogen's; her front door key had been in the pocket — she'd always been careless with keys. They had explained to him that she had been wearing the strap of her handbag around her neck and although he found this slightly odd, it nevertheless ruled out the possibility of the handbag found with the body belonging to anyone else.

Although he'd pushed the tiny gold ring in its cardboard box to the back of his desk drawer he could not dismiss it from his mind. The niggling memory of it returned to haunt him with uncertainty. He considered the likelihood of the funeral director being mistaken about it and grasped the notion. Mistakes were made. Bodies were sometimes mixed up. His eyes snapped open again. *Not this time.* Of the other five fatalities, three had been male and the other two, much older women. They had all been brought to St Aubrey's, and all had been identified. There was no mistake about that.

The body he had identified had been the same age, height and build as Imogen. The hair colour — as far as he could tell, had been the same too. But if he had been mistaken, if the woman he had buried this afternoon wasn't Imogen, then who was it? What the hell was going on?

'Are you awake?' Carole reached out to touch his cheek. 'What is it? You've been very quiet since we got back this afternoon.'

He pushed her hand away. 'It's nothing. Go back to sleep.'

'You're not fretting about her, are you?' She pressed herself close to him. 'She's dead, William. You're free now. We can be together as much as we like. Try to look on the bright side.'

He turned to look at her. 'You shouldn't have stayed here tonight. It looks bad. What will your father think?'

She laughed. 'Daddy thinks what I tell him to think. I've already told him we're getting married as soon as a decent interval has elapsed.'

'You've told him *what*?' He raised himself on one elbow to stare down at her. 'My God, Caro. Sometimes you overstep the mark. What on earth made you tell him that?'

'Why not? He already knew we were seeing each other. Anyway, it's true, isn't it?'

'I don't remember making any such decision.'

'*I* do. It makes sense. Look, you'll have Imogen's money now to pay off what you owe on the house. And when Daddy retires he's going to move down to Cornwall. He's giving me the house, which makes sense as I'd inherit anyway. I can sell it and move in here with you when you get his job. We'll pool our resources. What could be more perfect?'

William lay back and closed his eyes. He had no intention of marrying Carole. Once he had safely been appointed to Edward Mayhew's consultancy he planned to dump her. It would never work. They were far too alike. Together as husband and wife life would be a constant battle for control, something he'd already begun to recognise.

'Darling . . . ' she whispered seductively. 'Relax. I know how to make you sleep. Let me show you.' Her hand was caressing his chest, moving slowly downwards over his abdomen and groin with tiny feathery motions that made his stomach muscles contract. He snatched at her hand and held it.

'Don't! Not now. Better get some sleep. It's late.'

'When did the time ever bother you?' she said petulantly. 'Oh all right then, have it your way.' She turned her back to him, taking most of the duvet with her. 'Don't pretend you're actually mourning the loss of that silly little bitch! I know damned well that you couldn't wait to be free of her! Still, never mind. Just don't expect me to roll over and oblige next time you happen to feel randy.'

He smiled wryly to himself. Carole rolling submissively over was something he'd like to see! He did not respond to her snide remarks but waited till he heard her breathing deepen and felt her angry body relax beside him. Nothing ever bothered Carole for too long. She was too sure of the power she thought she had over him for that. Well, she'd find out.

For now he had to have time to think this problem through carefully. There was no way he could confide his suspicion to anyone. He'd already collected Imogen's life assurance, taken out when they first married. And although she had died intestate, the money from her entire estate would come to him too before much longer. She had no other relatives to claim it. And he needed that money like he needed air to breathe. His creditors were beginning to get decidedly restless.

Imogen had asked for a divorce. Was this her way of escaping? But how? She couldn't have planted that bomb herself. And there was no way she could have foreseen it. Who *was* the woman he had buried today? And why had she been wearing Imogen's coat and carrying her bag? Was it Imogen or someone else? Well, whatever, Imogen had presumably achieved her aim — to escape from him one way or another. But for how long? What would she do without money to support herself? Might she come back and try to blackmail him?

The sky was already beginning to lighten when he finally dropped into an uneasy sleep. He'd already decided that it couldn't be left like this. Somehow he would have to find out the truth. If Imogen was alive, then he would have to discover where she was and put a stop to any nasty surprises she had up her sleeve.

★ ★ ★

New Year passed and Imogen began to wonder how much longer her job at The Imperial would last. Finally she plucked up the courage to ask Mac. She tapped on the door of his little cubby hole of an office one afternoon before she went off for her break.

'Yes?' The chef sat at the desk from which he did his ordering and paperwork. He was a big man; broad and tall, with beady dark eyes and a neatly trimmed beard and moustache, French style. He got up to glower down at her from beneath bushy eyebrows.

She cleared her throat. 'It's almost a fortnight now since New Year and I need to know how much longer my job will last,' she said. 'Because if I'm going to be out of work I ought to be looking round for something else.'

'So — you're eager to be away then?' When he spoke you could cut his Glaswegian accent with a knife and fork. He raised one eyebrow at her.

'Oh no,' Imogen said hastily. 'Only the job was supposed to be temporary and I just — just need to know how much longer I'll be needed.'

'Well, it's up to the boss really,' Mac said. 'But if I'd my way I'd make it permanent. You're a good wee lassie. One o' the best workers I've had for a long time. You get on wi' it and you don't burst into tears when I yell at you.' He looked at her speculatively, his head on one side. 'We've a few functions booked for this month and next. Will I have a word wi' the boss on your behalf? Would y'like to stay on for a wee while longer?'

Imogen blushed with pleasure. 'I would. Thank you, Chef,' she said.

He laughed. 'Dinna kid yourself, lassie. Kindness isni' one o' m'features. I need help and you're it! Better the devil ye know, if y'see wha' I mean.'

But that evening when she got home to Acacia Avenue there was a shock in store. Mrs Perkins had given her a front door key in case Imogen ever returned after her landlady had gone to bed. As she unlocked the door and tried to open it, it stuck. There seemed to be something on the other side, restricting it. She pushed harder and her blood chilled as she heard a groan from the other side.

She managed to get the door open enough to squeeze through and soon found the light switch. When the hall was illuminated a sorry sight met her eyes. Mrs Perkins was lying just inside the door, a nasty cut on her head and one leg lying awkwardly twisted under her.

Imogen administered what first aid she could, covering Mrs Perkins with a blanket and reassuring her. It was clear that the woman had broken her hip and she was in considerable pain.

She told Imogen that she had been hurrying down the stairs to answer the telephone when she tripped and fell heavily.

The ambulance arrived promptly and Imogen went with her landlady to the hospital where the duty officer in Casualty confirmed her suspicion about Mrs Perkins' injury. After ascertaining that there was a bed free he announced that she must be admitted at once for surgery.

Once she was tucked up in the ward it was clear that the older woman was worrying about her house and business.

'I shan't be able to look after you now, dear,' she fretted.

'Don't worry about that Mrs P,' Imogen said. 'Just tell me if there's anything I can do for you.'

'Well . . . ' The older woman hesitated. 'I'd really like to have everywhere locked up while I'm not there,' she said. 'But what about you?'

Imogen knew that Mrs Perkins would not ask her to leave but that she would obviously prefer to shut the place down while she was away. 'That's my problem,' she said. 'I'll find somewhere. And I'll see to it that everywhere is secure first thing in the morning. You're not to worry about anything but getting yourself better.'

'Oh dear, it seems so ungrateful to turn you out,' Mrs Perkins said. 'If it hadn't been for you, goodness knows how long I could have lain there.'

Imogen patted her hand. 'You're not to worry. I'll be fine,' she said. 'You're going to be up and about again in no time and then maybe I can move back again, eh?' But for all her reassurances she couldn't help wondering just what she was going to do as she took the bus back to Acacia Avenue.

The following morning when she reported for work Mac called her into his office. 'I've had a wee word with Mr Bennett and he's happy for you to stay on for a while,' he told her. Bending down he peered into her preoccupied face. 'Oh dear, you're ni looking too happy about it. Isn't that what you wanted?'

'Oh yes — thank you,' Imogen said. 'It's just that my landlady had an accident last night. She's in hospital with a broken hip and I have to look for somewhere else to stay.'

'Is that a fact? Hmm.' Mac rubbed his bearded chin thoughtfully. 'I believe there's a room vacant upstairs in the staff quarters,' he said. 'Staff don't care to live in any more and Mr Bennett was thinking of refurbishing some of the staff rooms for other purposes.' He cocked an eyebrow at her. 'Would you like me to ask him for you?'

'Oh, would you?'

It was after lunch when Adam Bennett sent for her. She combed her hair in front of the staffroom mirror and nervously applied a little lipstick. She had only seen Adam from a distance since her first interview with him and she felt apprehensive. Did he want to get rid of her? Was he going to tell her there wasn't a room vacant after all — or even a job? It was with some trepidation that she knocked on the door of his office just after lunch.

Responding to his call of 'come in' she found

155

him seated behind his desk. He motioned to her to take a seat.

'I hear you'd like to stay on with us here at The Imperial for a few more weeks,' he said.

'I would — if you need me.'

'Mac tells me you're a very good worker. He also told me this morning that owing to your landlady's accident you're unfortunately homeless. Is that right?'

She nodded. 'She fell downstairs and broke her hip. She's likely to be in hospital for some time, so obviously I can't stay there.'

He was studying her carefully. She looked much better since the last time he had seen her close-to. Her bruises had disappeared and she looked more relaxed — happier somehow. In fact very attractive. His quick eyes took in the shining fair hair and the delicately boned face. He also noticed with some regret how red and sore her hands looked.

'Well, Mac was right when he said that there is a room free,' he said. 'But it's in a part of the building I'm thinking of refurbishing as a family flat. My son and his nanny already have rooms there because the present flat is too small to accommodate all of us.'

Imogen tried hard to conceal her surprise. She had no idea that Adam had any children. She wondered where his wife was.

'I see. Well, that would be very convenient — until I can find something else.'

'Of course, with my refurbishment plans it could be only a temporary measure, and I'm afraid you might have trouble finding anything to suit you. It won't be long now before the hotels and guest houses will be booking up for the season. They won't want their rooms cluttered up with low-paying permanent boarders. Even flats are let for the summer — at expensive rents.'

'I see,' she said unhappily. 'I had hoped that Mrs Perkins — when she's well again. But now that you mention it . . . '

'You won't find anything affordable on what we pay you for kitchen work,' he said frankly. 'Sylvia,' he leaned forward. 'I may call you Sylvia?'

'Yes — yes, of course.'

'I have to confess, Sylvia, that to hear you asking to continue as kitchen staff puzzles me,' he said. 'You're obviously well educated and one only has to look at you to know that you haven't been used to that kind of work. Wouldn't you prefer to look for something better?'

She swallowed. 'A job's a job, isn't it? Especially nowadays.'

'Well, yes. All the same . . . I was thinking — if I get a vacancy for a receptionist, would you be interested?'

She felt herself blushing. 'Oh yes, I would.'

'Well, there isn't anything just at present, but when there is I'll keep you in mind.'

'Thank you very much, Mr Bennett.' As she rose to leave he glanced at her. 'Perhaps you'd like to make out a CV for me?'

Her heart missed a beat. 'Oh — yes, I will. And thank you for letting me have the room.'

'Find Mrs Lane, the housekeeper,' he said as

she got up to leave. 'Her office is on the first landing, next to the lift. Just explain that you're moving in. Oh, and Sylvia . . . '

'Yes?' she turned at the door.

'If you could find a couple of people who'd vouch for you . . . ? I'm sure you must know someone.'

'Yes,' she said, her heart sinking. 'Yes, of course.'

Imogen moved her few belongings into the room at The Imperial that afternoon. Mrs Lane, the cool, efficient woman who had been housekeeper at the hotel for almost twenty years, seemed happy that someone would be occupying the room.

'I hate to see rooms lying empty,' she told Imogen as she helped her make up the bed. 'They tend to get so damp and musty. But these staff rooms will make a very nice flat when Mr Bennett gets the plans passed by the local council.' She tweaked at the curtains. 'These could do with renewing, but I suppose it's hardly worth it.' She glanced at Imogen and lowered her voice confidentially.

'I'd better tell you — Mr Bennett's little boy, Simon, is in the room next door,' she said. 'He's four, and a dear little boy, but you might find his nanny, Clare Thomas, rather — well — difficult.'

'Oh, in what way?' Imogen asked.

'She's a distant sort of woman. Keeps herself very much to herself,' Mrs Lane said. 'It's nothing to do with me of course, but she seems an odd choice for a nanny. Very tight-lipped if you know what I mean.'

'Is Mr Bennett a widower?' Imogen asked.

Mrs Lane shook her head. 'Bless you, no. Mr Bennett's father, Mr Richard, used to own The Imperial. He was here when I first came. Mr Adam managed a large hotel on the outskirts of London. His wife, Ann-Marie, was French; very clever and high-powered. She was a management consultant. When they moved here she gave up her job, but she hated the place and couldn't settle so she left Simon with the nanny and went back to London to her old job again.'

'Did she commute?' Imogen asked.

'Yes, at first; most weekends, but it never worked. Six months later she ran off with one of her clients, another Frenchman.' She sniffed. 'If you ask me it had been going on for some time. She and Mr Bennett divorced and she went back to France to live with her new husband.'

'What about her child?' Imogen asked. 'Didn't she want custody of him?'

'Seems not. From what I can gather she was never very interested in him, poor little scrap.'

'How old was Simon when she left?' Imogen asked.

Mrs Lane shrugged. 'He was just two.' She sighed. 'Still a baby, bless him.' She looked at Imogen. 'I'm not gossiping, telling you this,' she said. 'It's just that with you being here in the staff wing it's only right that you should know the circumstances.'

The story brought back the pain of Imogen's own loss and, as she unpacked her things, she wondered how any woman could walk away from her own child, especially at such a tender age.

Before she went on duty that evening Imogen chose a quiet moment to ring Chris from the pay phone in the staffroom.

'Hi, it's me, Sylvia.' It was what they'd agreed — that she would always use her new assumed name.

'Hello. How are you?'

'I'm fine. Listen, Chris, I'm living here at The Imperial from today.' She explained about Mrs Perkins' accident. 'There's a chance I might get a better job here at the hotel,' she went on, 'but I need a CV and a couple of references. I thought I could ask Mrs Perkins and — and you. Would you mind if I gave your name?'

'Of course not.'

'It's asking a lot. If we were to get found out . . .'

'It's no use thinking like that,' Chris said firmly. 'You've decided to go along this road and now you have to take all the chances that go with it.'

'I know. Chris — what shall I put on the CV?'

'Just be truthful about yourself — it's all you can do.'

'But if they check on the school or St Aubrey's?'

'I've never heard of anyone checking on a school or training college.'

'I suppose it's possible to trace the police record,' Imogen said fearfully. 'Suppose they found out about the prison sentence?'

'Just remember that as far as you're concerned personally, you've only taken the name,' Chris reminded her. 'You haven't turned *into* the woman. You don't have to assume her guilt as well. As for the rest, like I said, you'll just have to take a gamble on it.'

'Right. Thanks, Chris.'

'Are you all right?'

'Yes.'

'Sure?'

'It's a bit lonely. I miss you.'

'Me too. Maybe when the weather warms up I'll come and stay for a few days.'

'Oh, that would be wonderful.'

'We'll have to have a talk — sort things out for you.' She paused. 'Im — er — Sylvia . . . '

'Yes?'

'There was a funeral. It was in the paper. I wasn't there, someone else covered it and there were only a few lines on the back page. I just — thought you should know.'

'I see. I'm glad it's over. Bye, Chris. And thanks.'

It was late that night when Imogen woke suddenly. At first she wondered where she was and she had no idea what had woken her up. She lay in the darkness with a vague uneasy feeling of anxiety. Then she heard it; the soft and unmistakable sound of a child crying in the room next door.

★   ★   ★

Chris had been working late, covering a book launch at Harrods by a woman cabinet minister-turned-novelist. There had been a

161

champagne reception for the press afterwards and Chris had managed to get a few private words with the woman. It was almost nine when she climbed the stairs to the flat. She was just fumbling in her bag for her key when a figure stepped out of the shadows, making her jump.

'Oh! Max.' Her heart turned a somersault and quickly sank. 'What do you want?'

'That's a nice welcome after I've waited all this time,' he said. 'I thought you'd never come home.' He watched as she inserted the key and opened the door.

'I don't actually remember inviting you,' she remarked as he followed her inside. 'Anyway, how did you get in?'

'Slipped in behind another visitor.'

She sighed. 'Look, Max, I've had a busy day and I'm tired. Can it wait — whatever it is?'

'No.' He followed her through to the kitchen. 'I need to see you, Chris, and I think you need to see me too.'

'I've got an article to write up.' She filled the kettle at the sink, feeling her throat tighten with tension. 'I've been at that bloody awful champagne reception to launch Madeleine Barnes's abysmal novel. It was more like a rugby scrum and I'm knackered. For God's sake why can't you get the message, Max? We're finished!'

'You know that's not true.' He was getting the milk out of the fridge, sniffing experimentally at the jug — looking in the cupboard for the coffee. Just as though he still shared the flat with her. Suddenly he turned and caught the resentful look on her face. 'Oh, Chrissie, don't look like

162

that.' He reached out and pulled her into his arms. 'Poor baby, you're really shattered, aren't you? Look, why don't you go and have a nice hot bath and I'll cook supper for you, just like in the old days.' He held her away from him and looked down into her eyes. 'No strings. Just mates, OK?'

She leaned her head wearily against his chest. He felt so solid and masculine. The familiar scent of his old leather jacket mingled with the healthy saltiness of male sweat filled her nostrils and tugged painfully at her heartstrings. He tipped up her chin.

'You haven't noticed,' he said. 'I had my beard trimmed and my hair cut today.' It had always been a bone of contention between them. He never found time to do either unless she nagged him. 'It was just for you,' he said with his familiar heart-stopping grin.

'Thanks,' she said flatly. 'But you needn't have bothered.'

He cupped her face in both hands and kissed her as though he was savouring a particularly delectable wine. 'Mmm,' he murmured appreciatively, eyes closed. 'That's so good. I miss you so much, Chrissie. I just can't get along without you.'

'Try harder,' she said, her voice muffled as he pressed her head close to his neck.

'Right.' He released her suddenly. 'Go and have that bath then. Supper'll be ready in fifteen minutes. If you're not out by then I'll come and get you.' He turned her round and gave her a push towards the bathroom, smacking her rear none too gently as he did so.

There was very little food in the flat. Chris had forgotten to go to the shops. All Max could find was a packet of mince and a tin of tomatoes, but with his characteristic resourcefulness he had turned out a very passable spagbol. He'd brought a bottle of Chris's favourite red wine along with him and as she ate and drank, wrapped in her warm velour dressing gown, she began to feel better.

'Tell me about Madeleine Barnes's book launch,' he prompted, refilling her wine glass.

She smiled. 'Let's just say that if the champagne had been as chilled and fizzy as she was it might have been bearable.'

'Ouch!' He laughed. 'I hope you did your homework and read the book.'

'I did.' She grimaced. 'It was ghastly, a chimpanzee could have done better. Cover to cover sex, cardboard characters and no plot to speak of. But I hear it's already a bestseller.'

He laughed. 'You should know by now my love; it's a powerful combination, sex plus a notorious political name. And any fool can write a book, or so one would believe by the number of has-beens who jump on the bandwagon.'

Chris pushed her empty plate away and leaned back. 'That was marvellous,' she said. 'I'd probably just have made myself a sandwich and dropped into bed.'

'Glad to have been of service, madam.' He gave her a mock bow, then crossed the room and slid a CD into her player. A moment later the luscious strains of *Music of the Night* filled the room.

164

'Remember this?' he asked. 'The night we went to see *Phantom*. It was our first date. You wore that blue dress and you looked stunning. I'll never forget it. It was so romantic. All the way home in the car we sang the tunes.' He took her hand and pulled her to her feet, his eyes dark as they looked into hers. 'You were done up to the nines that night, but you know what? I like you better like this, all warm from the bath with your face scrubbed and wholesome.' He kissed her. 'It's not finished, is it, Chris? It'll never be finished between you and me. We belong together. We always will.'

As the music swelled he kissed her again, deeply and searchingly, and she felt her body melt to his touch. She should have known she didn't stand a chance. Once she had let him over the threshold of the flat he was back into her heart; the marauding invader, ruthless and persistent and oh, so insidious.

When she felt his firm hands slip the dressing gown from her shoulders and felt his lips graze the skin of her breast she stood motionless, breathlessly trembling with a fearful anticipation. And when he bent to slip an arm behind her knees, swinging her up into his arms, she knew she had once again let him win. But she was past caring.

She woke when it was still dark and lay quite still. At first she thought she must have dreamed the events of the previous night. She often dreamed of Max; dreams that left her aching with longing and frustration. Then she felt him stir beside her and knew that it had been real.

Their love-making had been fiery and tempestuous, each of them driven by the parting that drove them both crazy. Her body tingled with the memory of it and she reached out to touch him. He was instantly awake, turning to her, his arms around her once again, his lips seeking hers.

'You're still here,' he whispered against her hair. 'Thank God. I thought it was another one of my wild fantasies. Never make me go away again, Chrissie. I love you.'

She snuggled close. 'I love you too. Max, we'll have to sort out all the complications and — ' He stopped her mouth with a kiss.

'Shh. Time for that later. Right now, you're here with me in bed. We're warm and sexy and we're wasting precious time.'

This time they made love slowly and sensuously, without the urgency of the previous night. Deeply satisfied, relaxed and happy, Chris fell asleep again immediately after and when she woke again Max was coming into the room with a breakfast tray. He was freshly bathed and dressed. She sat up, looking at the clock in a panic. 'God! What's the time?'

'Relax, it's still only half-seven.' He sat down on the edge of the bed and poured two cups of coffee. 'Sex gives me boundless energy — 'specially with you.' He grinned at her as he lifted his cup. 'When I've drunk this I'll have to go. I've got a story to follow up.' He buttered a piece of toast for her. 'Chrissie, can I have a spare key?' When she hesitated his eyes widened. 'Oh, come *on!* Surely you don't have to think about it that hard.'

'I don't know, Max.'

'What do you mean, you don't *know*? Didn't last night mean anything to you?' When she didn't reply he went on. 'I know, you're one of those girls who only want one thing from a man. Once you've had it you toss us poor innocent guys out like used teabags!'

She laughed in spite of herself and he bent to kiss her, licking up a blob of marmalade from the corner of her mouth.

'Yum yum, you're delicious. OK, so where's that key then?'

'All right, you win. You'll have to rummage in the bottom of my handbag for it. But it's only for occasional visits, mind,' she called out to his retreating back. 'You're not moving in — at least — not yet,' she added, half to herself.

In the living room Max located the handbag where Chris had dropped it last night, in the corner of the settee. He rooted around in the feminine contents. 'God, the stuff you women carry around with you!' he called out. 'It weighs a ton. It's a wonder you don't have arms like a gorilla!' He found the key, but the ring caught on something, pulling it up from the bottom of the bag. He looked at it curiously and called out, 'Hey, there's a giro in here. What are you doing with someone else's giro?'

There was a pause from the bedroom, then Chris appeared in the doorway. 'I'd forgotten about that,' she said truthfully. 'I — picked it up somewhere. I meant to post it.'

167

'Really?' He turned it over and looked at it. Sylvia Tanner. The name rang a bell somewhere but he couldn't remember why. 'OK, I'll post it for you,' he said, pushing it into his pocket.

'No, it's OK, don't bother. I'll do it.' She stepped forward and held out her hand, but he took it and raised it to his lips, kissing the fingers. 'It's all right. No sweat. I'll do it on my way out. Got to run, baby. Shall I see you tonight?'

'Well — all right. I might be late home again though.'

He waved the key at her. 'Doesn't matter. I've got this now. I'll do some shopping, shall I? Have something nice ready and waiting for you.' He grinned wickedly. 'Might even make supper too!'

When he'd gone she stood staring at the door. Why hadn't she done something about the giro? How stupid of her to forget. Perhaps he too would forget about it. She hoped so.

Max was getting into his car when it suddenly clicked. Sylvia Margaret Tanner. Of *course*. He snapped his fingers in triumph. The Morgan case. So Sylvia had done her time and she was out! Interesting that he'd found the giro in Chris's bag. Was she hiding something from him? He took the giro out of his pocket and looked at the address. Right. Maybe he'd look her up and see if she was still in touch with Phil Morgan. There might be a story in it.

10

Max knew better than to wait for permission. He walked straight in through the door of number 25 Canning Terrace and up the stairs. Flat 6, it said on the giro. He knocked on the door with a crude 6 painted on it and waited. Nothing happened. Maybe Sylvia had found herself a proper job. He hoped so. Hoped too that the poor kid was making a decent life for herself. She deserved better than that low-life, Morgan. But looking about him at the dingy surroundings, he doubted it. Somehow girls like Sylvia never seemed to climb out of the rut.

He was just turning away when another door opened and a woman peered out. He smiled at her.

'Hi there. I'm looking for Sylvia Tanner,' he said. 'Do you happen to know when she'll be back?'

'Wish I did,' the woman said. 'She's been gone since before Christmas. Her room's let to someone else now.'

'I see. Are you a friend of hers?'

The woman nodded. 'Used to be.'

'You've no idea where she might be, have you? Only I've got something for her.'

'Well — not really.' She hesitated, stepping forward to look over the bannisters. 'Come in a minute,' she invited with a jerk of her head. 'Bloody walls round here've got ears.'

169

Inside the cramped bedsit a grubby baby played contentedly in a playpen by the fireplace. The woman took a packet of cigarettes from the mantelpiece and offered him one.

'Thanks.'

She took one herself and as he held out his lighter for her she peered at him over the flame. 'You're not the police, are you?'

'No, I'm not the police.'

'Thought not. You don't look like a copper. The Social?' Again he shook his head. 'Only I don't want to say nothin' to make trouble for Sylv.'

'I'm not here to make trouble, I promise you.'

'You're not the first person who's been here asking for her.'

'Really?'

'Yeah. This bloke's kept coming round harassing her.' She drew hard on her cigarette and blew out the smoke. 'He was here again this week. Seems to think I know where she is.'

'And do you?'

She looked at him. 'I just told you — no! And if Rex Morgan sent you, you can tell him — '

'Who's Rex Morgan?' Max interrupted. 'And what makes you think he sent me?'

'It's him who came round harassing her.'

'Well I can promise you that I don't run errands for anyone,' Max said firmly.

She looked at him for a long moment, taking in the powerful shoulders and emphatic presence and seemed satisfied. 'OK, but you can't be too careful. I expect you know that Sylv's been inside.' She sighed. 'It was Rex's brother Sylv was tied up with. Ever since she come out he's never left her alone. You never seem to be able to shake it off, prison. Follows you round like a bloody great black dog.'

'I know what you mean. But I promise you I only want to help, Mrs — ?'

'Sullivan. Mo Sullivan. And it's Ms, not Mrs. So — what is it you got for Sylv?'

'I think that's really between her and me, don't you?' he said. 'But she must be hard up and I might be able to nudge something profitable her way.'

'Legit you mean?'

'Of course.'

'Well — there's nothin' much I can do about it, is there?'

'I suppose not — if you really don't know where she is.'

'Well . . . '

He raised an eyebrow at her. 'Yes?'

'It's nothin' much — just that there was this woman asking stuff about her a while back,' she said.

'Really? Who was she?'

Mo gave him a sideways look as she flicked her ash out of the open window. 'Dunno. *She* knew where Sylv was though.'

'She did?'

'Yeah — said she was stayin' with her. That she'd been hurt in that bombing up Regent Street just before Christmas. She said Sylv had lost her memory and she asked me to tell her as much as I could about her to help her get it back.'

'Didn't you get her address or a phone number?'

'No. I asked if I could go and see Sylv, but she said she didn't wanna see no one and that she was goin' away for a while to get well again.' She frowned. 'That was weeks ago though. I thought she'd have been back by now. I tried to talk the stingy old git downstairs into keeping the room for her, but he wouldn't.'

'Not really surprising after all these weeks,' Max said.

'Thing is,' she glanced at him, 'thing is, her giros keep comin' here.' She opened a drawer and took out a handful of envelopes. 'Why 'asn't she given the Social her new address? She must want the money.'

'Perhaps she's found herself a job.' Max thought about the giro he'd found in Chris's bag — nestling at this moment in his wallet. 'This woman who came asking about her — did you get her name?'

'Miss Knight,' Mo said.

'What did she look like?'

She pursed her lips, thinking. 'Tall; good lookin'. Nice clothes. Oh, and red hair — not dyed; natural, I'd say.'

'I see.' Max took out a notebook and wrote down a telephone number, tearing the page out and passing it to Mo. 'That's my number. It's a mobile so you can get me on it any time. If you hear anything from Sylvia or if she shows up could you let me know?' He opened his wallet and looked at the giro, then he took out a ten pound note and handed it to her. 'Get the kid something eh?'

Mo smiled. 'Thanks, I will. And I'll let you know if I hear anything.'

Back in the car Max sat thinking, tapping his front teeth with his thumb nail. Miss Knight? And red hair! Knight — *Knight and Day*? And the Regent Street bombing. It was one hell of a coincidence, surely?

At the offices of the *Daily Globe* he chatted to his old friend Bill Morrisey, the assistant editor who, on the quiet, often let him use the office facilities for his own work.

'About lunchtime, isn't it?' Max said. 'Come on, I'll buy you a pint and a sandwich.'

Bill grinned good-naturedly. 'OK, what do you want this time? The scanner — Internet?'

'No. I've just invested in a state-of-the-art computer,' Max told him. 'I've even got my own website these days. But now you mention it I could do with a peep at the archives. Want to look up something from a couple of years back — case I covered when I was still on the paper. It won't take a minute.'

'No problem,' Bill said. 'The old man's out this morning anyway, but I know he wouldn't mind.'

By the time the two men were walking into the bar of the pub round the corner from the office, Max had refreshed his memory of the Morgan case. Ever since he'd talked to Mo Sullivan this morning something had been niggling at the back of his mind. Now he

173

knew what it was. Although Phil Morgan and the girl, Sylvia Margaret Tanner, had been charged and Morgan convicted of manslaughter, the jewellery from the robbery had never been recovered. Morgan had insisted that the safe had been empty but that Tanner knew where they were; she had disclaimed all knowledge of them. And no trace of them had ever been found.

Max was quiet over his beer and sandwich. If Tanner did know where the jewellery was it would explain a lot; the reason Morgan's brother was harassing her for a start. He was obviously after more than revenge for his brother's betrayal. And where did Chris come into it? Was she on to something? Was she really hiding Tanner — waiting until she had enough evidence to back up a hunch? Was she on the scent of the story of a lifetime?

* * *

When Chris got home that evening it was late. She'd been to Heathrow to meet the plane carrying an American rock group. In the VIP lounge she'd been jostled and pushed by photographers and other journalists, and when she did get close enough to ask for a comment she found the group members almost as rude and arrogant as her male colleagues. She was bruised and weary; seriously questioning, as she often did nowadays, whether she was in the right job.

As she climbed the stairs she thought

174

longingly of Max's promised supper, waiting for her, but the moment she let herself into the cold, dark flat she knew it was empty. 'Typical!' she said aloud as she threw her bag on to the nearest chair. When she needed him he always let her down. Had she been weak and foolish, letting herself in for all this again?

She took off her coat and lit the gas fire, then went through to the kitchen to put the kettle on. Max had said he'd do some shopping. Now there was no food in! If she'd known, she could have gone to the supermarket on the way home. She seethed with annoyance. *If only he wasn't always promising to do things and then forgetting all about them!* It really was all she needed tonight.

The sudden buzz of the entryphone sent her hurrying to press the button. Max was hopeless, he was always forgetting his keys. A few minutes later the doorbell rang and she ran to answer it. 'You really are the limit — *Oh!*' She stopped, her blood suddenly turning to ice as she recognised the tall figure standing outside.

'William!'

'Might I come in for a minute?'

'Of course.' Reluctantly she stood aside, then peered out on to the empty landing, wishing even harder that Max was here. In the living room they faced each other. 'What can I do for you?'

'I wanted to talk to you,' he said. 'You must

175

have been one of the last people to see Genny — alive.'

She swallowed. 'I suppose I was.'

'You didn't come to the funeral.'

'No.'

'It rather surprised me. I thought that as her oldest friend — '

'I was working,' she said quickly. 'My editor isn't the sympathetic type.'

'I see.'

There was a pause, then Chris said, 'So — how can I help?'

'I'd like to know what she did — that last day. She was staying with you.' He looked at her hard. 'She *was* staying with you, wasn't she?'

'Of course she was. We were going to have a day together, you know, just relaxing. I'd taken a few days off work — to settle into this flat. Well, then I got a sudden urgent request from the paper to cover a bomb scare — in Islington. It turned out to be a hoax. As you know, the bomb was elsewhere.'

'Quite. So you left Genny here — alone?'

'Yes. She was going up to Regent Street to have a hairdo and facial at Dickins & Jones. It was my suggestion. I — felt terrible afterwards.'

'And you never saw her again?'

Chris felt herself turn ice cold at the look in his eyes. Could he possibly suspect anything? 'No, I — ' The door banged and suddenly Max stood in the doorway loaded down with supermarket carrier bags.

'I'm sorry I'm so late, Chris . . . Oh — sorry.'

He stared at William. 'I didn't know anyone was here.'

Deeply grateful for the intrusion, Chris spun round. 'Darling, you remember William Jameson, don't you? Imogen's husband.'

'Of course. How are you?' Max lifted the heavy carrier bags in an apologetic shrug. 'Excuse me. I'll get rid of this lot.' He made his way to the kitchen. 'Anyone like a coffee?' he called over his shoulder.

'Not for me, thank you.' William moved towards the door. 'I should be going. Thanks for your help.'

'I'm sorry I couldn't tell you more. I don't quite know how else I could . . . '

'It's all right,' he said abruptly. 'Goodnight.'

She closed the door with a sigh of relief and was coming back into the living room when Max returned with two mugs of coffee. 'What did he want?' he asked. 'Bit of a cold fish, isn't he?'

Chris was frowning. 'He wanted to know about Imo's last day,' she said. 'But he never asked what she *said* or how she *looked*; whether she spoke about him. None of the things you'd expect him to want to know about her last hours.'

Max shrugged. 'Like I said, he's a cold fish. The way he behaved that day when we went there to lunch! Man's a total shit if you ask me. I wouldn't care to put *my* life in his hands on an operating table. Can't think what a sweet kid like Imogen saw in him. Come on, drink your coffee before it gets cold. I've got

177

us some steak for supper and after that there's something I want to talk to you about.'

★ ★ ★

Imogen woke suddenly. It was just getting light and she was immediately aware that someone was in the room — standing by her bed. She sat up and groped for the bedside lamp switch, her heart in her mouth. Then, as the light came on she gasped. Standing a couple of feet from the bedside table stood a little boy in blue pyjamas. He had thick dark hair and enormous brown eyes.

They stared at each other, then he took a step forward and asked, 'Are you my mummy?'

Imogen's heart melted. 'No,' she said gently. 'I'm not your mummy. I'm sorry.'

'Oh.' He turned dejectedly and began to walk away.

'I'd like to be your friend though,' she said as he reached for the door handle.

He turned the wide brown eyes on her solemnly. 'I haven't got a friend,' he said.

'My name is Sylvia,' she told him. 'What's yours?'

'Simon,' he said. 'Simon Bennett.' He looked at her, his head on one side. 'Have you got a little boy?'

'No, but I wish I had,' she said, getting out of bed. 'Look, it's not time to get up yet. I expect you've been dreaming. I'll take you back to bed, shall I? And perhaps we can talk again tomorrow.'

She took his hand and went out on to the

landing, to be confronted by a red-faced woman in a dressing gown standing outside in the corridor.

'Simon!' she shouted. 'How many times have I told you? You are to stay in your room until I say you can leave it.' She took his hand and jerked him towards her. 'I'm sorry he disturbed you,' she said to Imogen. 'He's a very naughty boy. I'm afraid he's very disobedient.'

'It's quite all right,' Imogen said. 'We were just getting to know each other, weren't we, Simon?'

Simon didn't reply, his lip was trembling.

The woman shook him by the arm. 'Say you're sorry at once,' she commanded.

'S — sorry,' the child muttered.

'Please — it doesn't matter,' Imogen began, but the woman was dragging the child towards his room. The door slammed and a moment later she heard the sound of a resounding slap, followed by a wail of pain. Her heart contracted and she cringed inwardly. Poor little boy. Did his father condone that kind of treatment? Her opinion of Adam Bennett sank.

Most afternoons since Mrs Perkins' accident Imogen had visited her in the hospital. She had had her operation now — a hip replacement — and was doing well. Already, she told Imogen, she had been out of bed and had taken a few steps.

'They like you to get on your feet as soon as possible,' she told her. 'So's not to get any complications.' She popped a grape into her mouth and passed the bag to her visitor. 'Just as well. I'm sure I've already put on weight.' She sighed. 'They're very good in here and the food's not bad but I can't wait to get home. Nothing like your own bed and your own cooking, is there?'

'I'd stay and enjoy being waited on while you can,' Imogen advised.

The older woman's face creased. 'It's not just that though dear. I'm getting worried about the summer bookings. Enquiries must be coming in by now and there's no one there to reply to them. I'm going to lose business.'

'I'll go and get your post for you if you like,' Imogen offered. 'I could bring your books and some stationery and you could do your booking from here. If you can trust me to go to the house, that is.'

Mrs Perkins brightened. 'Trust you? Of course I do. And it's a wonderful idea. It would be such a help.'

'OK, give me your key and explain where everything is and I'll bring them tomorrow.'

Relieved, Mrs Perkins settled herself more comfortably. 'Tell me all your news,' she said. 'I'm getting out of touch in here.'

Imogen told her the news from The Imperial and made her laugh over Mac the Knife's latest volatile outburst.

'His language is quite blue at times, but deep down I know he's a kind man; quite a softie really, though he tries to make people think he's a hard man. Really it's just when he's cooking that he's on a short fuse.' She also confided to Mrs P the thing that had been troubling her ever since her first encounter with Simon.

'I'm sure that Miss Thomas woman who's supposed to be his nanny is too strict with him,' she said. 'Poor little boy has lost his mother and he hardly seems to see his father either. I had no idea there was a child till I moved into the staff quarters.'

'Well, perhaps Mr Bennett isn't aware of what's happening,' Mrs Perkins said. 'Running a hotel is a twenty-four-hour-a-day job, you know. You're always on call. No place for a kiddie with no mother. I can't help feeling sorry for the man.'

Imogen was thinking about this remark as she called in at Acacia Avenue after her visit to collect the things Mrs Perkins needed for her business correspondence. When she had located everything and slipped it all into a carrier bag she locked up carefully and looked at her watch. She'd have to take the short cut back to The Imperial or she'd be late for her shift.

The winding pathway that led out on to the cliff path was a place where people came in summertime to feed the squirrels that lived in the trees. Imogen was hurrying round a bend in the path when she came upon a woman violently shaking a crying child.

'No wonder your mother went away and left you!' she was shouting. 'Who'd want to stay with a naughty boy like you?'

With a shock Imogen recognised Simon and his nurse, Miss Thomas.

'Stop it!' She had shouted the words before she could stop herself. The woman let Simon go and turned to her angrily.

'Mind your own business,' she snapped, red in the face. 'You don't know what I have to put up with. He's impossible at times, forever whinging and whining.'

Simon ran to Imogen and slipped a small hand into hers. She bent down to look into his tear-stained face. 'What's the matter, Simon?'

'Daddy said he'd take me to the pantomime,' he said. 'But Nanny says I can't go now because I've been naughty.'

'What did he do?' Imogen looked at the nurse.

'Running away — refusing to come back when I called him. He's always doing it.'

'Can't say I blame him,' Imogen said half under her breath.

The woman's red face turned pale and stiff with anger. 'I told you — mind your own business! I don't need some *washer-up* to tell me my job. I'm a trained children's nurse. I know what I'm doing. He needs discipline, that one, and plenty of it. He could have fallen over the cliff and then what?'

Crouching beside Simon, Imogen was concerned to hear him wheezing, and she could see that he was having difficulty with his breathing. She looked up at the woman with a frown. 'Has he got a chest infection?'

'No he hasn't! Leave him alone.' The woman took Simon's arm and snatched him away. 'It's asthma — if you must know. He can turn it on and off like a tap. Take no notice. He does it to get attention.'

'If it's asthma it should be treated,' Imogen

called after them, but the woman just shot her a bad-tempered glare and hurried away, the child forced to run to keep up. Imogen followed slowly, deeply disturbed by what she had heard and seen. Asthma in a child so young could be very frightening and serious; and being afraid and unhappy would only exacerbate the problem. Not only that, when he had reached for her hand she had been horrified at the bruises on his arm.

★ ★ ★

Chris sat back with a sigh. 'I couldn't eat another thing,' she declared. 'That was delicious.'

Max pushed his chair back. 'It was rather good, though I do say it myself,' he said. 'Sorry I was late.'

'I wish you'd been here earlier,' she told him. 'I got the shock of my life when I saw William Jameson standing outside.'

He frowned. 'Odd, him wanting to know what Imogen did on her last day.'

'I thought so too. He was horrible to her. Certainly didn't act as though he cared — not when she was . . . *here*.'

He raised an eyebrow. 'Really? In what way?'

'He tried to get her to make all her money over to him. He was cruel — sadistic; I think he was trying to make her think she was going off her head. He used to hit her too. And when she was pregnant . . . ' She stopped, realising she was saying too much, but Max's curiosity was well and truly aroused by now.

'Go on — what did he do when she was pregnant?'

'He — wanted her to have an abortion,' she told him reluctantly.

'And did she?'

'No. She refused.'

'So — she was pregnant when she was killed?'

'No. She lost it anyway.'

'Poor kid. I'd no idea.' He refilled her coffee cup. 'Chris . . . ' He glanced at her. 'What do you know about a woman called Sylvia Tanner?'

She caught her breath. How did he know? Then she remembered. 'Oh — that was the name on the giro, wasn't it?' she said. 'Did you remember to post it?'

'No. I thought I'd deliver it in person as the address was on it. It seems she's missing — hasn't been seen since before Christmas.'

'Really?' Chris's heart was beating fast but she affected nonchalance as she got up and began to clear the table. 'You watch TV. I'll wash up, as you got the supper,' she said.

'Right. Chris — doesn't the name ring any bells with you at all?'

She was scraping the plates, avoiding his eyes as she put the cutlery in a neat pile. 'No.'

'Don't you remember that case a couple of years back. A burglary that went tragically wrong. A guy called Phil Morgan went down for manslaughter. His girl — Sylvia Tanner — got a lesser sentence for turning Queen's evidence.'

'Oh yes.' She was on her way to the kitchen now. 'I believe I do vaguely remember something about it now.'

184

In the kitchen she ran hot water into the sink and squirted washing-up liquid into it. To her dismay she felt Max follow her. Standing behind her he asked, 'Chrissie — you didn't go to that address yourself looking for Sylvia, did you?'

'Why would I do that?'

'I don't know. You tell me. Only I spoke to a woman called Mo Sullivan this morning and she said that a woman had been there, asking questions about Sylvia. A woman with red hair.'

'And am I the only redhead in London?' She laughed unsteadily.

'You're the only redhead in London as far as I'm concerned.' He slipped his arms round her waist and turned her towards him. 'Leave that till morning. I've been thinking about you all day. Let's go to bed.'

The following morning they overslept. Chris was angry with herself. She'd been determined to be at the office early to finish off her report on the rock group — something she should have done the previous evening. She informed Max that he would have to finish washing up the previous evening's supper things.

'It's your fault I'm so behind with my work,' she complained. 'You'll have to go back to your own flat for a few nights,' she added as she searched frantically for a new pair of tights. 'My career and your libido are like oil and water!'

He laughed. '*Fire* and water would be a better simile.' He looked at her thoughtfully as she hastily applied her lipstick. 'Chrissie — are you on to something hot?'

She laughed wryly. 'I should be so lucky! All I ever get are the boring bread and butter family stories and the feminist stuff.'

'I thought you were all for feminism.'

'For equal opportunities, yes, but that feminist lot!' She pulled a face. 'If you have to make an issue out of being a woman, forget it, I say. You are what you *are*!'

'I'm all for that in your case,' Max said with a grin.

'I mean, now that they haven't got the nuclear arms race to protest about all they can go on about is birthing pools and not shaving your armpits.'

He laughed. 'Anyone ever tell you how gorgeous you look when you've got a bee in your bonnet?'

She raised a cushion at him threateningly. 'You're in dangerous water, Lindsay. Don't patronise me.'

'It's true though. Your nose twitches.'

She threw the cushion at him and he fielded it neatly. 'Seriously, Chris, when I asked if you were on to something I meant something of your own; something sensational?'

'Huh! Chance'd be a fine . . . ' She glanced at her watch and gave a little squeak of dismay. 'Oh my God! Look at the time. If I'm going to get this thing typed up I'll have to go — *now*!' She kissed him briefly and snatched up her briefcase.

'See you tonight then?'

'Haven't you heard a word I said? Don't you have any work of your own to catch up with?

Max . . . ' She stood in the doorway. 'Look — why don't we go away somewhere this weekend, just the two of us? We haven't had a chance to talk yet — really *talk*, I mean.'

'Let's discuss it tonight — yes?'

She paused at the door, torn between duty and desire. 'Oh — all right then.'

He smiled as he turned back to the washing-up. What a girl! The smile quickly vanished as he reminded himself that he hadn't told her yet that he was spending this coming weekend with the boys; taking them away so that his ex-wife and her new fiancé could suss out some honeymoon hotel they'd heard about in Paris. He wasn't looking forward to breaking it to Chris, especially now she'd had this idea of the two of them taking a trip. Suggesting that she accompany him and the boys would be like a red rag to a bull. Still, never mind, he'd think of something.

He was on his way out through the door half an hour later when the telephone rang. He hesitated. It wouldn't be for him and anyway Chris had switched on the answering machine before they went to bed last night. He was checking that he had his keys when the machine clicked on and he heard a voice say, 'Hi, Chris, it's Sylvia. I thought I might catch you before you went to work. Just wanted to thank you for putting a good word in for me. I'll call you again this evening. Bye.'

He stood rooted to the spot for a moment, then he snatched up the receiver and punched out 1471. The impersonal voice gave out the time and number. Holding his breath, Max pressed three and listened to the ringing tone. Then . . .

'Good morning. The Imperial, Craybourne. How can I help you?'

11

At about three thirty, Imogen's sleep was disturbed by small fists banging on her door. She jumped out of bed and opened it to find Simon standing on the landing coughing and gasping for breath. He was wide-eyed and speechless with terror. Reacting instinctively, Imogen grabbed the duvet from the bed and packed the basket chair that stood in the corner of the room. Scooping Simon up in her arms she propped him upright in the chair. Kneeling beside him, she took his hand.

'Don't be frightened, Simon. Try to breathe slowly while I count. In, one — two. Out, one — two.'

The door burst open and Miss Thomas stood bristling in the doorway. 'What on *earth* do you think you're doing?'

Imogen turned to her angrily. 'He's having an asthma attack. Go and put the kettle on. Quickly! Bring a bowl of boiling water and a towel.'

'Don't you order me about. I — '

'Please. Just *do* it.'

Something about her tone made the woman turn and scurry off. Five minutes later when she returned Simon had calmed down and was breathing slightly easier, responding to Imogen's calm manner and reassurance. She nodded towards the woman.

'Thanks.' Pulling the bedside table closer, she put the bowl of hot water on it, holding out the towel.

'I want you to come inside my magic tent,' she said. 'Breathe the nice warm steam. It'll make you all better. Promise. Just you try it and see.' She looked at the nurse. 'Doesn't he have an inhaler?' she asked quietly.

The woman shook her head. 'I don't believe in them.'

Imogen seethed but she bit back a retort. Simon was upset enough as it was without finding himself at the centre of an argument. After a few minutes she heard the child's wheezing ease and took the towel and bowl away.

'Let's get you back into bed now, shall we?' she said gently. 'We'll prop you up with lots of pillows and your nasty cough won't come back again tonight, right?'

'All right.' The little boy submitted with obvious pleasure to being carried back to bed and tucked in. When he was settled with his teddy hugged close and his eyelids drooping, Imogen went out on to the landing where Miss Thomas was waiting for her, her face full of furious resentment.

'How dare you interfere with my charge?' she demanded. 'I am responsible for that child. If anything had happened to him I would have taken the blame.'

'Exactly,' Imogen said crisply. 'In which case you should be thanking me.'

Miss Thomas drew in her breath sharply. 'It's none of your business. I resent your interference and I shall speak to Mr Bennett about you in the morning. I intend to complain about your behaviour in the strongest possible terms.'

'You must do as you see fit,' Imogen said. She went into her own room and closed the door quietly. She would have her say too, she decided. After what she had seen she could not keep silent any longer, even if it meant losing her job.

Next morning she was up early and at a quarter to eight she went downstairs. Sandra, the receptionist, was just arriving, her hands full of envelopes.

'Good morning, Sylvia,' she said cheerily. 'It's beginning to feel really springlike. I met the postman as I was coming in. Quite a lot this morning. Shall I look to see if there's anything for you?'

Imogen shook her head. 'There won't be. I mean, I'm not expecting anything.'

Sandra began to sort through the post.

'Shall I get you a coffee?' Imogen asked. 'I was just going to get one myself.'

'Yes please.' The other girl looked up thoughtfully. 'Look, Sylvia, I suppose I shouldn't really tell you this but I'd say you were in with a good chance of getting my job when I leave to get married in June.'

Imogen stared at her. 'I didn't know you were leaving,' she said.

'It was a quick decision,' Sandra told her happily. 'Rob, my fiancé, has been offered a job in Saudi Arabia and we're going to bring the wedding forward so that we can go over together.'

'I see. Congratulations.'

'Thanks. Mr Bennett told me he'd got you in mind and I happen to know he's written to your referees and had replies.' She smiled. 'Quite glowing ones, apparently, especially from your journalist friend in London.'

Imogen blushed with pleasure. 'That's wonderful.' She looked at her watch. She couldn't wait to thank Chris for the favour she'd done her. It was still early. If she rang now she'd probably catch her before she left for work. 'Can I make a call from here?' she asked.

Sandra smiled. 'Help yourself. I'm just going to take Mr Bennett's mail through to the office.'

It was only as she was dialling the number that she remembered Miss Thomas's threat and winced. Maybe her chances of getting a better job had already been shattered.

Chris had obviously already left for work, but she left a message on the machine with a promise to ring later. Maybe she'd know more by then.

She was busy peeling the mountain of potatoes that always awaited her first thing each morning when Sandra came through to the kitchen and asked for her.

'Mr Bennett wants a word with you,' she said. As they walked through to the office together Sandra smiled at her. 'I've a feeling he's going to offer you the job,' she said with a smile.

Imogen said nothing. She doubted it. It was much more likely that Nanny Thomas had already carried out her threat. Well, she would have to stick to her guns and say what she felt.

After all, it was for the child's sake, not her own.

Adam Bennett stood by the window. He wore a navy tracksuit and his hair was wind blown and tousled. Imogen had never seen him look anything but well groomed in his immaculate suits and she was rather taken aback. He looked quite a different person; younger somehow and more approachable. He turned as she came in and must have noticed her look of surprise.

'You must excuse the attire,' he said with a grin. 'I've just come in. I always take a run along the beach first thing. It keeps me fit. Sometimes it's the only exercise and fresh air I get all day so I don't like to miss it.' He raked a hand through his brown hair and sat down behind his desk. 'I wanted to see you before I went upstairs to change. I have to go out later this morning and I won't be back until you've gone off duty.' He drew two letters towards him. 'I've had two very satisfactory replies from your referees and I wanted to ask you how you would feel about taking over from Sandra when she leaves in June.'

Imogen felt herself flush uncomfortably. 'Well — it sounds wonderful,' she said hesitantly.

'There'll be plenty of time for her to show you the ropes before she leaves, which is why I'm asking you now.'

'That would be fine, but . . . '

He looked at her questioningly. 'Yes — but . . . '

'I'm afraid you're about to get a complaint about me,' she said. 'So perhaps you should reserve judgement about me till later.'

He frowned. 'Complaint? Has Mac been blowing his top again? If so — '

'Not Mac,' she swallowed. 'It's Miss Thomas, your son's nanny.'

'Nanny Thomas? What can you have done to ruffle her feathers?'

She looked down at her hands, folded in her lap. This was very difficult. Just how far should she go with it? 'You must be aware that Simon has asthma,' she said carefully.

He sighed. 'Unfortunately, yes. It started soon after his mother left. We're divorced.'

'Last night he had a particularly nasty attack,' she went on. 'It was my door he came to.'

Adam leaned forward. '*Your* door?'

'Yes. Since I moved into the room next door to his we've met a few times. He seems to like me.'

'Please — go on.'

'Luckily I'd worked on a children's ward and I knew how to handle his attack,' she said. 'But I'm afraid Miss Thomas was very angry at what she saw as my interference. She seems to feel that the asthma is all in Simon's mind and that if ignored it will go away. I can assure you it won't.'

'I see. So you had a disagreement and fell out. Oh dear. Perhaps it would be better if — '

'Unfortunately that's not all,' Imogen interrupted. Her heart was beating fast, but now that she'd started she knew she had to go on.

'Yes?'

She moistened her lips. 'Have you seen Simon lately?' she asked. 'Do you ever put him to bed or give him his bedtime bath?'

'I haven't lately, I'm afraid.' He flushed and

194

raked a hand through his hair again. 'I know I should really make more time for him but — '

'Please — I'm not criticising you,' Imogen put in quickly. 'It's just that I — wondered if you're aware of the way Simon is being treated.'

He looked up at her sharply. 'What is it you're trying to tell me, Sylvia? I think you'd better say straight out, don't you?'

'Believe me I'm not telling tales or trying to make trouble,' Imogen told him. 'It's for Simon's sake that I'm bringing this to your attention.'

'If you're suggesting that Miss Thomas is abusing Simon, that's a very serious accusation.'

'I don't know what your views on upbringing are, or how much control you allow her,' Imogen said slowly. 'I'm sure you're in favour of discipline, but in my opinion Miss Thomas carries it too far. She's harsh and unkind, both mentally and possibly physically. I believe Simon is unhappy and frightened. But don't take my word for it. It's easy enough to see for yourself.'

'Oh, my God!' The healthy colour from his morning run faded. He rose from his chair. 'I shall do as you say,' he told her. 'I'll do better than that. I'll take Simon out with me today. Perhaps we can talk. Thank you for alerting me.'

She got up and followed him to the door. 'If you don't agree with what I've said I shall quite understand if you want me to leave,' she said. 'I realise that it looks like interference, but I couldn't see it happening and not speak up.'

★ ★ ★

195

William hated department stores. They always made him feel trapped. To get to the beauty salon he'd had to ride up endless escalators, jostled by silly chattering women. But it was something he had to do.

At last he was there, surrounded by the warm, perfumed, slightly claustrophobic atmosphere of the beauty salon. He walked up to the reception desk.

'Good morning.'

Cindy looked up. 'Good morning. Can I help you, sir? Are you waiting for someone?'

'Were you working here on the day of the bombing?' he asked bluntly. 'Before Christmas. Do you remember this woman?' He took a snapshot of Imogen from his wallet and passed it to her. The girl looked at it, glancing up at him sideways. Was he a policeman, she wondered. No. He looked too well dressed. The suit and shirt screamed Savile Row.

'Oh yes. That's Miss Kendrick,' she said. 'At least she used to be. I can't remember her married name.'

'You remember her then?'

'Yes, of course.' She looked at him and the smile left her face. She'd thought him handsome at first but he looked quite ugly when he glared like that. And surely there was no need to bark at her in such a way.

'So — was she here having her hair done on that afternoon or wasn't she?' he said. 'Come on, you must keep records of some kind. Can you look in your appointment book? Wake up, can't you?'

'Is there something wrong, Cindy?' A slightly older woman stepped forward. 'Can I help, sir?'

'I believe my wife was in here on the day of the bombing in Regent Street,' he said. 'I want to confirm it.'

The woman glanced at the photograph. 'I was on reception that afternoon,' she said. 'I'm not likely to forget it. And yes, this lady was here.'

'You remember her?'

'Of course.' She flipped back the pages of the appointment book and turned it round for him to see. 'Here's her name — Mrs Jameson, isn't it? I'd have remembered her anyway because of the incident.'

'What incident?'

'A girl snatched her bag as she was paying,' the woman told him. 'It was most unusual — bizarre almost. She just seemed to appear from nowhere, grabbed the coat and bag as it lay there on the chair and ran.'

William's stomach muscles tightened. 'What happened?'

'Well, your wife gave chase, naturally. We rang security and hoped they'd catch the thief before she left the store.'

'Yes — and . . . ?' William tapped his fingers impatiently on the counter.

'Well, I never found out because soon after that the bomb went off and everything else went right out of our minds. Some of the injured staggered back inside the store and there were police and paramedics everywhere. You can't imagine what it was like.'

'So you didn't see her again?'

'No — not personally. It was utter chaos. Windows shattered and broken glass everywhere. One of the . . . '

'Thank you.' William turned abruptly on his heel and walked away, leaving the woman staring after him.

'Well really!' she said under her breath. Some men had no idea of common courtesy at all! And often the well-dressed ones were the worst.

Travelling down through the departments on the escalator William's mind was spinning.

So it was true? The woman whose body he had buried was a total stranger — some common thief who'd stolen Imogen's coat and handbag and then got her head blown off for her pains. So where *was* Imogen? She hadn't been among the other casualties on that day — or had she? Luckily he was in a position to find out. At St Aubrey's he'd have access to the admissions records. He'd make a list. A number of people had been treated for minor injuries in Casualty and allowed home. He'd check on those too. If they had families, or at least husbands, he could eliminate them.

Could she have lost her memory and be wandering somewhere? He doubted it. Amnesia wasn't half as common as films and books made it out to be. His eyes narrowed. Much more likely she'd taken advantage of the so-called 'incident' to run away from him. She'd been trying to leave anyway — asking for a divorce. This would have seemed like a heaven-sent opportunity. But she must be mad to think she could get away with it.

Back in his office at the hospital he told his secretary to divert all his calls and postpone his appointments for the afternoon, saying that he had a migraine. To his frustration she fussed around like a broody hen, bringing him a hot drink and some of her favourite analgesic tablets and drawing the blinds.

All afternoon he sat deep in concentration, trying to work out what had happened. If she was still alive — and by now he felt in his bones that she was, she must have taken another name. Mrs Imogen Jameson was dead. He had the death certificate. So — where would she go and what would she live on? She would have little or no money. He himself had inherited all she had. Before long she would be obliged to come back. And when she did she would find that all her money was gone! Well, it would be no more than she deserved. He bit his lip as he remembered the insurance money he had claimed — and also spent! He could be charged with fraud if the company discovered she was still alive! They'd never believe he wasn't in on it. Damn her to hell for landing him in this mess! If — no, *when* he found her he'd make bloody sure she paid for the chaos she'd caused.

He tried to put himself in her shoes — to imagine what she might do. Could he just leave it and hope she'd gone for good? If he found her and forced her to return she might be bitter enough to try and avenge herself; might try to blackmail him for money he didn't have. She might go to the press, or — worse — to the hospital authorities with tales of mental and physical cruelty. Worst of all, to Carole Dean, who held the keystone to his future career. Carole was already becoming disgruntled by his mood swings and he was going to have to tread very carefully with her until after his appointment for the cardiac consultancy.

Reluctantly he had to admit that if Imogen chose to, she could ruin him — smash all his dreams of getting to the top of his profession and wreck all the hard work he had put in. He couldn't risk any of that. It must never happen. He vowed with ice-cold determination that he would not *allow* it to happen. He must find out where she was and make sure somehow or other that she never came back.

He took out his telephone directory and began to search for the name of a private detective agency he had heard of. Armed with the list of admissions, and the list of patients treated for minor injuries on the day of the bombing, an experienced detective would surely have a good chance of tracking her down. At all costs he must find out where she was. And once he had located her he would act swiftly and surely.

★ ★ ★

Imogen finished her shift and went upstairs to change. Mrs Perkins was recuperating at home now and Imogen was going to see her this afternoon. She was glad to be getting out of the hotel. Sandra had told her that Mr Bennett had taken Simon out with him in the car quite early. She said the little boy had seemed delighted at the prospect of having his daddy to himself for the day. Miss Thomas's accusations would have to wait until they got back and, knowing her vindictive nature, her complaints would have been simmering all day and be nicely on the boil by then.

It was five o'clock when she returned from Acacia Avenue. The moment she walked in she saw Miss Thomas, wearing her best tweed suit and sitting upright and tight-lipped in Reception. From behind the reception desk, Sandra beckoned her into the office.

'She's waiting for Mr Bennett to come back,' she said. 'Breathing fire and brimstone. Seems he took Simon out with him this morning without asking her. She said she was in the bathroom and he just took the child and left her a note saying that he wanted to see her on his return. She's furious.' The receptionist looked at Imogen. 'And she's really got it in for you. Do you know what it's all about?'

'I'm afraid I do,' Imogen told her. 'There's about to be a showdown and I'm afraid I'll be at the centre of it, but I can't say any more than that at the moment.'

They came out into Reception again just as Adam Bennett and Simon arrived back. The moment she saw them Miss Thomas got to her feet and made a beeline for them.

'Mr Bennett — I want this woman charged with assault,' she said, pointing accusingly at Imogen.

Adam stared at her and Simon retreated, wide-eyed behind his father's legs. 'I think we'd all better go into the office,' Adam said quietly. He looked at Sandra. 'Will you take Simon along to the kitchen and give him some tea, please, Sandra?'

In the office he faced them across his desk. 'Now — who is Miss Tanner supposed to have assaulted?' he asked.

'Your son. That's who!' she told him. 'Rushing into his bedroom in the middle of the night and manhandling him. It isn't the first time either. Ever since she moved into that staff room she's been undermining my authority — making my position here impossible.'

'I see. Perhaps I should warn you, Miss Thomas, that if I send for the police it will not be Miss Tanner who is charged with assault, but you!'

'*Me?*' The colour left her face as she stared at her employer. Then she turned on Imogen. 'What have you been saying? You're a poisonous, trouble-making liar!'

'Miss Tanner has made no accusations against you,' Adam said. 'But she did alert me about Simon's asthma and his unhappiness.' He looked at her and Imogen saw that there was real anger in his eyes. 'I saw the bruises on his arms and legs for myself.'

Miss Thomas's hand shook as she reached for the back of a chair to steady herself. 'He's so naughty,' she blustered. 'He wets his bed! I don't believe in pampering a child. He needs discipline.'

'Discipline is one thing — abuse is another,' Adam said. 'I think you'd better pack your things and leave at once. I shan't call in the police this time but I will be contacting the agency about you.' He opened a drawer and took out an envelope. 'You'll find a month's wages in there in lieu of notice.' As she opened her mouth to protest he said quickly, 'I'd accept it if I were you, Miss Thomas. I think you know the alternative!'

Miss Thomas stared at him, then at Imogen, but the fire in her eyes had been replaced now with uncertainty. She clearly knew she was beaten. With one last snort of defiance she turned and left, slamming the door behind her. Adam drew a sigh of relief.

'Sit down, Sylvia,' he said wearily.

'I only did what I thought was best for Simon,' she said, shaken by the encounter. 'I didn't mean you to dismiss her — and yet — '

'Precisely. I couldn't allow her to have the care of Simon for one more night after what I've discovered today. And I shall be eternally grateful to you for alerting me to the situation.' He leaned back in his chair, looking suddenly tired. 'Poor little Simon. If only I'd have known what that harridan was putting him through. I blame myself. Life has been so hectic here since I took over The Imperial. My father had let the place go and it's been an uphill struggle, getting it back on its feet again. Then there was my divorce — all so traumatic.' He sighed. 'I was too wrapped up in my own problems to see that Simon was suffering too, young as he was.' He looked at her. 'Do you know she actually told him his mother ran away because he was bad.

203

Can you believe that?' He looked at her. 'What can I do to make it up to him?'

'There is one thing I know he'd like.'

'Yes?'

'He was disappointed at not going to the pantomime,' she told him. 'Perhaps — '

He groaned. 'I know. I meant to take him. I really did. And now the local one is over. Maybe I could find one that's still running. Norwich perhaps. I'll get Sandra to find out and get tickets.' He looked at her tentatively. 'Sylvia — I was going to ask you an enormous favour. Would you take care of Simon until I find him another nanny? He knows you now and he obviously adores you. He's been talking about you all day.'

She smiled, blushing with pleasure. 'Of course I will. I'd love to.'

'You *will*?' He laughed with relief. 'You don't know what a relief that is.'

'What about my job in the kitchen though?'

He shook his head. 'Don't worry about that. I'll get on to the agency and have someone here first thing tomorrow morning. If it's all right with you I'd like you to start taking care of Simon right now.'

★　★　★

'Craybourne? Where's that? And why do we have to go there, Dad?'

Max's elder son, Richard, sat beside him in the car, his face as dark as a thundercloud.

So far the weekend had been a complete failure. Max had taken his sons out to a

McDonald's on Friday evening, but apparently their taste for burgers had diminished since his last meeting with them. Afterwards, back at his flat, he proudly showed off his new computer. They were unimpressed. Apparently they had an even more state-of-the-art model at home, bought for them by their mother's fiancé. They didn't think much of Max's bachelor flat either, especially having to share his tiny spare room.

On Saturday he'd planned to take them to the Queen's Club to see the tennis. The last time he'd seen the boys Tim Henman had been their hero. He'd bribed a friend to get him three tickets at enormous expense. But when he proudly produced them the boys' faces had dropped. It seemed they'd set their hearts on going to Wembley for the football.

He hadn't been able to do anything right all weekend. What he thought of as their favourite food was no longer edible and the T-shirts he'd managed to get for them, emblazoned with the name of their favourite pop group, were — it seemed — abysmally out of date.

'No one likes *them* any more, Dad!' they'd wailed in unison.

It was all very depressing. Since he'd last seen them sixteen-year-old Richard, dark-haired like his father, had actually started shaving, and his voice had gone from a two-tone squeak to a dark brown baritone in a matter of weeks! They were growing up without him and he hated it.

But overshadowing everything was the row he'd had with Chris when he'd been forced to confess that he'd made domestic arrangements for the weekend. He should have told her earlier, he knew that now. Waiting till she'd set her heart on a romantic away-from-it-all weekend to talk about their future before dropping his bomb-shell was guaranteed to touch her on the raw. He should have known. Somehow, he told himself glumly as he drove, he was going to have to wheedle his way back into her good books. And this time it wasn't going to be easy; just when he thought he'd patched things up with her nicely . . .

There had been a lot of girls in Max's life since his divorce and when he and Chris had split up he'd told himself he was resilient — he'd get over her. Plenty more where she came from, he'd told himself. Now he knew he'd been kidding himself. There'd never be anyone for him like Chris. No other woman came anywhere near her. He had to admit that he was well and truly in love with the girl and the thought of losing her again through sheer crass insensitivity — his own pig-headed stupidity — was driving him mad.

All in all, Max was not having the happiest of weekends.

'So where is this dump, Dad? I've never even heard of it,' Richard asked.

'It's on the Norfolk coast.' Max concentrated his eyes determinedly on the road ahead. Nothing he'd done so far had been right so he might as well be hung for a sheep as a lamb and do something *he* wanted today!

'The seaside!' twelve-year-old Paul shouted

from the back seat. 'Wowee! Candyfloss and dodgems!'

Richard turned to look pityingly at his brother. 'Don't be daft. There'll be nothing open this time of year. The place'll be deserted — nothing but an empty beach.' He glared at his father. 'It's Sunday too. There won't even be a fish and chip shop open. Great!'

'Look, I'll take you for a slap-up lunch in a hotel,' Max said with a hint of desperation in his voice.

'Mum and Harry have gone to Paris,' Richard said. 'Why couldn't we have gone too?'

'Because you're going to bloody Craybourne with me,' Max snapped. 'And if you don't like it you know what you can do!' He turned to them. 'Look, it's work — someone I have to find. I'm — acting on information,' he added in the vain hope that the terminology would tempt their interest.

Paul leaned forward, his arms on the back of his father's seat. 'No kidding, Dad? Who is it? Is it a murderer?'

Max pulled the car on to the forecourt of a roadside cafe advertising coffee and doughnuts. 'We'll stop here,' he said. 'Don't know about you but I'm gasping for a coffee.'

When they were seated at one of the formica-topped tables, Max with his coffee and the boys with Cokes and doughnuts, Richard said, 'Are you going to let us in on this then, Dad? At least it would make this dump you're taking us to a bit more interesting.'

'I don't think you'd be . . . ' He broke off,

suddenly seeing a way to regain their respect and admiration. They'd talked non-stop all weekend about their prospective stepfather who was a detective with the Met. According to them, responsibility for the entire CID rested easily on his muscular Schwartzenegger-like shoulders. 'It's to do with a case I covered when I worked on the *Globe* a couple of years back,' he said nonchalantly.

'Really? Was it a murder case?'

'As a matter of fact, it was.' At least he had their attention now. 'Though the charge was reduced to manslaughter. It was a robbery that went wrong — an old lady died.' He thought they looked a bit disappointed. Maybe they'd hoped for something more gory and sensational. Kids nowadays! 'The thing was, the stolen jewellery was never found,' he added with a sudden stroke of inspiration.

'Wow! And are you on the trail of it, Dad?' Paul asked, his eyes round.

'Not exactly,' Max admitted. 'But I think I might have found someone who is.'

It worked. Their mood greatly improved, the boys followed him out to the car again and they continued on their journey.

They had lunch in Craybourne's quaintest hotel. The Lobster Pot was situated right on the seafront and had stone-flagged floors, oak beams and a blazing log fire. It was quite busy, but he managed to get a table close to a window with a sea view. One or two brave windsurfers were out and the boys watched, entranced, deciding that Craybourne wasn't quite as boring as they'd imagined.

They ate their way steadily through three courses, and as he paid Max inquired discreetly at the reception desk about the whereabouts of The Imperial. The girl gave him directions.

He took the boys for a walk down to the seafront and along the beach, then they went back to the car and he asked them to wait for him.

'I've got this errand to do,' he explained. 'Better if I go alone. Just stay in the car and look after everything for me, will you? I won't be long.'

They nodded eagerly. 'You will tell us about it when you get back, won't you?'

'Of course I will,' he promised. 'But it may be a red herring, so don't expect action and excitement.'

They watched him go. Richard said scathingly, 'I bet it's not true, all that guff about stolen jewellery. He's just trying to impress us.'

'Oh, d'you reckon?' Paul said, disappointed.

'Yeah, I mean — why would anyone give a stuff after all this time? Anyone who's got valuable jewellery insures it so they'd have had the money by now. And anyway, if the old lady died . . . '

'See what you mean,' Paul agreed. 'Still, Dad never used to lie to us, did he?'

'Lied to Mum though, didn't he? She said.'

Paul was silent. 'So — why do you reckon he's gone to this Imperial place then?'

'If you ask me — ' Richard's words were interrupted by the bleeping of Max's mobile phone. He'd seen his father push it into the glove compartment when they got into the car that morning and he retrieved it quickly. Flicking the switch, he held it to his ear.

'Hello.'

A woman's voice said, 'Oh — Mr Lindsay?'

'Speaking.' Richard winked at his younger brother.

'He's been here again.' The cockney voice was shrill and panicstricken. 'The man I told you about. Rex Morgan. He seems to think I know what Sylv did with the stuff from the robbery. *I* don't know, Mr Lindsay. Straight up. I ain't got a clue, but he don't believe me. He's started threatening now — hinting that something nasty might happen to my kid if I don't tell him.' There was a pause and she said, 'You still there?'

'Yeah,' Richard said.

'I wouldn't have bothered you, only you did say to ring your number if there was anything.' She went on. 'I wondered if you'd heard anything from Sylv — if you know where she is, 'cause if I don't find her soon . . . '

Richard took a deep breath. Then — 'Try The Imperial, Craybourne,' he said and switched off quickly.

His brother stared at him, his mouth an astonished O. 'Rick! Why did you do that?'

'Felt like it,' Richard said defiantly. His hands were sticky in spite of the bravado he affected. 'That woman was dead scared. It's obvious, isn't it? Dad said he was on the trail of someone who knew where that stolen stuff was, then after lunch he asked for this Imperial place.'

210

'And you said it was all lies!' Paul gasped. 'Hey — are you going to tell Dad when he comes back?'

Richard coloured. 'No, I'm not! And if you dare breathe a word to him you'll be sorry!'

★ ★ ★

Max stood on the opposite side of the road and looked at the white façade of The Imperial. Nice place; quiet and select. Just the kind of place to get lost in — become anonymous. Chances were she was working there. He wondered where Chris came into all this. How had she come to be in touch with Sylvia? And just what were they cooking up between them?

He could see a telephone kiosk further along the road. Inside he dialled the number then waited.

'Good afternoon. The Imperial, Craybourne. Can I help you?'

'Yes.' He took a deep breath. 'Do you have a guest by the name of Sylvia Tanner staying there?'

There was a pause, then the girl said, 'Not at present, sir.'

'Is there anyone of that name working there?'

'I'm sorry sir, but we don't give out information about our staff.'

'Of course. I quite understand,' Max said. 'Perhaps I should explain. I'm a relative — from abroad. I haven't been in England for some years and I lost touch with the family. A mutual acquaintance told me there was a Sylvia Tanner working at The Imperial and I thought it might be worth checking out.'

'I see. Well, if you'd like to give me your name and a telephone number perhaps I could make enquiries and get back to you . . . '

'Thank you for your time. It doesn't matter.' Max hung up, smiling triumphantly. Sylvia *was* there, otherwise the receptionist would just have said she'd never heard of her. If he went along to the hotel and sat in the bar for a while, chances were she'd show up. Then he remembered the boys, waiting in the car — and chewed his lip. Damn! He hadn't got time to hang around. He'd promised to have them home by six this evening and it was a long drive back to London. Maybe he'd have to give up for today. Now that he knew she was here he could always come back another day.

He was walking back towards the hotel when he saw a young woman and a child come out of the front entrance and walk down the steps. He stopped dead in his tracks, standing back in the shadow of a tree so as to be inconspicuous. There was something very familiar about the girl. If he didn't know he could have sworn . . . Then she turned in his direction and the breath stopped in his throat.

There was absolutely no mistaking who she was. But how could it be? The girl he was looking at had been killed almost three months ago in an explosion, so how could she be walking down the steps of The Imperial right in front of his eyes — alive? Very much alive.

212

He'd come here looking for Sylvia Tanner. But it wasn't Sylvia Tanner he was looking at. It was Imogen Jameson.

Wait till Chris heard about this!

12

Simon sat between his father and Imogen in the front row of the stalls. Adam had managed to get tickets for the mid-week matinee. He'd been lucky; the panto, *Jack and the Beanstalk*, at the Maddermarket Theatre was in its last week and the front row seats had been a cancellation.

Imogen glanced at Simon's face as the giant chased Jack across the stage. His mouth was open and his eyes as wide as saucers. Without looking at her he reached for her hand and she squeezed it reassuringly.

'It's all right,' she whispered. 'I'm sure he'll get away.'

At the finale when each of the characters walked down to take their bow, Simon clapped enthusiastically and when the curtain came down his face dropped.

'Is it over?' he asked.

Adam smiled. 'Afraid so old chap. But we're not going home just yet. Sylvia and I are taking you out to tea at McDonald's and you can have anything you like.' He winked at Imogen over Simon's head. 'Within moderation.'

Simon took full advantage of his father's offer and ate a hearty tea. Later, on the way home, strapped securely into his child seat in the back of the car he fell asleep, tired but happy.

'He enjoyed every minute,' Imogen said. 'It was a joy to watch his little face.'

Adam nodded. 'He's had too few treats since we moved to Craybourne. I've neglected him and now I mean to make it up to him. If it hadn't been for you I'd never have known what he was going through.' He smiled at her. 'He's been a different child since you took over, you know.'

'He's no trouble,' she told him. 'So good in fact that caring for him is more like a pleasure than work. Have you had any suitable applications from the agency yet?'

He shook his head. 'I haven't asked them to send any through yet. To be honest, I've lost confidence in that agency since they sent me Miss Thomas.'

'So you'd like me to continue for the time being?'

'If you wouldn't mind.' He glanced at her. 'He'll be going to school after Easter. He won't need so much attention then. Which brings me to something I've been meaning to talk to you about.'

'Yes?' She looked at him.

'Well, say if you think it would be too much, but I wondered if you'd like to think about taking the job of part-time receptionist and living in — caring for Simon too.'

Imogen bit her lip. It sounded too good to be true.

'Of course I'd get someone else to cover the hours when Simon would need you and I'd pay you for both jobs,' Adam added hurriedly. 'I don't want you to think I'm trying to exploit you.'

She smiled. 'I know you'd never do that. It sounds ideal. I'd love it.'

'There's something else,' he said. 'A slight snag. The planning permission to convert the old staff quarters into a family flat has come through at last. I've had a builder lined up for ages, so the work will begin almost at once. That means I'll have to ask you to move into the small flat I occupy now, on the top floor. I'm afraid it will be a bit cramped, but it will only be temporary. Once the job is finished you can have a bedroom and sitting room of your own if you like.'

'That would be perfect.'

'And now that you're about to be a permanent member of my staff I'll have to have your P45 and so on.'

She bit her lip. 'Oh! I haven't got one.'

'Not from when you were nursing?'

'That was a while ago and I . . . must have lost it — what with moving about and so on.'

'Oh well, it's not a problem. We'll have to get you started off afresh then.'

Adam didn't seem at all suspicious but Imogen was quiet for the rest of the journey. In the few weeks she had known Simon she had grown very fond of him. Losing her own baby had affected her deeply and Simon filled the aching void in her heart as nothing else could. But she felt so guilty about concealing her identity. If Adam were to find out that Sylvia Tanner had a police record — had been to prison, how betrayed he would feel. He trusted her, and there was an empathy growing between them, born of their mutual love for his child. How would she ever explain? While she had been a casual kitchen worker it hadn't mattered. But now ... Perhaps she should get out before things became too complicated. Before she grew too attached to Simon — and his father.

Back at the hotel Adam carried Simon upstairs and helped Imogen undress him and put him to bed.

'Once he's settled will you come down and have a nightcap with me?' Adam asked. Imogen looked doubtful and he said, 'Please say yes. It's been a happy day and somehow I don't want to let go of it just yet.'

The bar was deserted. Adam poured two brandies and brought them to the corner table where Imogen sat. He watched her thoughtfully as she took her first sip.

'Tell me about yourself, Sylvia,' he invited.

She felt herself freeze. 'About myself? There's nothing much to tell,' she said.

'I think there is.' He reached out and took her left hand. 'This for instance.' He touched her third finger gently. 'You've been married, haven't you?'

For a moment, she couldn't breathe. Staring down at the finger she noticed for the first time that there was a tell-tale band of pale skin where her ring used to be. There was no denying it. She nodded.

'I thought so. I'm not going to pry, but I'd like you to know that any time you need someone to talk to I'm here,' he said. 'No one understands the trauma of a broken marriage better than I do.' When she didn't reply he asked, 'Was there a child?' She shook her head. 'I wondered — because you're so good with Simon.'

She looked up at him. 'My mother and father were killed in a road accident when I was quite small so I know how it feels to lose a parent,' she told him. 'I know how it feels to be bullied too.' At least that was something she could tell the truth about. Then she surprised herself by adding, 'There would have been a baby too, but . . . I lost it.'

His fingers curled round hers sympathetically. 'Oh my dear, I'm so sorry.'

'It's all right. I'm over that now,' she said quickly. 'But when I saw Simon being mistreated I couldn't stand aside and say nothing.'

'Of course. I'll always be so glad you spoke up.' He looked at her for a long moment. 'Sylvia — you said you'd been bullied. Did your husband abuse you?' She made to pull her hand away but he held on to it firmly. 'I know I have no right to ask. It's just that when you first came you had bruises — marks.'

'I was in an accident,' she said. 'That was how I got those injuries. But since you ask — yes, he was violent sometimes. Mentally cruel too. But if you don't mind I'd rather not — '

'Your name isn't Sylvia either, is it?'

Once again she froze. Her eyes widened as they sprang up to meet his.

'I thought not,' he said with a smile. 'You just don't *look* like a Sylvia.'

'I wanted to make a fresh start,' she said.

'It's all right. You've every right to call yourself whatever you like. I'm not going to ask you any more questions. But if you want to tell me about it some time — well, I said, didn't I?'

'This isn't right, is it?' she said, her heart beating fast. 'You trust me with your child, yet you know nothing about me. For all you know you could be making a terrible mistake. Perhaps I should leave. Perhaps . . . '

'Perhaps nothing!' he said, grasping her hand firmly. 'I trust you because you're kind and capable and you clearly love my son. I think I know enough about human nature to be able to see that there is a deep personal tragedy in your past, but that is none of my business.'

'Yes but — '

'Sylvia — listen; Miss Thomas came to me with excellent references, from one of the most reputable agencies in the country. Well you know how she turned out. This time, I'm trusting my own gut feeling. Is that good enough for you?'

She smiled. 'I'll always be so grateful to you,' she said.

'It's mutual.' He grinned at her. 'I hope we're friends.'

'Of course.'

'And another thing,' he said, smiling at her ruefully. 'Everyone needs to talk at times — me as much as anyone. Would it bore you to bits to listen to me sometimes?'

She looked at him and realised for the first time that for all his busy life and being the host of people all around him, he was as lonely as she was. 'Of course not,' she said. 'No one has talked to me — *really* talked to me I mean — for ages.'

★ ★ ★

'You knew, didn't you? You knew she was alive.'

'Oh — just drop it, can't you?' Chris turned away and busied her trembling hands with filling the kettle. 'I've told you, you must have been mistaken. You know it couldn't have been Imogen.'

She'd been horrified when he told her that he'd taken his sons to Craybourne and had seen Imogen. It was the last place she'd have expected him to take the boys for a Sunday out.

'Anyway, what on earth were you doing there in the first place?' she asked.

'Put that kettle down and look at me when I'm talking to you!' He took her shoulders and turned her to face him. 'I went there on purpose. Last week, when I was alone here one morning after you'd left for work, there was a phone call. Someone called Sylvia left a message.'

'So?' She looked at him defiantly, trying not to let him see her dismay. But Max knew her too well.

'It was too much of a coincidence, Chris. You'd been to see her flatmate, Mo Sullivan.' He waved a hand at her. 'No, don't bother to deny it again. It was you. You told her Sylvia Tanner was staying with you. Then you get a phone call from someone called Sylvia.'

'I don't see what this has to do with Imogen,' Chris blustered, pulling away from him.

'Anyway, what made you think that that call came from Craybourne?'

He pushed an exasperated hand through his hair. 'Come *on*, Chris. How do you think? I dialled 1471 for the number that morning, and when I rang it I found it was a hotel in Craybourne.'

'Brilliant! Isn't technology wonderful?' she said sarcastically.

'It certainly is.' He reached out for her again. 'Chris — come clean, can't you? You know bloody well what all this is about. You're in it up to your neck and it's no use denying it. Imogen's alive, isn't she? She's gone into hiding in this hotel in Norfolk. But what I don't get is the connection between her and Sylvia Tanner.'

'You and me both! I keep telling you, Max; you must have been mistaken.'

As she turned away from him he caught her shoulders and swung her round to face him. 'You do realise that you're sitting on a red hot story here, don't you?'

'Oh, stop talking rubbish!'

'You're a journalist, Chris. You complain at being given all the boring mundane jobs. Well, this is your chance to prove yourself! Can't you see it? You could make the front page with this one if only you'd — '

'Front page!' she shouted. 'Is that all you can think about?' She stared at him furiously. 'You'd sell your own grandmother to get that all-important by-line, wouldn't you? Imogen is — *was* — my friend. I can hardly remember a time when she wasn't around and I miss her.

221

Even if what you say were true, do you really think I could do that to her?'

'You'd probably be doing her a favour.'

'Oh yes, that's how you justify everything, isn't it? All this just points out the difference between us, Max.' She rounded on him. 'You'd expect me to rat on my best friend, yet your ex-wife crooks her little finger and you jump through hoops!' She shook her head. 'Why don't you leave? Just go away. Apart from anything else, I resent you prying into my private business like this — playing the poor man's Hercule Poirot. Look after your own problems. God knows you've got enough of them.'

'Chris . . . '

'Just go! It's over. It's obvious that all I'm ever going to be to you is second best — first reserve. Someone to bolster your ego and mop your brow. Tea, sex and sympathy, that's me! Call me selfish if you like but I can't — I *won't* — settle for that.'

'It's not true. You're anything but second best, Chris. You're the best thing that ever happened to me. I've never felt for anyone what I feel for you. It's only till the boys are grown up.'

'And then what?'

'What do you mean?'

'It'll never end. There'll be graduation parties, engagements, weddings. They'll have kids of their own. Your grandchildren!' She turned to face him, her eyes blazing with hurt and longing. 'You'll always be their father first, Max. But I want children too; *our* children. You don't, do you? You've made that all too plain. You've been there — done that — got the . . . ' She turned away, swallowing hard at the lump in her throat, unable to complete the trite saying.

'Kids aren't everything,' he said quietly, standing behind her.

'To *me* they are.' She felt his hands on her shoulders and shook him off. 'No! Not this time, Max. You can't weaken me by getting me into bed this time — not any more. This is crunch time.' She turned to look at him and he flinched at the direct look in her eyes. 'Either make a commitment to me; a proper commitment, or leave now. I'm not prepared to compromise any longer.'

'So you want it to end? You really want me to go?'

'Yes!'

'If I do it'll be permanent this time. Is that really what you want?'

'I've said, haven't I? Do you want it in writing?' She stood with her back to him, looking out of the window, gritting her teeth as the silence seemed to go on and on. Then she heard the door quietly close and turned to find the room empty.

'That's it then,' she said softly. 'It really and truly *is* over this time.' Tears welled up and spilled over and she tried in vain to swallow the sob that rose in her throat. It's for the best, she told herself, angrily dashing away the tears. His family would always come between them. Better to end it now than go through the trauma of a parting later. If only it didn't hurt so much. She sank into a chair, bent double, devastated by the pain that was almost physical.

After a while she went back to the kitchen where the kettle had long since boiled, and made herself a strong cup of coffee. Then she began to worry about Max's insistence that it was Imogen he had seen. Knowing Max, he wouldn't rest until he got to the truth. He couldn't stand mysteries and when the bit was between his teeth he had the tenacity of a bulldog. Instead of denying it and going on the defensive she should have confided in him and begged him to keep it to himself. If he loved her as he said he did he would have done it for her sake. Now . . . She bit her lip. Now all she could do was contact Imo and warn her to take special care. She couldn't telephone her at the hotel. It was too dangerous. She would have to write her a letter. And the sooner, the better.

★   ★   ★

Max had paced the floor of his flat till the small hours, unable to cope with the thoughts that chased themselves round and round in his head. Chris meant it this time. He'd never seen her so determined. He'd known her views on his domestic problems and he knew that she'd been upset at his sudden announcement that he was spending the weekend with the boys. Yet he couldn't dispel the uneasy notion that the row they'd had was partly a diversion to get him off the subject of Imogen Jameson. What was it she was hiding? He was certain that the woman he had seen in Craybourne had been Imogen. He'd stake his life on it. Yet Chris had denied it so vehemently. And where did Sylvia Tanner come into it all?

He'd been on the scene of the bombing that afternoon very shortly after it had happened. Some of the victims' injuries had been stomach-churningly terrible. And Imogen had been identified conclusively enough by her clothing and handbag. And yet what he saw with his own eyes could not be denied.

⋆ ⋆ ⋆

'Wait for me, Daddy!'

Simon trotted along behind his father, Imogen following. It had been the little boy's own idea. He'd woken early that morning and insisted on accompanying his father on his morning run.

Imogen had been hesitant, afraid to intrude on Adam's solitude and spoil his enjoyment. She knew he treasured his early run in the fresh morning air. It helped to invigorate him and clear his head, preparing him for the day ahead. He'd told her that he did a lot of his thinking and problem solving on these morning jaunts and it was with misgivings that she approached him with Simon's request.

But he'd been happy for them to go with him. In fact he'd seemed delighted that his small son wanted to go along too.

'I don't always enjoy solitude,' he told her as he tied the laces of his trainers. 'In fact there are times when I'd give anything for a friend to talk things through with. If you can get him ready quickly we'll go right away.'

It was a beautiful spring morning, bright and clear, and as they jogged along the cliff path, the sea below them was a pure milky blue with frothy wavelets breaking on the sand. They paused for a moment so that Simon could rest and sat down at the cliff edge.

'Can we go down there to that little beach, Daddy?' Simon asked, looking down.

'If you like,' Adam said. 'We'll take the cliff path and go down to the cove. It's all right this morning because it's low tide.'

They went down the roughly hewn path in single file, slipping a little on the loose stones. At the bottom they scrambled over the rocks to the sandy cove Simon had seen. Imogen gasped with delight. The rugged sandstone cliffs towered above them, a glowing russet red in the morning light. And the sand, newly washed by the tide, shone like silver, reflecting the azure morning sky.

Seeing her shiver, Adam glanced at her. 'Are you warm enough, Sylvia?'

She nodded. 'It's so beautiful. It takes your breath away.'

'It might be, but it's also quite dangerous,' he warned. 'I know the tides on this coast and just at this point it can come in quite suddenly and cut off the unwary.' He pointed to the two spurs of rock jutting out into the water on either side of them, forming a small sheltered bay. 'If you're cut off here the only way is up the cliff.'

'What about the path?' she asked.

He pointed. 'That's cut off too when the tide

comes in; see, it's beyond the place where we climbed over the rocks.'

'Can I paddle, Daddy?' Simon capered at the edge of the water, the wavelets lapping at his feet temptingly. 'Shall I take off my shoes and socks?'

'Not today. It's too cold still. You'll have to wait till summer for that.'

'Oh! When will it be summer?'

Adam laughed. 'Soon, very soon.' He held out his hand. 'Come on now, Simon. Time we went home for breakfast.'

They climbed the steep cliff path again and when they reached the top Adam held out his hand to help Imogen up the last few feet. He looked at her when she drew level with him, his face serious. 'I want you to promise me you'll never go down to the cove without me,' he said. 'Several people have drowned down there. It looks so tempting yet it can be treacherous.'

'I won't,' she promised.

He smiled. 'Thanks for coming with me this morning,' he said. 'It's been fun. I hope you'll join me again.' He grinned, looking down at her unsuitable shoes. 'Though if you intend to, might I suggest that you get yourself some suitable footwear?'

She laughed with him. 'I will.'

When they got back to the hotel there was a letter waiting for Imogen. She saw at once by the writing that it was from Chris. Alone in her room she opened it and read the hasty words of warning her friend had written. On a visit to Craybourne, Max had been convinced that he had seen her.

She sat for some time with the letter in her hand, wondering what she should do. Chris said that she had insisted to Max that he had been mistaken. And Imogen certainly had not seen him. But surely it was too much of a coincidence not to be true. The obvious thing for Chris to do would be to take Max into her confidence, but in her letter she said she didn't trust him enough. He was too keen a journalist not to be tempted to use the story. *'I think I have convinced him that it wasn't you he saw,'* she wrote. *'But to be on the safe side better keep a low profile.'*

★ ★ ★

To avoid the risk of being seen by someone who knew him, William had arranged to meet Lesley Hemsby, the private detective whose services he had hired, in a pub called the Dog and Duck on the fringe of an Essex village. He'd been surprised at first to discover that the detective agency was run by a woman. But once they'd met and he'd seen for himself how capable and experienced she was, he forgot his misgivings. After all perhaps a woman with a woman's illogical, devious mind would be better equipped to deal with this case, he told himself. Though of course he hadn't told her what his true suspicions were. Only that he wanted to trace the thief who had stolen his wife's handbag.

He arrived early and parked the car, waiting until he saw the grey Ford Escort swing into the gravelled car park and stop. He got out of the car and greeted Lesley coolly and together they walked into the bar.

'You said when I rang that you'd got a result.' William said impatiently as they sat down with their drinks at a corner table. Lesley nodded, opening her briefcase.

'There's only one name on the list you gave me that doesn't seem to be accounted for and that's this one.' She pointed to a name on the list she had spread before them on the table. William read the name aloud.

'Sylvia Tanner.' He looked at her. 'Right. So what have you found out about her?'

'I traced her to an address in the East End.' She handed him a slip of paper torn from her notebook. 'That's it for what it's worth but when I called she was no longer living there. However, a neighbour gave me the lowdown on her. Apparently she's been missing since before Christmas.' She glanced at him. 'I didn't get this without persuasion; quite expensive persuasion.'

William waved a hand dismissively. 'Just put it on the bill. So — what makes you think that this is the woman we're looking for?'

'Seems that Tanner's absence coincides with the date of the Regent Street bombing,' Lesley said. 'I looked into her background and I find that she's got form — a police record, petty thieving, shoplifting. But she was convicted a couple of years ago for something more serious; aggravated burglary — assisting a guy who killed an old lady during a robbery that went wrong. She went down for a two-year stretch.'

'Really? That's interesting,' William said thoughtfully.

229

'Apparently several people have been around since she disappeared, asking questions about her,' Lesley told him. 'A woman and a couple of men. By the sound of it Ms Tanner is a much sought-after lady!'

William was silent, a ray of hope curving his lips into a smile. It looked as though Imogen had chosen the wrong person to swap places with. Perhaps if he left things alone someone else would solve his problem for him.

'Looks very much as though she could have been your opportunist thief,' Lesley was saying. 'It's my guess that she snatched your wife's bag and ran out of the store — straight into the explosion. And ended up in hospital.' She looked at William. 'Do you want me to go and check her out for you?'

'No.' William shook his head. 'I'll go myself. And if I find you've made a mistake I'll have to come back to you.'

'Naturally, but I don't think I have. Call it intuition if you like but I've got a gut feeling about this one. Somehow I feel there's more to it than meets the eye. I could come with you if you like,' she added hopefully.

'No! If you're right and this is the woman who stole my wife's bag I'd like to deal with her myself.'

Lesley drained her glass. 'Well, I wish you luck.' She looked at him curiously. 'Bag snatching isn't a major crime, and from what you say I assume you got the valuable contents back, so — off the record — why are you so anxious to find her?' She looked at him. 'You wouldn't take

230

the law into your own hands, would you?'

'I shall do what's necessary,' William said. 'The police are so lax these days. Most of the time they ignore it when you report a crime. I hope I'll be able to teach this woman to respect other people's property.'

She shrugged. 'Well, it's up to you. I've done what I can. Let me know if you need me again.' She paused. 'I take it you'd like to settle up now then?'

'I'll pay you when I know you've got it right,' William said. 'Meet me here again after I've checked.'

'All right — when?'

'I'll ring and let you know.'

Her eyes narrowed. 'If you don't mind I'd rather have your address. Or a phone number will do if you prefer.'

'No. I'll be in touch.' William picked up the list of casualties, typed on hospital paper, and pushed it into his briefcase. 'For heaven's sake, what kind of business do you run, Miss Hemsby? Can't you tell when a person is trustworthy? You've had your advance and expenses and you'll get the rest of your money when I'm satisfied!'

As he let himself back into his car William was jubilant. He'd bet everything he owned that this woman calling herself Sylvia Tanner would turn out to be Imogen. But he'd sit on it for a while — bide his time. Maybe one of the other people looking for this Sylvia character would hire someone to catch up with her. He'd wait for a bit and see. If not, it would be down to him. But it wouldn't do to jump too hastily. Imogen's come-uppance was something that would need very careful planning. He smiled grimly. It would be something to savour and look forward to.

He waved as Lesley Hemsby drove her Escort out of the car park, then he turned the key in the ignition and nosed his own car out on to the road. So busy was he with his own thoughts that he failed to notice the Mercedes sports car concealed in a shadowy corner of the car park, or the woman at the wheel, watching him with baleful intensity.

★　★　★

Imogen was happy. Happier than she could ever remember being. The accommodation in the tiny flat on the top floor of The Imperial was cramped, as Adam had said. The room she slept in was hardly more than a cupboard leading off Simon's bedroom, but Adam had promised her a sitting room and bedroom of her own once the new flat was completed. Even the disturbing news in Chris's letter hadn't worried her for too long.

When she and Mrs Lane had moved all Simon's and her own belongings over the day before the builders were due to start work, the housekeeper had congratulated her.

'I don't know what you've done dear, but I've never seen that child look so well and happy,' she said. 'And it's not only little Simon either,' she added with a knowing smile.

Imogen had looked at her sharply. 'Oh?'

232

Mrs Lane smiled. 'Perhaps it's not for me to say but Mr Bennett looks better too. More relaxed like; younger even!'

'I didn't enjoy having to tell him about Miss Thomas,' Imogen said with a sigh. 'I felt like a sneak. But I couldn't stand by and see the child so miserable.'

'I wouldn't lose too much sleep about her if I were you,' Mrs Lane said. 'I saw what she was from the moment she had charge of the child. Nice as pie to Mr Bennett's face but when she was alone with Simon it was a different story. Several times I saw things I wasn't too happy about and now I only wish I'd had the nerve to speak up myself.'

Since the morning that she and Simon had shared Adam's morning jog, the three of them had begun to have breakfast together. It had been Imogen's own idea and each morning she prepared the meal herself.

'It will mean that even if you don't have time to see Simon again all day at least you can start the day with him,' she'd told Adam, and he had agreed delightedly.

Breakfast each morning in the sunny little kitchen was a delight and, as Mrs Lane had observed, Simon quickly developed into a happier and less nervous child as a result. Adam seemed to benefit too; on most evenings he managed to find time to come upstairs and read Simon a story when he was in bed and after hearing him say one evening that he'd enjoy a home-cooked meal instead of the restaurant food he was accustomed to, Imogen decided to prepare a meal for him as a surprise. She did it one evening a few days after she and Simon had accompanied him to the cove. His delighted surprise was almost embarrassing.

'You've done all this — for me?' he asked incredulously, looking at the table she'd laid with flowers and a single candle. He looked at her. 'It's not my birthday, is it?'

She laughed. 'I wouldn't know. It's just that I heard you mention that you'd enjoy a home-cooked meal for once, so I thought you might like it.'

She brought in the cold starter she'd prepared and the chicken casserole and vegetables. 'There,' she said, putting them on the table. 'You can help yourself. I hope you enjoy it.'

His face dropped. 'You mean you're not going to stay and share it with me?'

'Well, no. I thought . . . '

'Are you going out? Do you have something booked?'

'No. I was just going to watch TV in my room.'

He smiled. 'You'll do no such thing! I'll fetch another plate. If you think I enjoy eating alone, you're very much mistaken. The whole point of a home-cooked meal is sharing it with the person who cooked it!'

Imogen blushed. 'That wasn't my intention.'

'Oh. Well of course if it would bore you . . . '

'Oh no! I only meant . . . '

He laughed. 'I'm teasing you, Sylvia. Please sit down before all this lovely food gets cold.'

He was so easy to talk to. She had wondered if he might probe further about her past, but he didn't. They found they had so much in common. Adam liked the theatre and the same kind of music that she did, though he complained that he didn't get much time to indulge his pleasures since taking over The Imperial.

'Suppose I asked Mrs Lane to babysit one evening and took you to a concert?' he said suddenly. 'Would you like that?'

Her heart leapt. It would be so lovely to go out. William had hardly ever taken her anywhere and since she had been in Craybourne she had been afraid to venture too far on her own, especially since Chris's letter.

'I'd love it,' she said enthusiastically.

He looked at her for a long moment. 'You know, when you smile like that it completely alters your face,' he told her softly. 'It takes all the sadness away. I've watched you so many times with Simon and wished I could bring a look like that to your eyes.'

His eyes held hers for what seemed an eternity, then desperate to break the tension between them she rose quickly to her feet. 'I must clear away these dishes,' she said shakily. 'The washing-up — '

'Leave them!' Standing up to face her, he took both of her hands in his. 'Sylvia, please — look at me.'

Slowly she raised her eyes to his and her heart quickened at what she saw in them.

'I don't know what happened in your past, but as the days go by I find myself wanting more and more to make up to you for whatever it was,' he told her. 'Before you arrived here life was mundane; all work and no play. It seemed to me that there was no light at the end of the tunnel. Since you came the sun has come out for me again.' Very gently he drew her towards him and kissed her very softly on the mouth. 'All I hope is that coming here has meant something to you too,' he went on.

'Oh, it has,' she said. 'More than I could ever begin to tell you. In fact I can't remember being so happy.' Reaching up she put her arms around his neck and he pulled her close, kissing her deeply and searchingly.

Later, as she lay awake in her room, Imogen's happiness was tinged with guilt and fear. She was falling in love with Adam, and he had made it plain that what he felt for her was deeper than friendship. But the fact that she was still married to William filled her with guilt at the deception she had created. Every day it seemed to get worse — more convoluted and complicated. One lie was never enough. More and more must be invented to cover the first. And she hated it. Soon she would have to tell Adam the truth about herself. He had a right to know now. But when he did — when he knew what she had done and that she had been living a lie all this time — could he ever trust her or feel the same about her? Would the happiness that seemed within her reach be shattered for ever?

She had just put Simon to bed the following evening when the telephone rang. She picked up the receiver.

'Hello.'

'Sylvia.' It was Sandra from Reception. 'There's a call for you. I'm putting you through now.'

Imogen felt her heart quicken with apprehension. It could only be Chris. But why was she ringing her like this, through Reception when they could so easily be overheard? Their arrangement had always been that Imogen should ring her. Was she ringing to warn her again?

But the voice that came through was unfamiliar. It was shrill and nasal with a strong cockney accent, and it sounded panicky.

'Sylv — that you love?'

'Y — yes?' Her heart began to thump.

'It's Mo. Thank God you're all right. Listen love, I'm gonna have to talk quick 'cause I ain't got much change and I'm in a phone box. I've let you down. Sorry, but I couldn't 'elp it. Rex come round. He threatened my Darren's life if I didn't tell him where you was. I had to get your address from that Mr Lindsay. Rex has got it into his head that you know where that stuff from the *you-know-what* is stashed. Maybe it's time you moved on. You know what Rex is like and . . . ' The line went dead leaving Imogen staring at the receiver.

Mo? Then she remembered — that was the name of the woman Chris had met when she went to Sylvia Tanner's address. But who was Rex? And why was he so anxious to track Sylvia down? 'Move on,' Mo had said. But where would she go? Just why, and from whom, was she running?

Her heart plummeted. What had she got herself into? And worse — by staying on here might she be putting herself and those around her in danger?

13

William was on the shortlist for the cardiac consultancy at St Aubrey's. Being appointed was, of course, a foregone conclusion. The interview had been arranged for Wednesday. Just three days to go and he would be St Aubrey's new cardiac consultant. It was in the bag! He was quite confident of that.

Edward Mayhew had hinted many times that he would put in a good word for him. He had a lot to be grateful to William for. They'd worked well together. In fact for the past year William had been doing most of Edward's work while the older man spent more and more time sitting on his many committees and playing golf. Not only that, but since Imogen's death William had given Edward every reason to believe that he would become his son-in-law as soon as a decent interval had elapsed.

He was in his study working on some notes for an article he was writing for the *BMJ* when he saw Carole's car draw up on the drive outside. He hadn't seen her for days. Every time he'd telephoned her lately she seemed to be out. He wasn't expecting her this afternoon and it was inconvenient when he wanted to work, but in spite of that he put down his pen and went to open the door. It was important to keep her sweet at the moment.

As he opened the front door he carefully

adjusted his smile. 'Darling! What a lovely surprise. Come in. I was just looking for an excuse to stop and make myself some coffee.'

'Hello, William.' She pushed past him into the hall, her shoulders stiff with indignation and her high heels tapping on the parquet floor. It would have been abundantly plain to all but the most insensitive of people that there was trouble brewing. She peeled off her gloves and coat, threw them on to a chair and stalked through to the drawing room without another word or glance in his direction. Frowning he followed her.

'Carole — is something wrong?'

'You tell me!' She turned to face him, her eyes glinting.

He laughed uneasily. 'There's nothing wrong with me?' His stomach muscles tightened. Surely she couldn't have found out about Imogen?

'Oh yes?' she challenged, her head thrown back. '*She* tell you that, did she?'

'She? Who are you talking about? I don't understand.'

'No? Come off it, William. You've been seeing someone else, haven't you?'

'No!' His eyes widened. As if he'd be so foolish, especially at this stage in the proceedings! 'What on earth gave you that idea?'

'You've been acting so strangely lately. I thought there was something going on, so I followed you.'

'You what? You followed me — where?'

She laughed. Her harsh cackle echoed unpleasantly round the room. 'Followed me

— where?' she mimicked. 'Where do you *think*? I saw you with her. Don't bother to deny it, William. Tall, dark — driving a tatty old Ford Escort. Ring any bells, does it?'

He felt the blood leave his face. Lesley Hemsby! Christ! How did he explain her? 'You've got it all wrong,' he blustered. 'It was business. She was — '

'Business! Oh, very good. That's a new name for it. Tell me her name then and who she works for. Tell me what this — this *business* was about. And I might believe you.'

'I can't. It's confidential.' He decided to bluff it out. 'She's a solicitor. It — it has to do with Genny's estate.'

'So why drive out to meet her in some remote pub at the back of beyond?'

'That's my business,' he snapped. 'What I should be asking is why you were following me!'

'Why not? I told you, you've been acting very oddly lately. You wouldn't open up and talk to me.'

'I don't have to tell you everything.'

'I don't like secrets, William. They make me suspicious. Now, are you going to tell me what this is all about, or do I have to advise Daddy against appointing you on Wednesday?'

'You *what*?' He stared at her, his anger flaring hotly. 'Don't you try to blackmail me, Carole. If I get this consultancy it'll be because I'm worthy of it. Not because *you* advise your father!' he raged. 'I happen to be a damned good surgeon. Who the *hell* do you think you are?'

'I happen to be Edward Mayhew's only

241

daughter,' she said. 'He adores me and he'd do anything for me. If I say you've been two-timing me he'll be influenced all right. You'd better believe that, William. Anyway, there are at least two other applicants who are as good as you. Probably better. It's far from a foregone conclusion that you'll get it.'

He stared at her, holding his temper in check with difficulty. He'd worked damned hard for this consultancy and he was damned if he was going to let her foul everything up for him. 'St Aubrey's owes me that post,' he growled. 'Not to mention your father. I've covered for him when he wanted to be elsewhere or when he wasn't up to operating. I've done most of his work for him over the past year.'

She shrugged. 'So what? It's what you've been paid for, isn't it?'

'*Paid* for? I've done the work I've been paid for and a hell of a lot more besides.' He stared at her, his eyes bulging ominously. 'I wasn't paid to tolerate you for instance.'

'What?'

'Yes, *tolerate* you, Carole!' He laughed. 'Don't tell me you thought I actually enjoyed your amorous advances.' As she turned away he grasped her wrist. 'Why do you think I endured your greedy sex-starved body in my bed — forced myself to make love to you when all the time the very sight of you made me want to puke!'

She wrenched her wrist from his grasp and took a step backwards, her eyes wide with shock. 'How dare you! How *could* you?'

He laughed. 'That's something I often asked myself. You threw yourself at me and I danced to your tune. I made myself cooperate because I wanted that job. But why on earth I put up with you and your voracious sexual appetite I don't know. I could get any job I wanted, anywhere in the country — the *world*.' He looked her up and down. 'You're past it, Carole,' he said brutally. 'Well past it! From those grabbing scarlet claws of yours to your revolting sagging body. Do you know something? You disgust me. You've always disgusted me!'

'Oh!' Tears of fury sprang to her eyes. 'You — you *shit*!' She lifted her hand and struck him hard across the face.

Her ring caught him, scratching his cheek painfully. He roared an obscenity and instinctively lashed out at her with the back of his hand, hitting her so hard that she staggered off balance, tumbling backwards over a chair and collapsing against the wall with a cry.

The moment he'd done it he knew that it was a bad mistake. As she struggled to her feet he could already see her eye swelling and a trickle of blood seeping from the corner of her mouth. With a frightened glance at him she ran into the hall and hurriedly gathered up her coat and bag, making for the front door.

William followed. 'Carole! Wait — look, I'm sorry. I lost my temper. But you shouldn't have hit me — shouldn't have accused me. It wasn't true you know. You should — '

She rounded on him. 'I should never have had anything to do with you!' One hand safely on the

243

handle ready for flight she spat the words at him like an enraged cat. 'I saw how you treated poor Imogen. That should have given me an idea of the kind of man you are. You're not fit to have sick people's lives in your hands. You can say goodbye to that consultancy, William.' She fingered her face tenderly. 'When Daddy sees what you've done to me you'll be bloody lucky to keep the job you've got! It'll be a miracle if you're not struck off by the time I've done with you!'

He stood in the hall, listening as she revved the car furiously and roared off down the drive as though the hounds of hell were in pursuit.

She'd get over it, he tried to convince himself. Carole had always liked a rough and tumble. In the past she'd found it a turn-on. But even as he was reassuring himself he knew he would not be forgiven. Not this time. By morning she'd have a black eye and a fat lip. He'd marked her for all to see. She'd never forgive him for that. Hell hath no fury . . . The quotation might have been made for Carole. She had a devious mind and a vindictive streak. She was the last person to make an enemy of. And, yes, she meant what she said all right. By the time she'd finished with his reputation it would be in tatters. All he'd worked and schemed for — to end like this. It was infuriating.

But surely he could still get that consultancy. He was a good surgeon. They knew it at St Aubrey's. The staff liked him and the patients adored him. Yes, he was still in with a chance. Edward was away for a few days. By the time he got back the heat would have cooled. Anyway, his was only one voice when it came to a consensus.

Just as long as no one found out about Imogen. His heart quickened. All this was her fault of course. She could land him in it right up to his eyes if she chose to reappear. His nostrils flared and his fists clenched and unclenched at his sides. If she came back and began making claims ... She had to be stopped, he told himself. He daren't risk it. It would have to be very carefully planned, but she definitely had to be silenced for good. His future depended on it. His chest was so tight that he could hardly breathe and he could hear his own heart beating as the adrenalin pumped around his body. He'd go and see that woman Lesley Hemsby had told him about — make her tell him where Imogen was. He'd have to be careful not to arouse any suspicion, although there was absolutely no reason why he should be suspected. After all, as far as the world knew, his dear wife had died in the Regent Street bombing. All he'd have to do was to make sure she stayed dead!

* * *

It was Paul's birthday. Max had been mildly surprised when his ex-wife had agreed to him taking the boy out for tea and the cinema. They went to see a lurid sci-fi romp that bored Max rigid, but Paul seemed to enjoy it enormously. Over Big Macs and fries later, he chattered on about it animatedly until suddenly he looked up at Max and said, 'Dad, there's something I think you should know.'

Max looked up in surprise. 'Really? What's that?'

'You know that day we went to Craybourne and you were on the trail of that stolen jewellery?'

'Yes.'

The boy looked uncomfortable. 'Well, while you were gone something happened.'

Max frowned. 'What was that?'

Paul sucked at the straw in his milkshake till it made the guzzling noise that set Max's teeth on edge. 'While you were at that hotel place your mobile went off.'

'Really? I thought I'd switched it off. So — did you answer it?'

'Rick did.' Paul looked up at him, his face reddening a little. 'It was some woman who said she was looking for someone called Sylv. She said that a man called Rex was looking for her. She sounded really scared.'

'Oh?' Max looked up, his interest suddenly aroused.

'Yeah. The thing is, Dad . . . '

'Yes, what?'

'Well, I'm not telling tales, but I thought you should know in case it was important.'

'Come on, Paul You thought I should know what?'

The boy bit his lip. 'Rick told her to try that hotel where you went. The Imperial, wasn't it?' He looked anxiously at his father. 'Would it have messed things up for you, Dad?'

Swallowing his concern, Max shook his head. 'Oh, no. Don't worry about it.'

'You won't tell Rick I grassed him up, will you?'

Max smiled. 'No. I won't.' His mind was racing. He'd have to call on Mo Sullivan again — ask her if she had passed the information on to Rex. Once he knew where to find her, Sylvia would be in danger. Maybe Mo knew what the connection was between Sylvia and Imogen. He had to find out once and for all.

★ ★ ★

'Sylvia, you won't go away and leave me, will you?' Simon asked.

They were sitting at the top of the cliffs looking down into what Imogen called the forbidden cove. She looked at him in surprise.

'Darling, of course not.'

It was uncanny, almost as though the child could read her mind. She'd been thinking about the telephone call from the Mo woman, wondering how she had known where to contact her. It had to be Max who had given her whereabouts away and it was very worrying. With each day that passed since the call, she had expected something to happen and she knew that she should really leave Craybourne and find another hiding place. But she couldn't bring herself to make the break.

She put an arm round Simon and hugged him close, hoping against hope that she wouldn't have to let him down. He'd been betrayed too many times already in his little life; first his mother and then the sadistic Miss Thomas. He trusted her and relied on her. And so did Adam. She hated the thought of disappointing them. As far as she could see she had two alternatives: confide in Adam, subject herself to his dismay and disillusionment; or pack her belongings and sneak off silently like a thief in the night. Neither prospect was inviting. And here she was promising Simon she wouldn't leave him.

She buried her face in the little boy's dark hair, breathing in his sweet scent, her throat tight with tears. It was so unfair. She loved him so much. She was falling very much in love with Adam too. And now she was facing the prospect of letting them both down. Perhaps nothing will happen, she told herself. But could she risk it? Was it fair to put those she loved at risk? Better to leave quietly and take her chances — alone.

'Look, the tide's out,' Simon said. 'Couldn't we just go down and have a paddle? It's a warm day.'

'Better not. Daddy made me promise not to,' she said. 'Not without him. The tide is dangerous. We don't want to get trapped, do we?' She shivered as she stood up and brushed down her skirt. It was odd but ever since she'd had that telephone call she had the feeling that someone was watching her. She looked around, but she could see no one acting suspiciously. Nevertheless she took Simon's hand.

'Come on, we'd better go back now. Tell you what, I noticed that the ice cream kiosk is open near the pier. If you're good I'll buy you one on the way home.'

Back at The Imperial she took Simon up to the flat and gave him his tea, then she went down to Reception again.

'Has anyone been in asking for me?' she asked Sandra.

The girl looked surprised. 'No. Why, were you expecting a visitor?'

'No — I just wondered.' As she went back upstairs Imogen still felt shaky. The feeling of being watched was eerie and unnerving, but she reassured herself that if she really was being followed it was hardly likely that her pursuer would make himself known to anyone.

Adam came into the kitchen as she was washing up Simon's tea things and stopped short at the sight of her white face. He looked at her. 'Sylvia. Are you all right?'

She turned, forcing a smile 'It's nothing. Something I forgot on my shopping list, that's all.'

He looked unconvinced. 'You're as white as a sheet. Are you sure it's nothing?'

'I'm sure. I'll have to go in now and see to Simon.'

He put out a hand to bar her way. 'Simon's fine. He's looking at his favourite TV programme. Sylvia, wait a minute.'

'Yes?'

'I came up to ask you. There's a concert on in Norwich tomorrow evening. I've got tickets and Sandra says she'll sit with Simon. Will you come with me?'

'Oh — I . . . ' She hesitated. How could she go out with him, talk and behave as though nothing was happening when all the time this threat was hanging over her?'

'There *is* something wrong, isn't there?' he said. 'I can see it in your face.'

She felt the tears gathering at the back of her throat. She longed to blurt out the truth and beg him to help her. But she had no right. She was in this alone. Somehow she must resolve it herself.

'It's just that I've got a bad headache,' she said. 'It'll be all right though. I'll take some aspirin.'

She retired to her room early that night, soon after Simon was in bed. For an hour she lay on her bed in the dark, racking her brain for the best solution to her problem. She couldn't walk out on Adam and Simon, yet she couldn't put either of them in jeopardy. But was this to be the pattern of her life from now on? Was her entire future to be spent running away?

For the first time, she thought about Sylvia, the woman whose identity she had taken. Had her life been like this? Always afraid; threatened and bullied into doing things that went against her nature? Constantly running away from some man — taking the blame for crimes she'd never intended to commit? Perhaps she'd been running away that day when she'd stolen the coat and bag. Perhaps someone had been following her and she wanted to disguise herself. And because of it she'd paid the ultimate price. Poor Sylvia. Never to have known real love — never to have had the chance to make a decent life, and then to have died so horribly. *But I'm still alive and I do have a choice,* Imogen said aloud. Suddenly she knew that if she ran away now she'd be running for the rest of her life. Now was the time to face up to reality. There might never be another chance.

At last she made up her mind. She owed Adam the truth and he should have it, whatever the outcome. She'd heard him come up to the flat and go into the living room about an hour ago. He liked to watch the news on TV at about this time. Getting up she smoothed down her skirt and ran a comb through her hair, then she went out into the corridor and tapped on the door.

'Come in.' When he saw that it was her he looked surprised. 'Sylvia! You don't have to knock. Come and sit down. Is your headache better?'

She glanced at the TV. 'Adam, I've got something very serious to talk to you about. Could we . . . ?'

'Of course.' He got up and switched off the set, looking at her anxiously. 'It sounds ominous. Please — sit down and take your time. Whatever it is I'm not going to eat you.'

She forced a smile at his attempt at defusing the situation, but she was shaking with tension and her teeth were almost chattering as she sat down on the edge of a chair. 'I'm afraid you're going to be very angry,' she began.

'I'm sure I won't,' he said. 'Not with you. Please, just tell me what's on your mind and let me be the judge.'

'I'm going to have to leave.'

He frowned. 'Leave? Surely not? What's wrong, Sylvia? Surely it's nothing we can't sort out.'

She swallowed hard. This was going to be even harder than she'd imagined. 'It's a long story,' she began. 'To begin with my name isn't Sylvia, but you've already guessed that. It's Imogen. Imogen Jameson.'

He nodded. 'You said you wanted to make a fresh start.'

'I did — do. And I've been happy here. So very happy.'

'But — you're not any more?'

She sighed. 'I think I'd better begin at the beginning. You guessed rightly that I was married. Well — I still am.'

'I see.'

'No. You don't.' The silence between them was almost tangible as he waited. There was no going back now. She took a deep breath.

'William is a doctor — a heart surgeon. I was a nurse when we met. I was very young and I let him sweep me off my feet. Naively, I thought he loved me but it turned out that it was the money I'd inherited that he wanted, not me. When I stubbornly held on to it he — punished me.'

Adam got up and moved across to sit beside her. 'In what way?'

'Many ways — oh, so many. He was cruel and sadistic, violent too at times. He accused me of infidelity, taunted me with my inadequacies; he was unreasonably demanding and he constantly undermined my confidence.'

Slowly and haltingly she related the painful story of the drowned kitten and William's insistence that she had done it herself while sleep-walking.

'Then, when he knew I was pregnant he tried to make me have an abortion,' she said. 'I refused, but I fell down some stairs and lost the baby anyway.' She swallowed hard at the lump in her throat. 'He tried to make me believe that that was my fault too.'

'Oh, Imogen.' He reached for her hand.

'William was — is — ambitious, obsessively so,' she went on. 'He had a lover; the daughter of the consultant surgeon he worked with at the hospital. I believe he intended to get rid of me somehow and marry her to further his career.'

She paused and Adam nodded encouragingly. 'Go on, Imogen. I'm listening.'

'I put up with it all for so long. I was even forced to entertain his lover in my home, but losing the baby almost finished me. A close friend asked me to go and stay with her in London for a few days. I went to the West End to have my hair done. It was the day of that huge car bomb explosion in Regent Street.' She looked at him. 'Last Christmas, remember?'

'I remember.'

'While I was paying, someone — a woman — grabbed my coat and handbag, leaving her own in its place. I picked them up and chased her through the store into the street. Then the bomb went off and I was injured.'

He held her hand tightly, remembering the bruises and cuts he'd wondered about when she first came looking for a job. Suddenly he guessed what she was about to tell him. 'My God! You swapped places? She was killed and — and they thought it was *you*?'

She nodded. 'When I came round in the hospital they were calling me Sylvia. When I eventually worked out why, it was like a revelation. It seemed I was being given the perfect opportunity to escape.' She shook her head. 'I must have been mad to think I could get away with it. I think I must still have been a bit disturbed after losing the baby. All I could think of was that it was a way to free myself of William. He wouldn't give me a divorce, you see. I suppose he thought it would damage his reputation and anyway he knew a divorce would cost him money. He kept grinding me down, hoping, I suppose — just hoping that I'd . . . '

'Don't.' He pulled her into his arms and held her close. 'Don't think about it. I wish I'd known all this before.'

'I didn't dare tell anyone,' she said. 'It all seemed so perfect here, but I suppose I knew all along that it would have to end eventually.'

He held her away from him. 'Why are you telling me now? And what do you mean about it having to end?'

'Someone who knows, or rather *knew* me, saw me here and realised that I'm still alive,' she told him. 'My best friend — the only other person who knows where I am — wrote to warn me. The man is a friend of hers — a journalist, and he might not be able to resist looking into it as a possible story. Then, a few days ago I had a telephone call from a friend of Sylvia Tanner's, warning me — or rather *her* — that a man was looking for her. You see, Sylvia had been to prison. She was mixed up in a particularly nasty robbery. Then this afternoon — maybe it was my imagination but I felt sure someone was watching me.' She looked at Adam, tears now in her eyes. 'I know now that I can't go on like this. It's all such a terrible mess. If all this got into the papers it would only be a matter of time before William found out what I'd done and when he knows I'm still alive . . . ' She broke off, her blood chilling at the prospect. 'It could make trouble for you — ruin your business and all you've worked for. It's best if I leave. I'll pack and go first thing in the morning.'

'You'll do nothing of the kind.' He was on his feet, taking her hands and holding her fast.

'But if William did find me — what would I tell him?'

'Tell him the truth. What could he possibly do?' He drew her close. 'Listen, Imogen, you can't believe I'm going to let you go now. You don't know what life was like for me before you came into it. You've made such a difference. I can't lose you now. There has to be a way out of this and we'll find it. We'll go and see a solicitor; get the legal facts straight. You'll get a divorce easily on the grounds you've told me about and as long as you're here, you're safe. We'll take care of it all together.'

She opened her mouth to protest but he put his fingers against her lips. 'Please, Imogen. I love you,' he said softly. 'Just let me take care of you. Everything is going to be all right. Trust me.'

She gave herself up to his kiss and leaned against him gratefully. The relief was so enormous that she wanted to cry. It seemed she had carried her burden alone for so long. Being able to share it with Adam, even to be called by her own name once again, was like having a great weight lifted from her shoulders. Like coming home. She looked up at him.

'I don't want to be alone tonight,' she said.

He kissed her. 'You needn't be. You needn't be alone ever again.'

* * *

Max took Paul home and headed for the East End. Parking the car in Canning Terrace he fed the meter, but as he was walking towards number 25 he saw a man come out through the front door. He drew back into a doorway for a moment, watching. The man was quite a long way off but there was something familiar about him. Max watched as he approached a gleaming BMW and unlocked the door. Then he knew. He might occasionally have trouble remembering faces but Max never forgot a car registration number. And this one belonged to William Jameson! What the hell was he doing here? What possible connection could *he* have with Sylvia Tanner?

He walked slowly back to his own car and sat inside, thinking hard. Then an idea occurred to him; a notion so bizarre and unlikely that he almost dismissed it. But the more he thought about it, the more credible it seemed. He got out again and ran into the house and up the stairs two at a time to knock loudly on Mo Sullivan's door. She opened it quickly, glaring angrily at him.

'What the bleedin' 'ell do you want? I just got my Darren off to sleep. First that other geezer, now you!'

'I'm sorry, Mo. I won't keep you a minute. I just wanted to ask you one or two questions.'

'Oh yeah? And what if I don't feel like answerin' them?'

'What did that man who just left want?'

She glared at him. 'What do *you* wanna know for?'

'Please, Mo. It could be important.'

She shrugged. 'He never give me his name. Wanted to know where Sylv was. He don't give up easy. It was the second time he'd been round.' She laughed. 'First time I told 'im to get in the bleedin' queue!'

'What about this time? Did you tell him?'

'Well, yeah. I did in the end — when he told me why.'

'What reason did he give you?'

'Says he's got some good news for her. He's a lawyer, see. Some old auntie died and left her some money.' She smiled. 'Looks like Sylv's luck might be on the up at last. That Rex Morgan got nicked last night; caught red handed robbin' an off-licence so we don't 'ave to worry about him no more. Best news I've 'ad for ages.'

'Mo. Have you seen Sylvia since she left here?'

'No.' She shook her head. 'I spoke to her though.'

'You did? When? How?'

'On the phone. You told me where she was, remember? I phoned to warn her about Rex after I gave him the address of that hotel.'

'And you're sure it was her you spoke to?'

'Well — I asked for her and they put me through.'

'What did she say?'

She frowned. 'What *is* this? Why do you wanna know?'

'Because — I believe that Sylvia is dead, Mo. I believe she was killed in the Regent Street bombing last Christmas. I think someone else might be impersonating her.'

'Oh! Oh my God!'

'I'm sorry to shock you with it like this, but someone — another girl — could be in grave danger. Now what did she — what did the person you spoke to — say?'

She bit her lip, trying to remember. 'Well — not much really. I was in a phone box, see, and I wanted to warn her. The money ran out before she could answer prop'ly. Anyway, I wasn't really listenin'.'

'So it might easily have been someone else?'

'Well — I s'pose so.'

'Thanks, Mo. You've been a great help.' He turned, then paused. Taking out his wallet he handed her a note. 'Treat yourself, eh?'

'Thanks, Mr Lindsay.'

'And I'm sorry — about Sylvia.'

'Me too. I'm gonna miss her. She was a good mate.'

⋆ ⋆ ⋆

Chris was working on an article when the entry-phone buzzed. She got up and lifted the receiver.

'Who is it?'

'Chris — it's me, Max.'

She sighed. 'Go away, Max. There's nothing to say.'

'Chris, please. I have to talk to you. It's vital.'

'No!'

'It's about Imogen.'

She froze. What could he have found out now? 'All right,' she conceded. 'Come up. But if this is some cheap trick . . . '

'I assure you, it isn't.'

His tone convinced her and she pressed the button and waited. A few minutes later he walked in. In spite of herself her heart flipped at the sight of him, but she kept her voice level.

'What is it, Max? It's late and I have work to do. You'll have to be quick.'

'Right.' He closed the door firmly behind him and turned to face her. 'I'm going to ask you one question, Chris, and I want one truthful answer. Then I'll go — if you want me to.'

'Go on then.'

'Has Imogen taken on the identity of Sylvia Tanner?' When she didn't reply he went on. 'I've got this theory, you see. I think that Sylvia was killed in the bombing that day and somehow

Imogen has assumed her identity. OK, I know it's bizarre in the extreme and I hope to God I'm wrong. If I am, just tell me. That's all I want to know.' He watched as the colour left Chris's face. Crossing the room, he took her by the shoulders and bent down to look into her eyes.

'Chris! It's true, isn't it? I can see it in your face. But how did she do it? And *why*? I mean, I know she was unhappy with Jameson but this — '

'Max — if I tell you, you've got to promise not to sell the story.'

'What? What the hell do you take me for? Of course I promise.' He sighed. 'Not that it wouldn't make a hell of a splash. But no, of course I wouldn't use it.'

As briefly as she could, she told him about the bag-snatch and the chase and confusion that followed; Imogen's realisation that there had been a mix-up and her impulsive decision to let everyone believe that she had died in the bombing.

'No one could have been more shocked than I was when she turned up here at the flat a couple of nights later,' she told him. 'Bruised and battered, but adamant that she still wanted everyone to believe she was dead.'

'And that was when you went and sussed out Mo Sullivan?'

'Yes. Somehow we had to find out some details about Sylvia. I mean, she could have had a husband and kids for all we knew.'

'Instead of which she had a whole lot of far worse baggage.' He drew up a chair and sat astride it facing her. 'Listen, Chris, Rex Morgan — Phil's brother — has been looking for Sylvia and Mo inadvertently got hold of the address of The Imperial and gave it to him.'

'But Sylvia isn't there and he'll soon find that out.'

'It's not him we need to worry about now. He's been picked up for some other crime. It's Jameson Imogen needs to be afraid of.'

'What do you mean?'

'I went to visit Mo yesterday. When I arrived at the house, who do you think was just leaving?'

Her eyes opened wide. 'Not William? Oh God! Are you sure?'

'Positive. He kidded Mo that he was a solicitor and spun her some yarn about Sylvia being left some money. And I'm afraid Mo gave him the Craybourne address. You see what it means, don't you? It means he's on to Imogen. He knows where she is. Somehow we've got to warn her — get to her before he does!'

14

As Imogen watched Simon at play on the swings her thoughts were with Adam. His suggestion that they go to see William together had terrified her. The thought of it still brought a chill to her heart, in spite of the logic he had tried to bring to his argument.

'What can he possibly do to harm you?' he asked. 'We'll see a solicitor first and go armed with the legal position,' he went on. 'You have ample grounds for divorce and no one could blame you for running away after the bombing. As you say, you were still traumatised after losing the baby and your fall. Bullies always cave in when they're made to face the truth.'

At last she'd allowed herself to be reassured, comforted by the fact that she was no longer alone. Adam loved her and for the first time in years she felt cared for and protected. With his help she would see it through and be able to start a new life.

Last night had been like a revelation. She had been so tense at first with Adam. But he had made love to her so tenderly, stroking and caressing her until he coaxed her to relax. Finally the touch of his lips and hands aroused her so that she responded to him passionately, the memory of William's loveless brutality erased for ever.

This morning she felt free, light as air and happier than she could ever remember being. Early this morning, before Simon was up they had talked again, deciding to go to London and meet William as soon as they could get away. The prospect of the coming meeting made her stomach quake but she knew it had to be done and, as Adam said, the sooner it was done and out of the way, the sooner they could get on with their lives. Meantime, he reminded her, there was the concert to go to in Norwich that evening.

'It's just what we need; an evening out, away from everything, just the two of us,' Adam said. 'Sandra will sit with Simon and just for tonight we won't think about William, the past or the future. Tonight we'll just think of us; you and me.'

'I need something to wear,' Imogen said. 'I don't know if you've noticed but all my clothes are second-hand cast-offs — things that Chris gave me. I had nothing but what I stood up in when I left London and I've never felt quite right, wearing someone else's things.'

'Go into town and buy something this afternoon,' Adam suggested. 'I've got appointments all morning but I'm free this afternoon. Simon can stay with me.'

The memory of the conversation made her look at her watch. Seeing that it was almost twelve o'clock she called Simon to her. 'Better go home and get some lunch now,' she said. 'You're going to spend the afternoon with Daddy and we mustn't keep him waiting.'

263

'Can I help him in the office?' Simon asked as he trotted along beside her. 'Will he let me play with his computer?'

She laughed. 'I don't know about that. You'll have to wait and see.'

As she took his hand and walked towards the park gates she was too occupied with her thoughts to notice the man on the other side of the playground, intently watching her every move — even when he stepped out from the cover of the bushes and began to follow them.

★ ★ ★

Although Craybourne was quite a small town, it was also a holiday centre and therefore the shops were of quite a high standard. As soon as she got into the centre of the town Imogen made an appointment to have her hair done before she began looking round for a new outfit. Sandra had recommended a hairdresser and to Imogen's delight they could fit her in at Michelle's at four o'clock. In Galloway's, the town's one large department store, she lingered in the dress department, looking along the rails for the kind of thing she wanted. Not too dressy, but smart; suitable for an evening out but not too formal. She wanted to look nice for Adam — wanted him to be proud to be seen with her. She tried on one or two things but wasn't entirely happy with them. Thanking the assistant she turned to leave, but as she did she caught sight of her reflection in a mirror and a chill went through her as another reflection — some distance behind her own — caught her eye. A man was standing near the escalator and just for one fleeting second she thought it was William. She spun round to look — but there was no one there.

Going down on the escalator Imogen tried to calm her racing heart, assuring herself that it had all been in her mind; someone who looked like William, a trick of the light or a distortion of the mirror. After all, there was no way that William could know she was here. But the feeling of shock and fear persisted as she walked through the store's ground floor and into the street. Outside, she stood on the pavement, looking right and left, scanning the faces of the afternoon shoppers, but she saw no one who remotely resembled William.

In a small exclusive boutique two streets away she found just what she was looking for, a delphinium blue dress in wild silk; perfectly plain, but with a stylish matching jacket to wear over it. Paying for it, she moved on to look for shoes and a handbag which she found quite easily a few shops further along the street. Her purchases completed, she looked at her watch and saw that she still had half an hour to go before her hair appointment. Time for a cup of tea.

She should have been enjoying the freedom and the luxury of spending some time and money on herself for once. She would have been if only she could shake off the unnerving feeling that she was being followed.

Slipping into a nearby coffee bar she queued

for a pot of tea and a bun. She was paying for them at the end of the counter when something made her look back. That was when she saw him. There, at the far end of the queue — she was sure it was the man she had seen in Galloway's. He was a long way off and there were people between them, partly obstructing her view, but she was certain it was the same man. And this time she was positive that it was William.

She thrust her money at the cashier and ran in a panic to the only place she felt safe. In the ladies' room she stood staring at her white, stricken reflection in the mirror. What was she to do? She was safe enough in here but she would have to go out there again, pass all the tables to get out of the place. He would still be there — waiting; confident now that she could not escape. There was no way she could avoid him.

Her stomach churned and she felt physically sick with fear and dread. She looked around her frantically, even wondering whether she could squeeze out through the one small window. Suddenly the door opened, making her jump and spin round, her heart in her mouth.

'Is anything wrong dear? Are you all right?' The middle-aged cashier had come in and was eyeing her with concern. 'When I saw you leave your tea and come rushing in here I wondered if you were ill.' She peered at Imogen. 'You're dreadfully pale. Can I get you anything?'

'Is there another way out of here?' Imogen asked. 'You see there's someone out there — a man — who's been following me.'

'A stalker? Do you want me to call the police?'

'No. I'll be all right if I can just give him the slip.'

'Well . . . ' The woman looked doubtful. 'Well — if you're sure. Better come with me.'

She led Imogen out through a side door and into an alleyway. 'Just turn left and walk along to the end and you'll find yourself in the street again,' she said. 'Now, are you sure you'll be all right dear?'

'I'll be fine, thanks.'

At the end of the alley she cautiously looked both ways. To her relief he was nowhere to be seen. She made straight for Michelle's. She'd be safe at the hairdresser's and when she was finished she'd ask them to call her a taxi back to The Imperial. He couldn't touch her, she told herself. She was safe now.

By the time her hair had been shampooed and she had settled in the chair to have the cut, Imogen had convinced herself once again that she was being paranoid. Surely she must have imagined the whole thing. She'd hardly been out on her own since coming to Craybourne and the telephone call she'd received, plus yesterday's incident, had unnerved her. It was easy to imagine that any tall dark man was William.

She watched as the girl expertly cut and shaped her hair, then blow-dried it. She looked and felt so much better and she smiled, anticipating Adam's admiring look when he saw her dressed in the new outfit, ready to go out.

As she paid she asked the receptionist to order

her a taxi. The girl picked up the telephone and made the call.

'He'll be about five minutes,' the girl told Imogen. 'They're not allowed to park outside, but he'll wait for you just round the corner of the next street.'

She waited, standing close to the door. People passed, early holiday-makers, housewives out shopping, schoolchildren on their way home. No one remotely sinister or suspicious looking. When five minutes had passed she stepped out into the street. She could see the corner from where she was. And, yes, there was a car waiting.

She hurried towards it and climbed into the back. As she did so she heard a hooting from behind and out of the rear window she saw another car with a taxi sign on its roof. Too late, she realised that she was in the wrong car! She reached for the door, but before she could open it, she was flung violently backwards as the car roared into life and sprang forwards into the traffic, to the angry hooting of other cars and the shouts of irate pedestrians.

'Stop! What do you think you're doing?' she called out in alarm. Then her blood froze as she caught sight of the driver's face in the rearview mirror. This time there was no mistake. It was William!

His eyes rose to meet hers. 'I thought I'd surprise you, Genny,' he said coolly. 'Like you surprised me — by being alive.'

'Stop! Let me out!' She tried to open the door but he'd used the central-locking device to fasten all four.

'Not yet. We've got a few scores to settle first.'

'Where are we going?'

'Just shut up. You'll find out.'

'Stop!' She threw an arm around his neck and pulled his head back, making him swerve dangerously. The car mounted the pavement, bringing shouts from people waiting at a bus stop. He grabbed her wrist and flung her arm away furiously.

'What do you think you're doing you stupid bitch! Do you want to kill us both?'

Shaken and breathless, she collapsed on to the back seat. Surely someone would have contacted the police by now, if only to report a dangerous driver. Any minute now a police car would surely come alongside.

But no police car appeared and soon the built-up area and suburbs had given way to a country road with no houses in sight. William was still driving heart-stoppingly fast. She looked out, frantically trying to recognise the location, but it was totally unfamiliar to her.

About a mile further on he turned right abruptly on to a rough track and drove on for about half a mile, bumping over potholes and ruts till she thought her teeth would rattle. Eventually the car came to a stop outside a derelict cottage. He switched off the engine and turned to her.

'Well, well. You've had your hair done,' he said sarcastically. 'I'm flattered.'

She shrank back on the seat. 'What is this place? Why are we here?'

'You'll find out.' He clicked off the locking device. 'Get out!'

She wrenched open the door and stumbled out of the car, taking to her heels to run along the track, but it was hard going in her town shoes. The rough track was slippery from recent rain and a few minutes later she turned her ankle painfully and went sprawling in the mud.

William grabbed her arm and yanked her to her feet. 'Get up! God, you're pathetic.' Pushing her arm up her back he frog-marched her back towards the cottage, kicked open the door and pushed her inside. Slamming the door shut, he leaned against it.

It was dim inside the cottage with its boarded-up windows, but she could see the malevolent look on his face as he said, 'Don't worry, we're not staying here long, just long enough to give you the chance to explain your actions. If there is an explanation.'

She took a deep breath, looking round her for some means of escape. He laughed.

'You can look all you like. You won't get away. You'll never get away this time, Genny.'

'How did you know where I was?' she asked.

He laughed. 'I saw you bolt into the ladies' and I guessed there'd be a back way out of the place. I followed you to the hairdresser's and it was a pretty fair guess that you'd order a taxi. You were always so predictable, Genny. I can read you like a book.'

'I was coming to see you next week,' she told him. 'To explain — to ask you — '

'It's too late for that,' he interrupted. 'The

damage is done. You've ruined me. *Ruined* me, do you hear?'

'This isn't the way, William,' she argued. 'You — you won't get away with it. I'm expected. When I don't arrive people will be out looking for me. Someone back there must have seen you abduct me. There'll be witnesses.'

'No there won't. People don't give a damn nowadays. Too occupied with their own problems. They don't want to get involved. Anyway, it will be too late by then.' He stepped up close to her, glowering down into her face. 'You're going to pay for what you've done. You're going to have an unfortunate little accident. They won't find you till tomorrow morning and by then I'll be miles away. Anyway why should anyone suspect me? After all, my wife is dead!' He folded his arms and regarded her. 'But first things first. You say you wanted to explain, so go ahead. The floor's all yours. I'd like to hear why you did it. It's not very nice, is it, letting your loved ones believe you've been killed?'

'How did you know?' she whispered. 'How did you find out?'

'When the undertaker gave me this.' He produced a tiny gold ring from his pocket and thrust it under her nose.

She stared at it, shaking her head. 'I don't understand.'

'I knew your body intimately enough to know that it had no adornments of this kind,' he said harshly. 'Body-piercing is hardly your style. When he told me where it came from I knew immediately it wasn't you I'd just buried. But I didn't tell anyone. No. I kept up the pretence — went along with it all until I found out where you were.'

'If you've known that long, why — '

'Why! Because I've been biding my time, planning what I'd do when I caught up with you. You didn't seriously think I'd let you get away with it, did you? It suited me to let everyone think you were dead. And now, very soon you will be.'

Her heartbeats seemed to fill her chest, drumming in her ears deafeningly. 'What can you gain by this, William?' she said. 'You never loved me. You married me for the money and you've had that. Just divorce me and you can marry Carole. That's what you always wanted, isn't it?'

'Carole!' he snapped. 'Because of what you've done — because of *you* — Carole and I have split up.'

'Because of *me*?'

'I'd engaged a female private detective to track you down. Carole jumped to the wrong conclusions — thought I was seeing someone else. Ironic, isn't it? I've lost the consultancy too — *and* my job at St Aubrey's. You've ruined my career and my life, Genny!'

'No!' She stared at him. 'How could any of that be my fault?'

'But it is! You've spoiled everything for me.' His eyes suddenly glazed. 'Just like he did — Michael. All those years ago.'

'Michael?'

'My brother.' His lip curled. 'The brother I

never wanted. He took my mother away from me and ruined everything. I had to get rid of him just as I'm going to get rid of you.'

'William!' She gasped. 'What are you *saying*?'

But his eyes were still far away. For the moment he seemed to have forgotten she was there. 'A lot of people tried to take her away from me,' he went on, almost to himself. 'Her friends clamoured for her attention too.' In the dimness she could see that his eyes were tortured and bloodshot, the pupils two black pinpoints. He seemed to be in another world and the look on his face brought an ice-cold chill to her heart. 'People loved her you see, because she was pretty and clever and vivacious — just like you used to be.' He looked at her accusingly. 'Till you changed too like she did — like they all do.'

'William — '

'My father hated me,' he went on, unheeding. 'He never wanted kids you see — always wanted her all to himself,' he said. 'But Michael — the baby — even my father liked him. That was the last straw. She called him Michael and after she had him she hardly knew I was there — always holding him, cooing and fawning over him.' His lower lip protruded in an almost childlike pout.

'So I decided to get rid of him.' He smiled. 'It was so easy. I was surprised how easy. I only had to hold the pillow over his face for a little while and he stopped breathing.' He sighed and the corners of his mouth drooped reminiscently. 'She cried. I didn't like that. But to make her better I told her my secret.'

'What secret?' Imogen whispered.

'I told her my father had done it,' he said. 'She believed me. She knew I'd never lie about a thing like that. After all, I was only a child.'

The thudding of her heart was so loud that she was sure he must hear it. 'But — you told me that he believed *she* had done it,' she said.

'He *did*! That was the clever part.' He laughed. 'You see, I told him I'd seen *her* do it. Oh, they were so angry with each other. You never heard such a row. I sat on the stairs and listened. It was so exciting it made me shiver. In the end he packed his things and he left, just as I'd hoped and I knew then it had worked. I had her all to myself again.' The smile left his face. 'Only then she got ill and they took her away to that place where I couldn't go.'

He closed his eyes in pain and when he opened them again she saw that he had remembered where he was — and why. He glared at her. 'It always happens to me. Women! They're never satisfied. One person to love is never enough. No matter how much you give them they always want more — friends, babies, lovers. And in the end they always let you down. Patients don't do that. They're grateful. They respect and appreciate you for your skill and what you are.' He looked at her with pure venom in his eyes. 'You let me down, Genny. You changed. You wanted things — things that had nothing to do with being married to me.'

'I just wanted a life, William. To be a person in my own right,' she protested. But he wasn't listening.

'But the way you left! Making me believe you

274

were dead — letting me think I was free again when all the time . . . ' His breathing quickened and she saw his hands clench at his sides as he directed his glare on her again. 'Do you like being dead, Genny? I hope so because now you're going to find out what it's really like.'

'William — let me go,' she begged. 'No one need ever know. You've got the money. You'll be all right. You can sell the house and go away — start again.' She made a move towards the door but his hand shot out, grabbing her by the throat and pinning her against the wall so that she could scarcely breathe.

'Shut up and stay where you are,' he rasped. 'Why should I go away, just because of you? I had a promising career. I should have had that consultancy. It was mine. I worked hard for it. And now you've messed everything up for me with your meddling.'

'No, William. I asked you for a divorce. If only you'd agreed, none of this would have — ' She struggled to free herself but he pressed harder on her throat, making her cough and gasp.

'Shut up! You're going to listen to me now. I'm not going to make it easy for you. It won't be quick. You're going to have to suffer a bit for what you've put me through.'

★ ★ ★

By the time Chris and Max started out it was almost eight o'clock. Chris sat silently beside Max as he weaved in and out of the busy London traffic, glad for once that she wasn't

275

driving herself. She knew she'd be far too worried to concentrate properly. Before they left her flat she had rung The Imperial in Craybourne and asked to speak to Sylvia. The receptionist had asked her to hang on and a few minutes later a man's voice came on the line.

'Hello. I'm Adam Bennett, the manager of The Imperial. I understand you were asking for Sylvia.'

'That's right. May I speak to her, please?'

'I'm afraid she isn't here at the moment.' There was a pause and then he said. 'May I ask who is speaking please, and what it is you want with her?'

Chris looked across at Max, biting her lip with indecision. 'I'm sorry but it's private. Can you tell me when she'll be back?'

'I'm not sure. Can you give me your name? I'll ask her to call you back.'

There was something about the man's voice. He sounded worried — desperate almost. She decided to risk it. 'My name is Christine Day,' she said. 'I'm Sylvia's best friend.'

There was a pause and then he said quietly, 'I think you mean Imogen's.'

Chris almost fainted. He *knew*! She gestured wildly at Max and he crossed the room to lean close and listen to the conversation.

'How much has she told you?' she asked.

'All of it, I think. I know that she's not Sylvia Tanner but Imogen Jameson and that her husband thinks she was killed in the Regent Street bombing four months ago. We've talked. She's confided in me about her

276

marriage and the reason she did . . . what she did. I think she trusts me. I've persuaded her to go and see her husband and make a clean breast of the whole thing.'

'Oh no!' Chris gasped. 'That really isn't a good idea. You don't know what he's like.'

'I do. She's told me about him. And I wouldn't let her face an ordeal like that alone. I intend to go with her.' There was a pause then, 'Imogen and I have become close since she's been here — very close.'

'I see.'

'Look, I think I should tell you,' he went on. 'I'm worried. Imogen went shopping this afternoon and she hasn't returned.'

Chris gasped. 'But it's . . . ' She looked at her watch. 'It's almost seven. The shops . . . '

'Exactly. The shops have been closed for over an hour. Not only that but I was taking her to a concert this evening. She was looking forward to it. I know she wouldn't be late unless something had happened.'

'Oh my God!'

'Have you heard from her? Do you know anything?'

'No, but I think you should know why I was ringing her.'

Max grabbed the receiver out of her hand. 'Hello. This is Max Lindsay. You don't know me but I'm a friend of Imogen's too. I don't want to alarm you unnecessarily, but we have good reason to believe that Imogen's husband might have found out where she is. It's too long a story to go into now, but you can take it from me that he definitely has that address.'

'Oh my God! You've confirmed my worst fears. This is what I've been so afraid of.'

'Look,' Max went on. 'We — Chris and I — could drive over there right now if you want us to,' he said. 'I'm not sure what we can do, but three heads are better than one and I know Chris would like to be there.' He pushed up his sleeve to look at his watch. 'It's seven now. We could probably be with you by nine.'

'Thanks. I'd be glad of your support. Meantime, should I contact the police?'

'I don't think they'd be very interested at this point,' Max said. 'She's only been missing a couple of hours. Besides, there might be some rather awkward questions to answer.'

Now they were in the car and on their way. 'Was it wise to stop him from notifying the police?' Chris asked. 'Is what Imo did against the law?'

Max shook his head. 'Whether it is or not, I think it's better to keep them out of it for the time being.'

'I suppose so. Max — how did you find out about this? What made you go to see Mo Sullivan?'

He sighed. 'It was Paul's birthday yesterday. I took him out and he told me about something he'd obviously had on his conscience since the three of us went to Craybourne — that Sunday when I spotted Imogen.'

'What was it?'

'I left the two of them in the car while I checked out The Imperial. Richard was a bit pissed off because he hadn't wanted to go to Craybourne. I left my mobile in the car and when it rang he answered it. The caller was Mo Sullivan. She assumed it was me answering. She wanted Sylvia's address. Out of pure devilment Richard just told her to try The Imperial, Craybourne.' He shook his head. 'He couldn't have known what he was doing of course, but it was so irresponsible. I could murder the little sod. Over the last couple of years he's grown really spoilt and bolshie.' He glanced at Chris. 'Sometimes I feel I don't know those boys any more, and as for what they feel about me; I'm not the dad they used to love. I'm just a boring old fart they can't get out of seeing — someone to be tolerated.'

Chris reached out to cover his hand on the steering wheel. 'I'm sorry. It must be very hurtful.'

'It is.' He looked at her. 'And soon they'll be off, leading their own lives; Richard to his sixth form college and Paul to this bloody public school that's going to cost me an arm and a leg. I'll just be a back number.' He glanced at her. 'That's why it was so wonderful to know you were always there for me. Believe me, Chris, I wasn't just using you as a convenience.'

'I know. I suppose I've always known really.' She swallowed hard, determined not to soften too easily. 'Max — if you knew about William yesterday, why did you wait till this evening to come and tell me?'

'I couldn't be sure you'd believe me.' He shot

her a wry smile. 'After all, you were adamant that it couldn't have been Imogen I saw. Besides, I wasn't sure you'd even let me into the flat, never mind listen to what I had to say!'

'No, I see.' She looked at him. 'I'm sorry.'

'It hurts, you know.' He looked at her. 'I mean why couldn't you have confided in me? You just couldn't trust me not to use the story, could you?'

She looked at him. 'After what you said? No, not really.'

He was silent for a moment. 'It's just that I always found it frustrating — the way you hold back on any kind of human story.' He sighed. 'The truth is, you really don't think much of me deep down, do you, Chris?'

'It isn't that. I promised her, that's all.' She looked at him. 'It wasn't my secret, it was hers. And it was vital to keep it; vital for her safety. Surely you can see that.'

'Of course I can. I do have feelings you know.'

She glanced at him. 'As for what I feel about you . . . '

'Yes?' The hopeful look in his eyes wrung her heart.

'I love you, Max. You know that. I always have and nothing can alter it, more's the pity. It's just that I never felt I came first and I'm selfish enough to want to.'

'You *do* come first,' he told her. 'It's just so hard when you have other commitments. Put it this way, you're my priority — but they're my duty.'

'I know. I understand.'

'Do you though? Do you really?'

'Yes! In a way. Look, I'll try to, Max. From now on I'll really try.'

'From now on? Does that mean we get another chance?' He drew the car into the verge and turned to pull her into his arms, kissing her hungrily. 'Oh God, Chrissie, I've missed you so damned much,' he murmured against her hair. He took her face between his hands and looked into her eyes. 'Look, I promise that if you come back, from now on you come first — whatever.'

She stroked his cheek. 'Don't make promises you won't be able to keep. I know how hard it is for you — being torn two ways. I'll be more tolerant in future. At least I'll try to be.'

He looked at her for a long moment. 'I think we should get married,' he said firmly. 'What do you say?'

She laughed. 'Watch it, Lindsay! It's not like you to be rash! You've always said you'd never do it again.'

'Well, I've changed my mind. It's allowed, isn't it? Promise me you'll give it some thought. It could be so good, Chris, you and me.'

She sighed. 'Oh, Max, you choose the weirdest times to propose. I'm sorry but right at this moment all I can think of is what's happening to Imo.'

'I know. We'll go.' He turned the key in the ignition again. 'Look, don't worry. Surely Jameson wouldn't really do anything to harm her, would he?'

'I wouldn't like to bet on it. Oh God, Max, where can she be?'

★ ★ ★

It was dark now. Imogen was cold and hungry. They seemed to have been at the cottage for hours. William had tied her hands and feet, just in case she tried to make a break for it again. He'd passed the time by telling her stories — stories she'd rather not have heard; about the little dog his mother had loved that he'd dropped over a railway bridge on to the line below. About the time he'd laced his mother's best friend's tea with bleach, causing her to be rushed to hospital in agony. He told her about Kate, a ward sister at his Edinburgh hospital, who broke off their engagement because of his possessive jealousy. He seemed to enjoy telling how she'd finished up in hospital with a broken arm and four cracked ribs. With relish he described his row with Carole.

'Being with her was no fun after you'd gone anyway,' he said. 'To begin with it was to make you jealous and I never meant to marry her. I just thought she might help get me the consultancy. If only she hadn't been so stupid and demanding. I was so sick of her silly face.' He smiled. 'It was so satisfying, swiping that smug look off it. What I did to her was almost a work of art.' He calmly recounted Edward's description of Carole's injuries.

'But that's nothing to what you're going to

282

get,' he told her, pushing his face close to hers. 'Just you wait till you see what a treat I've got lined up for you. I've been watching you since yesterday. I've had a good look round Craybourne and I've planned it all so carefully.'

She knew now with chilling certainty that he was mad and that she'd be lucky to escape with her life. When he forced a gag between her teeth she fought him with every ounce of strength she had, struggling even more wildly when he tied a blindfold over her eyes and she could no longer see. But she was no match for his manic strength as he bundled her into the boot of the car. Lying in the airless darkness, she tried hard not to panic as she heard the car start up, and seconds later they were bumping back along the track the way they had come.

★ ★ ★

It was almost ten when Chris and Max arrived at The Imperial. Adam was waiting for them, pacing up and down in Reception. When he saw the headlights of Max's car he went out to meet them, enormously relieved to have someone with whom to share his anxiety. He took them up to the flat and made coffee for them.

'You say that Imo went shopping,' Chris said. 'What time was this?'

'About two. As I told you, we were going to a concert in Norwich this evening. She wanted to buy something to wear — said all her clothes were second-hand.'

Chris smiled. 'That's right. They were mine.

283

Did she mention anywhere else she might go?'

'The hairdresser's. She was going to try Michelle's in Quay Street. Sandra, our receptionist, recommended it to her. I rang there just as they were closing and she had been there. She left at half past five — asked them to order her a taxi.' He lifted his shoulders helplessly. 'Heaven only knows what happened after that. But I'm sure she would have rung if some emergency had cropped up.'

'Have you tried the hospitals?'

He nodded. 'All of them, within a fifty-mile radius. Nothing.'

Chris looked at Max. 'Shall we take the car and drive round — look for her?'

He shook his head. 'Where would we look? She could be anywhere. It's a needle in a haystack.'

Chris sighed. 'You'd have to try to think like William. Might he have masqueraded as a taxi driver? And if he did pick her up where might he have taken her?'

The three of them sat looking at each other, totally at a loss. Chris thought she had never in her life felt so helpless and useless.

★　★　★

When William opened the boot of the car Imogen felt light-headed from lack of air. She inhaled the cool fresh air as hard as she could and knew at once that she was near the sea. Swiftly he untied her feet and heaved her out of the boot.

284

'Walk!' he commanded, grasping her arms and pushing her from behind.

She stumbled forward and soon realised that she was on a steep downward path. Her feet slipped on loose stones and several times she almost fell, but he jerked her back on to her feet and continued to guide her forward and downwards, till at last she felt soft sand beneath her feet.

The thud and roar of the sea was loud in her ears now as the waves crashed on to the shore, and her blood chilled as a horrible suspicion began to form in her mind.

'The tide will soon be in,' he told her, pushing her down into a sitting position on the sand. She felt him crouch beside her. She could feel the warmth of his arm next to hers and feel his hair touch her cheek as he leaned close to whisper.

'Do you remember when you were depressed? I brought you some medication — valium. Remember? But you wouldn't take it. It's a pity because it would have made you forget. Just as it's going to make you forget now.' She felt him fumble in his pocket, then she felt something hard and cold press against her skin. 'Feel that? Know what it is? It's a syringe. You're going to have some valium now, Genny,' he told her. 'But not tablets; this time an injection. This time you don't get a choice. After tonight nothing will ever matter again. The tide will do the rest for me. No one will suspect anything. Valium is widely prescribed. You took too much, that's all. And by tomorrow morning I'll be back in London and it will all be over.'

'No!' Her voice was muffled by the gag as she tried to get away from him. But he held her fast, pushing up her sleeve to expose her arm.

'It won't take long to work,' he told her softly. 'It's quite kind really. No pain. No suffering. A damn sight better than you deserve so stop fighting it, Genny. You can't win.'

As she felt the needle go in she tried to scream, but the only sound that escaped through the gag was a thin squeal, lost in the sound of the incoming tide.

The blood sang in her ears and her head pounded as the drug slowly took hold. William held her fast until he felt the life drain out of her body, then he removed the gag and blindfold and untied her hands.

'Goodbye, Genny,' he said dispassionately.

She was aware of the chilly sea air on her face — of the rattle of the shingle as the waves lashed the shore and the sea drew nearer. Clouds hid the moon and she couldn't see much but she knew now with chilling certainty where she was.

She heard William's footsteps receding. Already the tide was in so far that he had to clamber over the rocks to get at the cliff path. She heard the skitter of the small stones that he dislodged as he went. With an almighty effort she managed to raise herself on to her hands and knees and move a few feet, but the drug was too strong for her and she sank back on to the damp sand again, tears of fear and frustration streaming down her cheeks as she realised there was no escape.

'We've got to do something!' Chris said. 'I can't just sit here any longer.'

'I think we should call the police,' Adam said. He got up and went to the telephone. 'I know it's only a few hours but surely under the circumstances . . . '

At that moment the door opened and a small figure in pyjamas stood in the doorway. Simon rubbed his eyes as he looked bemusedly round at the two strangers.

'Where's Sylvia?' he asked. 'I woke up and looked for her in her room but she isn't there.'

Adam put down the receiver. 'Simon. What are you doing awake at this time of night?'

'I had a dream. I want Sylvia. She said she wouldn't go and leave me, but she isn't there.' His face crumpled and two large tears slipped down his cheeks. Adam crossed the room and picked him up, sitting down with him on his knee.

'She had to go out for a little while,' he said, trying to keep the desperate concern out of his voice.

'Can I stay up till she comes back?'

'I don't know about that old chap. It's pretty late you know.'

'Who are they?' Simon pointed at Chris and Max.

'This lady is Sylvia's friend,' Adam said.

'Has she come to take Sylvia away?'

'No. Of course not.'

'Did she go away with that man?'

'What man?' Adam looked at his small son. 'What are you talking about?'

'This morning. We were at the park. He was hiding in the bushes. I thought he was playing hide and seek, but he didn't have any little boys with him.'

The three adults looked at each other, suddenly riveted by the child's words. Was there anything relevant in what he was saying or was it just childish imagination?

'It was the same man as yesterday,' Simon went on. 'He was there when we went to the cove. I wanted to go down and paddle but Sylvia said no, because you said we mustn't. The man was watching us.'

Chris and Max exchanged glances. 'What did he do?' Chris asked. 'Did he speak to you?'

Simon shook his head. 'No. He just watched,'he said. 'He didn't say anything.'

'What did he look like?' Max asked.

Simon thought for a moment. 'Big,' he said, holding his hand up above his head. 'Black hair.'

'Did Sylvia see him?' Adam prompted.

'I don't know,' Simon said solemnly. He looked round the room at the three serious faces, catching some of their fear and anxiety. 'Where is she? I want Sylvia!'

'She'll be back soon.' Adam stood up and hoisted Simon on to his shoulders. 'Tell you what, we'll go and find Mrs Lane and she'll read you a story and stay with you till you fall asleep. All right?'

'Why can't you read to me?'

'Because I have to go out for a little while.' Adam looked at the others. 'I shan't be long.'

The minutes ticked by, but when Adam came back he looked more positive. 'If she is with him I've got an idea where he might have taken her,' he said. 'If I'm right there's no time to lose. Can we go in your car?'

In the car, as Max drove, Adam explained about the cove and the dangerous tides. 'If he's been around exploring the place for a couple of days it's just the kind of place he might have sussed out.' He looked at his watch. 'I've just checked with the coast guards and high tide is due at eleven, so we'd better hurry.'

* * *

The moment the car drew up on the cliff top Max let out a yell. That's it! His car. He's here.'

They got out and Max went over to the car. There was no one inside and the bonnet felt cool.

'It's been here some time,' he told the others.

They stood at the cliff's edge looking down into the darkness of the cove below. It was cloudy and too dark to see anything, but they could see the dark glimmer of the water and hear the waves breaking on the beach. Suddenly the moon came out from behind the heavy clouds and Adam leant forward with a cry.

'There's something down there!' he shouted. 'There — can you see? At the bottom, close to the cliff.'

Max leaned forward, straining his eyes. 'Yes, there's something there all right. It could be anything,' he said. 'But whatever it is it's going to get carried out by the tide pretty soon. Is there any way we can get down there?'

Adam shook his head. 'There are two spurs of rock on either side of the cove. That's what makes it so dangerous. Once the tide is in it's cut off.'

'We have to do something!' Chris cried. 'If he pushed her over — if she fell all that way she could be seriously injured and unable to move.'

But Adam was already punching the buttons on his mobile phone. 'The coast guards,' he said as he waited for a reply. 'I'll try to persuade them to get the helicopter out. That's our only hope.'

Suddenly there was a cry from Max, who had walked further along the path, looking for some way to get down.

'Quick! There's something — or someone — down there,' he said. 'Looks as though he fell from the path on to the rocks.'

15

Imogen opened her eyes and quickly closed them again. The light hurt them and for a moment she couldn't remember where she was. Inside her closed lids her world was confused. From the brief glimpse she had had of her surroundings she knew she was in hospital. Something had happened to her. What? Then she remembered the bomb blast, the girl who'd stolen her handbag, the chase and the explosion.

So — has everything else been a dream?

Disappointment overwhelmed her as she thought of Adam and The Imperial, of Simon and the wonderful new life she'd seen opening up for her. It had all been a figment of her traumatised mind and now — now what must she face? Mercifully she slept again.

When she next woke a face floated above her. She frowned — puzzled.

'Chris?'

'Yes, it's me.' Chris took her hand. 'I'm here love.'

'What time is it? How long have I been here?'

'It's six o'clock — in the evening, that is. You've been asleep for almost twenty-four hours.'

As Chris squeezed her hand reassuringly, the horrific events of the previous day began to filter mistily back into Imogen's mind. But which was real and which was a dream?

'I had a nightmare, the worst I have ever had,' she said haltingly. 'I thought I was with William,' she said. Her tongue felt too big for her mouth and she tried hard to control her slurred words. 'I thought the car was a taxi — he took me to a derelict cottage somewhere and then to the cove. He gave me an injection of something — valium.' She looked up with terror-filled eyes. 'Oh God, it was an awful nightmare, Chris. He meant to kill me. I couldn't stay awake — couldn't move. I thought I was going to drown.'

'Shhh.' Chris patted her hand. 'It was no dream, but don't worry about that now. Just rest. You're safe.'

Later, after more healing sleep, the fog in her mind cleared enough to realise that what she had thought a nightmare was in fact reality. She demanded to know the truth. 'How did you find me, Chris? How did you know where to look?'

'It was little Simon who gave us the idea,' Chris told her. 'He's a smart little kid. It seems he'd spotted a man watching you, at the cove and in the park, for a couple of days. He thought it was some kind of game, but he gave us a description and everything. We knew then that it must have been William and Adam guessed he might have taken you to the cove. After that we moved as quickly as we could. Adam got in touch with the coast guard and persuaded them to call out the helicopter. It was touch and go. They had a terrible job to reach you. The tide was coming in fast and you were too deeply unconscious to be cooperative.'

Imogen moved her limbs gingerly. 'Am I all right?'

'You're fine, thank God,' Chris assured her. 'When they first got you here they didn't know what you'd overdosed on, so they were a bit worried at first. But a blood test soon told them it was only a tranquilliser. William must have wanted to make it look as though you'd taken it yourself. You'd swallowed some sea water and you had slight hypothermia, but other than that you're fine.'

'William.' Imogen looked round the ward fearfully. 'He might come back — to make sure . . . '

'No, he won't.' Chris took her hand. 'Imo, love — William is dead. We knew he wasn't far away because his car was still parked at the top of the cliff when we got there. The coast guards recovered his body after they brought you up. In his hurry to get away he must have fallen from the cliff path on to the rocks. His neck was broken.' She squeezed her friend's hand. 'It's probably just as well,' she said gently. 'From all you've told me he was seriously disturbed and he would have been charged with attempted murder.'

'Oh God.' Imogen's eyes clouded. 'There was something dreadfully wrong with him, Chris. He told me some terrible things about his past — things he did as a child. Things I'll never be able to forget. And now, after last night, I know he was capable of anything.' She sighed, still feeling slightly fuddled. There was still a lot she didn't understand. 'But — how did you come to be here?' she asked.

Chris smiled. 'It's a long story and one you needn't bother your head with for the moment. It's Max you have to thank really. It's complicated but he came to Craybourne a couple of weeks ago and happened to spot you. Then he found out by accident that William knew where you were, too. Until then I'd denied all his suspicions but when he told me about William I had no choice but to come clean and tell him the truth. We rang Adam right away and when he told us you were missing we knew William must have found you. That was when we decided to drive up here.'

'Thank God you did.'

'The first thing we have to think about now is getting you home again and sorting it all out.'

'Home?'

'Yes. We had to tell the police the whole story, Imo — about you and Sylvia and the mix-up. And why. There's to be an inquest — post mortem and everything on William, and then they'll want to question you as soon as you're fit enough. I'm afraid it won't be pleasant, but you won't be charged with anything. But at least it seems now that poor Sylvia was innocent.'

'How do you know?'

'It appears that old Mrs Jarrold's solicitor tracked down a distant relative in Australia. This cousin or whoever was her only beneficiary and had access to a safe deposit box at the bank. In it was all the jewellery, so it looks very much as though Sylvia tipped her off, though of course we'll never know for sure.'

Imogen closed her eyes. 'I'm glad she was innocent. It's been odd, taking on her identity. I feel almost part of her now.'

'It's time to let her go now darling,' Chris said gently. 'Time for you to start living again. If you want, you can come home with me and stay at the flat for a while.'

'I'll come, but only for a while,' Imogen said. 'This is my home now, Chris,' she said. 'With Adam and Simon — if they still want me, that is. Goodness knows I've caused Adam a lot of trouble. He might be glad to see the back of me after all this.'

'I hardly think so. He's been here with you most of the time since they brought you in — worried out of his mind. They sent him home to get some rest, and he's going to be furious that he wasn't here when you came round.' She smiled. 'It's pretty obvious that he's in love with you, Imo. But I want you to be very sure this time. That's another reason I suggested coming home with me; to give yourself some time and space to think things through properly.'

'I see. Perhaps you're right.'

'I'm sure I am. The next few weeks are going to be trying for you, but you know we're all here for you.'

Imogen looked at her friend. 'You keep saying 'we'. Do I take it you and Max are back together again?'

'You do,' Chris said with a grin. She held up her crossed fingers. 'I think we're going to be OK from now on. In fact — he's asked me to marry him.'

'Oh Chris! That's lovely.'

'Hang on. I haven't said yes yet.'

'But you will?'

'I might — when I've given him time to sweat a bit first. There is one decision I've made though. I'm giving up journalism.'

'Oh, Chris, are you sure?'

'Positive. I'll never make a good newspaper woman. I just haven't got what it takes, Imo. Max has. He's got that knack of keeping things in separate compartments. I used to think he was hard — ruthless even — but the way he's behaved over this business of yours has shown me a different side of him and I know now that he does care deeply about people. He's actually quite vulnerable too; far more than I ever imagined.'

'And you love him.'

Chris smiled. 'Yes, God help me. I love him.'

'So — what will you do?'

'It's all arranged,' Chris told her. 'I'm going to start training for social work. It'll mean a drop in money and a lot of hard work, but it's what I really want.'

Imogen squeezed her hand. 'Good for you.'

Chris looked up and saw a nurse hovering. 'I'd better go,' she said, getting to her feet. 'Try to rest love. I'll see you again later.'

Imogen fell asleep again soon after and when she woke it was Adam's face she saw. He was sitting beside her and as she opened her eyes he reached for her hand.

'Hi there.'

She smiled. 'Hi.'

'Welcome back. Know what? They're going to let me take you home in the morning.'

'That's good news. I can't wait to see Simon.'

He raised her fingers to his lips. 'I can't tell you how distraught I was,' he told her. 'And when they brought you up from the cove and I saw how bad you looked, I thought I'd lost you for ever. It's not an experience I want to repeat. From now on I don't intend to let you out of my sight for more than a few minutes.'

'Chris has suggested that I go home with her to London, though, until the police enquiry is over,' she told him.

He looked at her with concern. 'Well — if that's what you want, you know I wouldn't stand in your way.'

'It's not that, Adam.' She sighed. 'I don't want the publicity to harm your business. Perhaps it would be better if I went with Chris — just until it all dies down.'

'We can come and visit you, though, can't we?'

She smiled. 'I hope you will.'

He squeezed her hand. 'You can bet on it. We're going to miss you dreadfully, Simon and me.'

She smiled. 'I'll be back — for keeps, if you want me.'

He leaned over to kiss her gently. 'Call me selfish if you like but I've been praying you'd say that.'

We do hope that you have enjoyed reading this large print book.

Did you know that all of our titles are available for purchase?

We publish a wide range of high quality large print books including:
Romances, Mysteries, Classics
General Fiction
Non Fiction and Westerns

Special interest titles available in large print are:
The Little Oxford Dictionary
Music Book
Song Book
Hymn Book
Service Book

Also available from us courtesy of Oxford University Press:
Young Readers' Dictionary
(large print edition)
Young Readers' Thesaurus
(large print edition)

For further information or a free brochure, please contact us at:
Ulverscroft Large Print Books Ltd.,
The Green, Bradgate Road, Anstey,
Leicester, LE7 7FU, England.
Tel: (00 44) 0116 236 4325
Fax: (00 44) 0116 234 0205